Cyber Sisters

KELLY CLAYTON

&

GRANT COLLINS

ISBN: 978-0-9934830-6-6

DEDICATION

To Drena and Clem, Mum and Dad, thank you for
your unconditional love and support.

BOOKS BY KELLY CLAYTON

The Jack Le Claire Mystery Series

Blood In The Sand (2015)
Blood Ties (2016)
Blood On The Rock (2017)
Blood Rights (2019)

Cyber Sisters (2018)

BOOKS WRITTEN AS JULIA HARDY

Fortune's Hostage (2018)

ACKNOWLEDGMENTS

Heartfelt thanks to Tom Rilko for sharing his considerable knowledge and experience.

Gratitude is due, as always, to Jenny Quinlan, a fabulous editor, who unfailingly gives her all.

To our beta readers – Claire, Suzie C, Ann, Suzie L and Elaine – thank you for taking the time to give that all-important first-reader feedback.

The final eyes belong to Kath Middleton, an excellent writer and eagle-eyed proof-reader. Thank you.

Our last thanks go to each other. We know what we have, appreciate it, and are ever grateful..

CHAPTER ONE

Marianne Sinclair delayed leaving the sanctuary of her office until the last possible moment. Her own private space was the coveted corner suite, its glass-fronted opulence fitting for the CEO of the successful investment firm MJS Securities. She checked her slim wristwatch—a recent thirty-fifth birthday present to herself. It was only a five-minute walk to where she needed to be.

She debated changing out of her dress and jacket into something more casual but didn't have time. She removed the clip from her tightly bound hair, letting it fall loose. Her scalp tingled at the release. She stared at her reflection in the mirror. She would have to do.

She imagined the others would be downtrodden losers, stupid enough to fall for the latest online scam. Not her. It had been the wheel of chance and pure bad luck. She didn't know why she was bothering to go except the bloody policewoman had kept insisting, and she was desperate to be left alone. She didn't need any hassle from anyone, so she would go to keep the peace and hope the police managed to find out who had done this. She doubted she'd learn anything tonight she didn't already know.

Her high heels clicked as she strode up the wide entrance steps, swerving to avoid a young couple, jean-clad legs entwined as they embraced. Her feet were starting to ache in her pointy stilettos; she'd been too busy to change into her walking flats before she left the office. Several of her traders—young, eager beavers—had looked up in surprise, their eyes blinking as they adjusted to looking at a real person and not their lit-up banks of screens. It was unheard of for Marianne to quit the office before 9:00 p.m. It wasn't exactly as if she could tell them where she was going. They'd have a field day. She knew what they said about her. Marianne was so damn smart. Ah, but she hadn't been clever enough.

She'd thought she was so in control, careful in everything she did, but she had taken her eye off the ball, had rushed, had obviously done something she shouldn't, and shame ate away at her. She had taken charge of her life almost two decades earlier and built a protective wall. She had toughened up, and now she had money and connections. He would never get to her.

She halted. Where had that come from? Was it the sight of the teenagers on the steps, so seemingly bewitched by each other the world around them disappeared? It had been several years since an unbidden thought had made it past her defences, and she wasn't letting it out now.

She paused outside room eighteen of the Westminster College and quickly reapplied her lipstick—Chanel Rouge Shine No. 62, Monte-Carlo. It was the only shade she had worn in years. The pinkish tone suited her fairness but was dark enough to not stand out at work. She wondered, fleetingly, if it was part of a uniform, that together with her designer suits, expensive shoes and good handbags she was sending out a message. Look at me—see what I have achieved, and all on my own. She wanted to laugh. Of course that's what she was doing. Mind you, few people would know exactly who she was. She kept a low profile, and no photographs existed of MJ Sinclair, the notoriously successful fund manager. You couldn't be too careful in these days of social media where lives were displayed online for all to see; especially when you had secrets. Secrets that could ruin several lives and draw a hell load of trouble to her door. She kept her head down and her life private.

Her stomach lurched in an unfamiliar way. Was she nervous? Surely not. Her eyes were drawn to the typed sign on the door: *7:00 p.m. Online Security and Social Media.* She grabbed the handle and threw open the solid wooden door, knocking into a woman who had apparently been loitering on the other side.

***

Anita Ferguson stumbled and let out an embarrassed gasp as the door behind her opened wide and banged into her. Several pairs of eyes turned her way. Her stomach was filled with a concrete block, and she was covered with a thin layer of sweat—not uncommon for her, but she knew it had nothing to do with the menopause. Not this time. In front of her were almost twenty chairs laid out in two rows. Almost all the chairs were occupied. There were more women than men, and they all seemed to be studiously ignoring each other as they sat, eyes glued to their phones.

A young man leaned against the wall. If he was the tutor, this was yet another reason to turn tail and run. She didn't want a handsome, carefree boy to see her shame, to ask how she could have been so stupid. A well of panic started to rise from her churning stomach, and she took one deep breath, exhaling slowly, and then another. It didn't work. She couldn't move. In her cowardice, she turned, ready to leave, only to have a hand placed against her back as a woman's voice rumbled in her ear, "Come on, in you go. We're late as it is." And the woman prodded her farther into the room.

**

Sue Wexford looked up from her phone as the tutor pushed away from the ledge he'd been leaning against and, gesturing at the two women by the door, said, "Come in and grab a seat. Okay. Let's begin."

With a start, she realised she knew one of them. Wasn't that just her damn luck? London was a city with over 8.5 million people, and she had to bump into an old work colleague. She hadn't seen Anita Ferguson since she'd left her part-time job over a decade before. Well, she hadn't seen her in the flesh, but Anita regularly posted on

Facebook. What had happened to her? She was a shadow of herself.

There were sounds of general shuffling as chairs were settled into, phones reluctantly shoved into handbags and legs crossed.

The tutor moved to the middle of the lecture area. He looked ridiculously young; a good-looking boy with a chiselled jaw and shaggy brown hair. His worn jeans and T-shirt were yet another stamp of his youth. "Hi, I'm Tom Capelli, and I'm your tutor for this course. I'll be giving you an overview of cybersecurity, and the aim is to provide you with the information to allow you to protect yourself online. Let's make it informal and interactive to get the most out of it."

Sue's heart sank; interactive wasn't something she enjoyed. She wanted to be anonymous, learn more than she already knew and try to make sense of the whole damn mess. Her tongue tingled, and she longed for another cigarette. She hadn't smoked since she'd found out she was pregnant with Jess. It hadn't been easy, not at first, but her little girl had been more important than anything else.

She hadn't even been tempted to start again when Dave died. They'd once had a good marriage, or so she'd believed, but they had fallen into a comfortable, almost dismissive midlife companionship. She had truly grieved when the unthinkable had happened, but she hadn't started smoking again, hadn't even considered it. Then she'd found out what Dave had done.

A month ago she bought her first packet of cigarettes in thirty years, together with a litre of gin and a dozen cans of slimline tonic. You had to be healthy, didn't you?

More fool Dave that she even needed to be here in the first place. Her motive for being here was perhaps fraudulent, but she wasn't going to let some swine take what was hers without understanding if there was anything she could do about it.

Tom's voice pulled her back to the moment. ". . . and let's begin by finding out why you're all here. Who wants to go first?"

Unsurprisingly, no one volunteered. A long moment passed, and the weight of the silence pressed down until Sue could almost taste it. She prayed, begged for someone else to speak first.

Tom smiled and shook his head. "Okay, I get it. It's awkward. But we need to start somewhere."

For a horrible moment, Sue thought he was going to pick on her to speak and then realised, with a palpable sense of relief, that he was merely waiting for a volunteer. The woman next to her had stiffened, and her elbow banged into Sue as she sank lower in her chair. Sue quickly glanced at her neighbour. She had mid-length, shiny, brown hair and a pretty face. Her skirt was a little too tight and had risen to mid-thigh, and she continually tugged it back into place. She stared as if caught in bright headlights, her eyes darting to the side as if in panic.

***

Emily Manning burned with embarrassment. There was no way she could stand up and speak in front of these people. Most were dressed in jeans and tops. They were casual and stylish. She was neither. Her confidence had taken a whack since the divorce, and since she rarely went out, she had no idea what was in and what was out. She feared she was nothing more than a woman a smidgen past forty dressed in clothes almost half a decade old. Her cheeks were on fire as she tugged at her skirt as it started to ride up her thighs again. It had once fitted her beautifully, but she had put on almost ten pounds in the last few weeks. Worry and stress had made her eat until she was busting.

How could she tell them what had happened? She didn't even understand it herself.

A brusque voice boomed from the front row as a tall blonde woman stood. Emily figured she must be in her mid-thirties. She was gorgeous, slender and beautifully dressed. Emily immediately disliked her. She was the one who had barged in last, right behind the nervous woman set to back out of the room. "Oh, for God's sake. We've all been bloody idiots. Why else would we be here? Right, I'll confess first."

***

Marianne had no time for faffing about. Whether in a classroom or a boardroom, it was better to speak first, ask the question, make a comment—get your voice heard. Tonight was no different. "My current account was emptied through online banking. They completely cleaned me out. I'd recently sold some shares, and the timing was impeccable. To do this right, I'm Marianne, and I've been scammed."

She glanced around the room to see if they got the allusion to groups like Alcoholics Anonymous; that's how they always introduced themselves at meetings in the movies. Were they a bit annoyed by the comparison? They should be. They weren't addicted to anything. They were simply naive. All of them, including herself.

Tom grimaced. "Identity theft is on the increase. The crooks get access to your system, have a good old root around and then pretend to be you. Have you changed all your passwords?"

"You bet." She sat down. It was someone else's turn now. A man stood at the back. "I'm Ted, and I bought some car accessories through an online advert. They took my money, but the goods never got delivered."

"This is increasingly common," Tom said. "Anyone else been conned this way?"

A flurry of hands shot into the air, and comment after comment was the same. Losing £50 here and £200 there on dodgy adverts. Marianne questioned why they had bothered to come to the class. This was peanuts compared to what had been stolen from her.

Tom walked to the back of the room and stood in front of a forty-something woman with wide-eyes who sat straight and rigid as if frozen in place. His voice was soft and low. "As you can see, everyone here has had a bad experience online. Can you tell us about what happened to you?"

Marianne turned round in her chair. The woman's face was scarlet, and she seemed to have puffed up in her ill-fitting skirt. She was a pretty girl or could be if she dropped a stone and bought some fashionable clothes.

"I'm Emily, and I've been scammed. I was buying a flat . . ." She paused and cleared her throat.

Her voice had shaken a little, and this was apparently an ordeal for her. Marianne understood why they all had to speak. You had to own the problem, acknowledge it and move on.

"I recently got divorced, and our home was sold. This enabled me to make an offer on a flat. I was paying most of the purchase price in cash with only a small mortgage. I got an email from the solicitor with the banking details to send the money to. I sent it straightaway."

Tom's voice was surprisingly gentle when he spoke. "It wasn't sent to the solicitor's account, was it?"

Emily took a moment to speak. "No. My lawyer sent a similar email the following week, again asking for the money to be transferred. I said I'd already sent the money. Long story short; I was defrauded and sent the money to someone completely unconnected with the solicitors."

Marianne snorted. "Swine. Can you get it back?"

Emily shook her head. "The police said they can't trace the money. Apparently, the account it was sent to has already been closed. Plus the cutbacks mean the police are stretched. They don't have the time to investigate online crimes. They suggested I hire a private cyber investigator, but I can't afford it."

A woman with sad eyes sighed. "I didn't even know that job existed. I'm Sue, and I got friendly with someone online. They needed money. I gave it to them."

"I'm sorry. That's an all too familiar story." Tom considered the last person in the room who had yet to speak and smiled, hopefully in an encouraging way. She was the one Marianne had crashed into when she arrived.

She seemed to brace herself and when she spoke her voice was pitched low. "I'm Anita. I became friendly with someone on Facebook and sent some money out on his behalf. I haven't heard back from him yet. I saw an advert for this class at the bus stop. I want to understand what went wrong. I didn't know Facebook and things were this dangerous. I don't know what I'll do if I don't hear from him soon." Her voice wobbled, and she cast her eyes downwards, staring at the ground.

No-one spoke. The evening was getting progressively heavier. Tom glanced away before commenting. "Social media platforms, Facebook and so on, are essentially safe. The problem is how we use them."

Marianne knew he was speaking to all of them but the woman's eyes filled with tears as if the words were meant only for her. "But all I did was befriend someone. I'm sure there is a reasonable explanation."

To Marianne, she was delusional, still hanging on to the hope it was all a mistake, that she hadn't been conned. Anita's optimistic words belied her dull eyes.

Tom walked towards the whiteboard. "You've all had a rough time, but I'm here to make sure it never happens again. Let's find out what not to do online, and we're specifically going to run through social media activity. And look on the bright side: it's usually the younger crowd getting swindled because they live online."

What bloody rot, thought Marianne. That was no comfort to a group whose ages seemed to range from mid-thirties to early seventies. They had all been taken for granted and shamed. At least they wouldn't be that naive again.

CHAPTER TWO

An hour later, Marianne knew more than she had thought possible about what stupid, trusting fools inhabited the planet. And she was one of them. Tom moved away from the presentation screen. Grabbing the back of one of the chairs, he turned it around and sat astride as he leaned forward. "That's us almost done for tonight. Now . . ."

It was like being back at school. A dozen chairs scraped across the floor as everyone rose to their feet and scrambled for the door. At least half the room had gone before Tom jumped up and said, "Wait! There is another session next week. We'll go into more detail on social media and email hacking. I need to recap. We've still got ten minutes to go." He sounded desperate.

She stood and pushed back her chair with a clatter. There were three other women left in the room in addition to her; the rest had scarpered.

"Thanks, Tom, but we've had enough of this room for one night, and I've had enough of the lecture as well."

"Look, I've not long started doing these courses. I work for a charity, and we hope the police and other official bodies will recommend people to us. We can help you work out where you went wrong and help prevent it from happening again." He paused. "Most of you were referred here by Cybercrime Liaison Officers from the Metropolitan Police. We've made a big push to get in the door with them, and I'd appreciate decent feedback from you. Obviously, I want to help you as well."

Marianne sighed. "There's a pub next door. Why don't we pop in there for a quick drink and you can recap to your heart's delight?"

The other women seemed surprised. No one said anything.

Marianne mentally rolled her eyes, grabbed her bag and headed towards the door. "Come on, the drinks are on me. We'll still be doing the course—only in better surroundings."

Tom laughed. "Well, if you put it that way. Come on, the Cybersecurity course is officially decamping to the Stag's Head."

***

Sue stood, unsure of what to do. The woman who'd been sent an email by imposters—Emily, she thought—seemed bemused as she gathered together her belongings and followed Marianne and Tom. Anita was rooted in place. Sue sighed. What was the saying? If you can't beat them . . . ? Well, she better join them in that case. She gathered her coat and bag and paused by the door. "Come on, Anita, love. You remember me, don't you? I'm Sue Wexford—from Johnson Ross Accountants. I haven't seen you in an age."

"Oh yes. Hi, Sue. I didn't recognise you at first." Her voice was a whisper, and she quickly turned away, staring at the floor.

"What harm can it do to grab a quick drink? And someone else is paying; makes it even better."

Anita didn't look up. She shook her head. "I'm truly not in the mood for company. I don't even know why I came here. I better go home."

Sue waited until Anita was about to walk past, then gently touched her arm. "We're all in the same boat, and I bet what we all revealed here is only the tip of our personal icebergs. I won't tell anyone I saw you here." If the truth were told, there wasn't anyone to tell; the only friends they had in common were on Facebook, which meant they probably never came into contact in person and their relationships consisted of liking and commenting on each other's often inane, styled photos. "Come on, we'll have a quick drink. Let Madam Bossy put her money where her mouth is."

Anita hesitated and shrugged. Sue figured it was the only concession she would get.

The Stag's Head was next door but one and it wasn't busy. There was a load of offices nearby, but at this time of night most commuters would have finished their sociable drinks with colleagues and be on their way home. Sue and Anita entered the pub shortly after the other three. Tom and Emily sat in a booth. Sue slid onto the plush red velvet seat and motioned for Anita to do the same. "Where's Marianne?" She'd better not be in the loo, trying to dodge out of getting their drinks.

A shamefaced Tom answered. "She's at the bar. I did try to say I'd pay, but she ordered me to sit down and be a good boy."

"Yep, that figures."

***

"What figures?" Marianne slid a tray onto the table and handed a pint of lager to Tom. She gestured towards the two bottles of wine on the tray—one white, one red—and said, "Help yourself."

Sue answered the original question. "You not letting Tom pay. I think that's more to do with getting your own way as opposed to championing equality."

Marianne chuckled; the woman had a point. "And you're right. We should all pay our own way, but I do like to be in control." She looked at Tom. "Right, let's get on with the recap."

Tom quickly sipped his lager and smacked his lips appreciatively. "Right, rule number one is don't give out personal details or passwords. A bank, for example, will never ask you for a password in full. They will only ask for a certain number of digits. But be careful if they ask for a couple of digits and then say they have to start the security check again because their system crashed. If they subsequently ask for two different digits, be on your guard. They could be trying to build up their knowledge of your password. By getting enough digits, they can run different permutations through sophisticated software until they find the right passcode."

"That didn't happen to any of us," Sue said. "We didn't give out our details."

Emily was quick to respond, her tone pained. "I didn't need to. I transferred them the bloody money myself."

Tom grimaced. "That brings us to email fraud. Remember that, when online, people may not be who they say they are. If you ever receive an email asking for a payment to go to an account you haven't paid before, do a double-check. Ring the person or company to check the details. And please ring the number you already have, from headed paper or something, and not the one given to you in the email."

Emily gulped her wine and set the almost-empty glass on the table. "That makes so much sense. I know that. Why was I so stupid? Christ, I could kick myself."

"Many people do the same. We are all busy, distracted and multitasking. Lack of attention is what fraudsters feed off. They need you to be trusting. Another tip—when you receive an email, hover over the sender's name, and the full email address should appear. A scammer's trick is to have an email address similar to the one you know and recognise but with a tiny difference. Perhaps it's the addition of an extra letter or number, or a slight misspelling, anything giving them a unique address that is similar to the legitimate one but will only go directly to them."

Marianne chimed in, "Yes, but how did they know she was about to send money to her solicitors? Or that I had recently sold some shares and had ready cash available? My money is usually tied up."

"Ah, and there is the question. The hackers must have got a virus or worm into your system. One that allowed them to access your emails, social media, account numbers—everything."

Marianne slumped in her chair. "Shit! That's what the police said to me, but they don't have a clue how anyone got access because it could have been a multitude of different ways." She appraised Tom. "Maybe you could have a look into this for me? I'll pay you."

Tom seemed to mull it over for a moment, before shrugging. "There's no need. I'm happy to take an initial look. Bring your laptop next time we meet. You should all do that. The police have asked for feedback on any viruses or stings we come across that could have a wider impact. We can make the next session focussed and interactive."

On second thought, Marianne wasn't too sure she wanted someone rooting about her personal business. She sobered as she realised someone already had. What had they seen? What did they know? She shrugged the worry aside. Her secrets were decades old and well hidden.

Sue nodded, but her eyes were downcast. Perhaps she didn't fancy someone poking about her computer either?

Anita was more direct. "There's no need for me to do that. I know what happened, and I have to accept that I've been taken for a bloody fool."

Sue patted her hand. "Come on, Tom can probably tell you loads about what happened."

Anita pulled back her hand as if scalded. She stood, and the table rocked, knocking over her half-filled glass. Tears were in her eyes as she backed away from them. "No. I'm sorry. I can't." And with that, she left.

Marianne spoke for them all. "What the bloody hell is her problem?"

***

Anita hit the refresh button for what seemed like the hundredth time, but the treacherous screen mocked her. There was no *ping* signifying a tantalising notification of a private, direct message. She flicked across to her emails—nothing. Her stomach was leaden, heavy, and her temples were starting to ache. She hadn't heard from him in almost two weeks. They had been in daily contact before. This couldn't be happening. It just couldn't. She tried to ignore the kernel of fear that seemed to have permanently taken root in her stomach.

She opened their message chain in Facebook and flicked through the hundreds of text chats they had exchanged over the last six months. Surely she was wrong? He'd been loving and caring and completely open about his circumstances. She can't have misunderstood. Perhaps something had happened to him. Maybe he was ill?

Her shoulders drooped, and she rested her head in her hands, her thoughts a chaotic muddle. What the hell was she going to do? A worm of sanity wriggled its way through her self-delusion, shining a light on her stupidity. She knew. She'd been taken for a fool and had acted like an even bigger one. She'd used money that wasn't hers, and she couldn't repay it on her own. He'd said the insurance money would come through soon and he'd pay her back. It was a temporary loan, he'd said. But now he wasn't responding to her messages.

Bile burned her throat, and she gagged as she swallowed the foul liquid. What the hell would she do? What could she do? The mantra ran through her head like a thundering train. She pulled the neckline of her top away from her sweat-soaked skin. She'd get found out soon. It was all over, and she was finished.

Or was it? A niggling thought crept through the jumbled maze of her mind. She searched through her emails, her fingers trembling as they flew across the keyboard. She exhaled, long and slow, as she found the one she needed. She had no other options. She couldn't fix this on her own. They would have to help her. If this didn't work, then there was nothing else she could do. She would be ruined.

CHAPTER THREE

The second session of the Cybersecurity evening class saw a vastly reduced attendance. Only Marianne, Sue and Emily had bothered to turn up. Well, some guy had put in an appearance, but he slunk out after the first half hour. Marianne wished she'd done the same as she concealed a yawn and willed her eyes to stay open. She couldn't help sneaking a glance at her watch as Tom concluded. "So we're already at the end of this second session. We've had a look at some online fraud case studies. Remember, these are real-life stories. These people exist, and they were duped into giving money to scammers they thought were someone else. Invariably, they're people they built a romantic connection with, and trusted, but, ultimately, that person didn't exist. Instead of a retired US marine, they'll be corresponding with a kid in a warehouse in Nigeria where the scams are being run."

Sue asked, "But what about the people they see online, you know, on video chats. They're real?"

"Sure, they're real people, but they are pretending to be someone else, playacting. These gangs make up whole other personas. It is rare for them to become involved in face-to-face chats, even online. Those communication lines are usually for when they want to get their hands on a bigger sum of money, and without exception, it's a honeytrap scam. You know, the person you've been falling for through their words, then you see them in the online flesh, and it all becomes much more real."

Marianne glanced at the others, catching Emily's eye. "You think Anita got scammed in a honeytrap, and that's why she didn't turn up tonight? All a bit too close to home, eh?"

Emily drew back. "It's not for us to speculate. She said she befriended someone and helped them out with money."

Sue butted in before Marianne could respond. "It doesn't matter what happened to her. We all got scammed in one way or another. It must be much worse if you not only lose money, but you also lose the person you thought the scammer was."

Marianne raised her hands in mock surrender. "Sorry. I didn't mean anything. You know Anita, don't you?"

"I worked with her ages ago, we were pretty friendly but lost touch when I moved on. We reconnected on Facebook a couple of years back. Whatever happened is her business."

Marianne sensed an undercurrent in her tone. Had Sue been involved in an online romance that went bad? She must be around fifty, but she had to concede the older woman didn't look any the worse for it. "I'm sure. Anyway, I figure we've seen the last of Anita. She was hardly the life and soul of the party anyway."

It was a throwaway comment, regretted the moment she uttered it, and delivered in her carefully modulated accent. An accent more cosmopolitan London than attributable to any particular area of the UK. She'd left her

Scottish burr far behind.

Sue snapped, "Look, we barely know each other, but Anita is obviously extremely upset about what happened. You could tell that by looking at her. I'm worried about her. She seemed edgy."

"Right, time's up. I hate to interrupt your chat, but the class is now finished. I'm afraid I'll need to look at your laptops next week at the final session." Tom's dry comment brought Marianne back to the moment.

"Okay, let's go and have a drink." She had nothing better to do. She had told her boyfriend, Adrian, she was working on an urgent project and wouldn't be seeing him tonight. Luckily, he was going to a work event. He didn't need to know about any of this.

Sue stood, shaking her head. "No thanks, I'm worried about Anita." She pulled out her phone. "Earlier tonight I sent her a private message on Facebook asking where she was. Give me a minute to check if she answered."

She flicked through her phone. "She hasn't replied. Tom, do you have a number for her?"

"I don't know. Let me check."

He pulled some papers from a battered leather satchel and flicked through them. "No number. Got an address though."

Sue pulled a notebook and pen out of her bag. "Give me the details."

Marianne jumped up. "You can't do that. What about GDPR?"

Tom looked blank, as did Sue and Emily.

Really, had these people been living under a stone? "It's the General Data Protection Regulation. You hold Anita's data purely concerning her attending this course. You can't use it for any other reason or pass it on to anyone else."

Sue stared at her. "I'm worried about Anita, and I don't give a damn about any funny laws. I have a weird feeling."

Marianne couldn't believe the attitude. "It'll be Tom that has a funny feeling if he gets fined for contravening the legislation."

Sue said nothing, but her stance was combative. Marianne knew she could take her.

Tom laughed. "Whoa, take it easy, girls. Oops—clumsy me."

He dropped the papers to the floor and bent to gather them together. One slipped out of his hand and floated to Sue's feet. Accidentally on purpose, no doubt. She picked it up and quickly read the contents before handing it back to Tom.

Sue was at the door before Marianne knew what was happening. "Right, I'm off to see Anita. See you next week."

Emily shrugged, before chasing after Sue. "Wait for me. I'm coming too."

Marianne stared after them. She'd been a bit of a bitch. What harm would it do to check on Anita?

She ran after them—well, as fast as she could run in five-inch heels.

***

Anita's heart raced as she climbed the stairs to her flat. The lift wasn't working, yet again, and she didn't have the strength to moan to the caretaker. The last thing she needed at the moment was additional service charges to fix the damn thing.

Another week had flown past, and she still hadn't heard from Tony. She had to accept the obvious; she'd been ghosted. She'd read about it on a Facebook post. How someone withdrew from contact with you and ignored you as if you didn't exist. That was her.

She'd put the flat on the market that morning, but it would take time to sell. Time she didn't have. She fumbled with the key and finally managed to open the door despite her shaking hands. She went straight to the kitchen, chucking her bag on the hall floor and kicking off her shoes. In moments, she'd opened a bottle of red wine and poured a generous glass. She took a long drink, the heavy wine burning her throat but, temporarily, numbing her pain.

Her laptop was on the dining table, and it sat silent, mocking her. She had refreshed her inbox all day long, her phone hidden under a pile of papers on her desk. She had checked on the tube, but there had been nothing. She needed the money badly, and the efficient girl at the bank had taken all her details and said they'd get back to her as soon as possible to let her know if the lending was approved. But that had been a week ago. She scanned her inbox and stilled as the mouse hovered over the email she'd been waiting for. She drank the rest of the wine, and her senses buzzed with anticipation as she opened the message.

She read it. Reread it for good measure, then pushed the laptop to the side and rested her head in her hands. They couldn't lend her any money. Said her credit-risk analysis wasn't good enough. Shit! She had nothing to sell apart from the flat, which would take an age, and no one to turn to.

Her mobile pinged, and she quickly grabbed it. The text message was from her boss. Short and sweet.

Finance has asked for an urgent meeting with the two of us tomorrow. Do you have any idea what this is about?

She stared at the words as dread froze her movements. She was finished. She laid her arms on the table and used them to cushion her head as hot tears of despair mixed with shame covered her face and blurred her vision. A black cloud descended as her thoughts threatened to deafen her. She stumbled to the counter and poured another drink. She downed it in one, the alcohol burning her throat, numbing the pain and robbing her of rational thought. She needed something stronger and eyed the open bottle of vodka on the counter. There were no options left.

CHAPTER FOUR

Marianne took a good look at her two co-travellers in the taxi. Emily was dressed in a similar fashion to the previous week, her top strained across her breasts, and her skirt rode a little too high. Comfort eating, perhaps? She must be in her early forties—a little older than Marianne, but worlds apart. Those nails hadn't seen a manicure in a while.

She moved her attention to Sue, who sat across from her in the pull-down seat. She was staring out the window. She was attractive, but there was something in her eyes Marianne couldn't quite figure out. Was it loneliness? She didn't wear a wedding ring, but a betraying red mark gave the game away. Was she divorced?

The cab driver's voice broke into Marianne's thoughts. "That's £32.50, please, love." They'd travelled clear across London, but Marianne had insisted they take a cab as opposed to the tube. Of course, the underground would have been much quicker, but this mode of travel was marginally more civilised.

"I've got this." She fumbled in her purse, shoving a twenty, tenner and fiver at the driver before exiting. The others followed close behind. She dismissed Sue's shocked, "Shit, that was expensive. We better split the fare", with a wave of her hand.

"I insisted we get a taxi. It's on me."

She had expected the small residential square to be dark and quiet; instead, lights were blazing, a few front doors were open, and a handful of people were standing on the street by a small, neat block of flats. It was Anita's address. An ambulance was parked up, and a uniformed paramedic waited by the open backdoors. An empty police car remained in front. There was a buzz of chattering gossip and anticipation, the kind that permeated the air when disaster lurked nearby, the kind that accompanied accident and crime scenes. The vultures waited.

Marianne pushed to the front of the small crowd where two track-suited women were gossiping and said, "Hey, what's going on?"

One turned around, a cigarette hanging from the corner of her mouth. She spoke without removing it, her voice a mumble. "No fucking idea, love. The ambulance and police turned up about twenty minutes ago. Oh shit, what is that all about?"

A blanket-covered body was being carried out on a stretcher. The light was fading, and the chatter increased. The woman with the cigarette said, "Who the hell is that?"

Her friend spoke, "Oh Christ, look, there's Chloe."

A pretty dark-haired girl was being led to the police car. A middle-aged policewoman had an arm around her and helped the girl as she stumbled along.

Marianne asked, "Who is Chloe?"

"Chloe Ferguson. Her mother, Anita, lives in one of those flats."

Marianne froze.

A teenager came rushing up and grabbed at the

cigarette woman. "Mum, it's Anita Ferguson. I heard some bloke say Chloe couldn't get in touch with her mum, so she came round to the flat. She found Anita collapsed on the floor. She topped herself."

Marianne closed her eyes as the paramedics loaded the covered body into the back of the ambulance, and stepped back. Sue and Emily were beside her, eyes wide and faces ashen.

Sue's hand shot to her throat, and she gasped. "Oh Christ, no." She stumbled to the side, and Marianne caught her as she collapsed into her arms, sobbing.

CHAPTER FIVE

Half an hour later, the three of them were sitting in Marianne's lounge. She'd hailed a cab, ushered them into her apartment and poured three large gin and tonics.

Sue hadn't said a word. She couldn't. She sat on the sofa, pale-faced and subdued, sipping at her drink. Marianne leaned forward as she faced Sue. "You certainly got upset there. Mind telling me why? It was a terrible thing to happen, but from the sound of it you barely knew her and hadn't seen each other for years."

With a shaking hand, Sue set her drink on the coffee table. She didn't have the strength to hide the truth, not anymore. Her voice was a hoarse croak. "I'm sorry; it brought everything back to me."

She drew a hand through her hair. Emily, who was sitting on the other side of the sofa, scooted over until she was close enough to put an arm around Sue's shoulders and made gentle shushing noises. What little energy Sue had deserted her, and she slumped against the cushions, clutching her drink to her chest.

Marianne said, "Something is obviously wrong. What is it?"

Sue exhaled a ragged breath, and when she spoke her voice trembled. "I'm afraid I lied to you. I didn't get scammed—well, not directly." She sipped her drink. She didn't flinch at the strong taste of the double measure but relished the numbness it would deliver.

"My husband died several months ago. I hadn't realised it at the time, but we had been living separate lives for years. He had his interests, and I had mine. Our daughter is mostly away as she works on the cruise ships, and Jess was, I guess, our only shared connection. We weren't unhappy—at least I wasn't. It was, well, it was comfortable."

There was silence for a moment as the words lay heavy in the air. Marianne asked, "What happened?" Her voice was soft and gentle, and that was Sue's undoing.

"Dave took his own life: I found him. I came home from coffee with friends, and he wasn't in his study. I called out, but there was no answer. I went upstairs. I saw his legs first. He hanged himself." Her voice hitched and tears she had thought long dried blurred her vision. "I was in shock. He left a note, but all it said was that he was sorry. I started sorting everything out; you know, the financials and so forth. That's when it all came crashing down. There was a chunk of money missing from our savings. It was almost cleared out. The money had gone into an account in Switzerland. The bank said they couldn't do anything about it. Dave and I were sole signatories, which meant either one of us could sign alone."

"If you don't mind me asking, who did he send the money to?" Marianne asked.

"It was a company account. I had never heard of it before. My lawyer has contacted the bank in Switzerland. They said there was nothing they could do as the account had already been closed. He made the payment of his own free will. No crime was committed."

"Except he was conned." Marianne's voice bit with indignation.

The silence grew heavy. Sue sighed, shook her head, and took a steadying drink. "There was a woman involved, of course. I found out later. I went through his emails, private messages and social media. She was young, pretty and foreign. She had a heavy accent. I don't know where she was living, but I'd say she was Eastern European."

Marianne reared back. "How did you know what she sounded like? Did you meet her?"

"No. Dave had some videos stored on his laptop. They were Skyping or using some kind of video communication. He recorded a few of their chats. The girl was young, with bouncy hair and a pretty face. She was thin, busty and everything I stopped being a long time ago." Her grief was wrapped in anger.

Emily asked, "How did he meet her?"

"They connected on Facebook. Half the people who do don't even know each other in real life anyway. I checked his Facebook messages. They started chatting about nothing much at all, and then it became progressively personal. I could hear the excitement in those words he wrote to her."

"And the money?" Emily prompted. "What happened?"

"She set Dave up beautifully. Talked about how she needed money for medicine for her son and she had nothing. He made small payments here and there. Then came the big one. Her kid was rushed into hospital and needed an operation. My stupid husband paid her straight away. He sent thousands of pounds in total because the requests kept coming. What was he was thinking? How could he imagine I wouldn't notice almost all our savings were gone?"

A pinprick of pity pulsed in Marianne's eyes. "I'm sorry. It sounds like you've been through hell. And I can see why what has happened to Anita has upset you."

"It was obviously a shock because I knew Anita, but it all seems so similar. After Dave sent the money, his little girlfriend disappeared into thin air. His emails were getting increasingly anxious. It was clear he wanted to leave me to make a new life with her. I guess that's why he wasn't bothered about me finding out the money was gone. He was planning a new life with her. Once we divorced, sold the house and split everything 50-50, he was going to begin again with his girlfriend and her kid."

"She did a runner?" Marianne was blunt but correct.

"Exactly. I'm left with little to live on, as we relied on Dave's income; my savings are gone, and the life insurance company won't pay out because Dave committed suicide."

"Shit! Pardon the language, but you're screwed."

"You could say that." Sue's voice was dry, and from Marianne's heightened colour she obviously realised she may have been too direct.

Emily said, "What now?"

Sue jiggled her glass in front of Marianne's face. "Why don't you get us another drink, and we'll raise a toast to Anita. I'll need to work out how we find out about the funeral arrangements because I, for one, am definitely going."

CHAPTER SIX

Marianne couldn't help but feel a little fraudulent as the choir's voices lifted high, soaring in a deep-felt rendering of "Jerusalem", as the pallbearers raised the coffin high on its final journey. The front pews emptied first as a sobbing Chloe, leaning heavily on the arm of a middle-aged man, led the way.

She glanced around the crowded church and reflected it would have been branded a right good turnout in the environment she had grown up in. She and Emily hadn't known Anita at all. Sue had barely seen the woman in a decade. They had heard snippets of gossip from whispering mourners. An empty pill packet and a drained vodka bottle gave testimony to how Anita had ended her life. The whispers also revealed that the why was still an unknown factor.

They were the last to file out of the church. There was no receiving line, and Anita's daughter was being comforted by the man who had escorted her from the church, presumably her father.

She turned to Sue and Emily with a sigh. "Right, I better be off. How about you?"

Sue shook her head, with a determined look. "Oh no, you're not." She waved a copy of the funeral order of service in front of Marianne's face. "The wake is at a nearby hotel. We're going to properly pay our respects."

Emily said, "Is that a good idea?"

"Anita is linked to us all through our shared experiences of online crime. I want to know if that has something to do with why she killed herself."

Marianne said, "It may be something else entirely. Who knows what goes on in someone else's life? You know what they say about behind closed doors. It's trite but true."

"She always looked happy enough in her Facebook posts." She held her hands out in an obvious attempt to stop Marianne and Emily from speaking. "Yes, I know. Everyone shows their best possible life on social media, but Anita was once more than a mere acquaintance. Please, will you come with me?"

Marianne shrugged, looked at Emily and dutifully followed Sue.

***

A gin and tonic later, Sue was slightly more up to the task of approaching Anita's daughter.

"I'm Chloe. Thank you for coming." The girl was red-eyed and pale, her words automatic. She cocked her head to one side. "How did you know my mother?"

"I'm Sue. I worked with Anita many years ago, and we met up again recently."

Emily spoke up in her soft voice. "I'm Emily. Marianne and I met your mum at a night class. We are extremely sorry for your loss."

"Thank you. I didn't even realise Mum was taking night classes. Mind you, it's becoming apparent she didn't tell me everything." There was an undercurrent of tension in her words. "What was the class about?"

Sue glanced at the others. Anita obviously hadn't told her daughter, but what harm could it do now? "Social media and safety online. We'd all had a few issues with that stuff."

Chloe frowned. "How odd. Why didn't she ask me? I sorted out her Internet, and I'm pretty techie."

Sue said, "Perhaps she was embarrassed. She said she'd been conned out of some money."

Chloe's gaze was intense, and she stilled. "Did she say how much?"

An odd question, thought Sue. "No, simply that it was her savings."

Chloe turned even paler. "You better come with me. We need to talk in private."

A small lounge was set to the side of the reception area, and they followed Chloe, who closed the door behind them and sank against it. "This is starting to make sense. Christ."

Marianne asked, "What do you mean?"

"The day after Mum died, the police turned up. There was money missing from the business she worked for, and it seemed Mum had taken £50,000 and paid it into her own bank account. She'd stolen it. The police talked to her bank and discovered the £50,000, plus her own savings, about £15,000, were transferred to a foreign account. The police have taken mum's laptop away, but I haven't heard any more. You mentioned scamming. Did someone coerce her into stealing and then passing the money on to them?"

Sue moved closer to Chloe, who now perched on the

small sofa. She tried to process the words as they battled through her chaotic thoughts. "We don't know. All your mum said was that someone she thought was a friend turned out not to be one at all, plus she'd paid over money she'd never get back."

Chloe stood and, plucking a tissue from a box on the table, blew her nose. Her dark hair was pulled back in a high pony-tail, her slight figure dwarfed in a black shift-dress and her pained eyes were testament to her grief and confusion. Sue ached for her.

"I'll have to tell the police about this. Mum didn't take the money for herself. She was conned."

"Yes, of course."

"Will you come with me to the police, tell them what you know? Let's go tomorrow. I don't want to waste any time."

Sue smiled her agreement. Surely the authorities would have to investigate this. Anita deserved justice.

***

Though it was only late afternoon, Marianne didn't go to the office. She'd headed home to get changed. She showered, brushed out her hair and styled it into a messy bun.

She turned and twisted in front of the mirror. Running her hands down her waist and over her slim hips, she smoothed the silken material of her evening dress. She was elegant and classy and precisely the sort of women that should be on Adrian's arm. She had met all of his friends and had already passed their tests, proving she was one of them. Or at least she assumed she had; no one gave her funny looks, winced at her pronunciation or giggled behind their mouth at her manners.

The doorbell rang, and she rushed to answer it. Adrian was early, which was unusual for him. Tall and dark-haired, he was the perfect foil for her fairness. His square jaw and patrician nose hinted at his impeccable lineage. Adrian was the second son of Viscount Shoreham, the owner of a trendy Mayfair art gallery and a man far removed from the world Marianne had escaped from. But they were together. That alone showed her how far she had travelled.

"You're early, but I'm ready." She grabbed her bag. "It's been an interesting day, so a good meal and some wine will go down a treat." She smiled at him. He was funny and knowledgeable and took her into a world utterly alien to the one she grew up in. They were good together.

Adrian came in and closed the door behind him. "I thought we could have a chat before we go out."

She laughed. "That sounds ominous." She was joking, but he didn't smile.

"Marianne, I have something to ask you. We've been together almost a year, and we get on fabulously. We're both successful, like the same things, and we have the blueprint for a damn good partnership."

He fumbled in his jacket pocket and pulled out a small velvet-covered box. He opened it to reveal a sparkling diamond ring. A sizeable pear-shaped centre stone was surrounded by flawless emeralds. "It belonged to a great-aunt of mine." He smiled, all nervousness gone. He presented the box to her. "Marianne, will you do me the honour of becoming my wife? Will you marry me?"

She hadn't been expecting this. Not at all. She was

blindsided and didn't know what to think. Yet there was only one answer.

"Yes, of course, I will marry you."

He placed the ring on her finger. It was a little too small, and he had to force it on. "There. That won't come off easily. You're stuck with me now."

He pulled her to him and kissed her. She sank against him, her mind whirring and buzzing. He hadn't mentioned love. But that wasn't important. She was gaining much more. She would be safe once she was Mrs Adrian Kempster and daughter-in-law of Viscount Shoreham. She would no longer have to fear the past. He could never reach her, never touch her. Never.

CHAPTER SEVEN

The police interview room was antiseptic. It was painted a stark white, devoid of all colour. A sturdy table was attached to the wall as were the plastic bench seats. There were no windows in the room. The door had a sliding panel to allow one to see in or out. It was currently closed tight. The walls were closing in on Sue as her claustrophobia took hold. She held her hands fast together, curled into fists, her nails digging into her palms. The last time she'd spoken to the police was when she'd found out Dave had transferred their money to what was undoubtedly a scammer's account. That conversation hadn't gone too well. Was she back for more of the same?

The door opened and banged shut with a metallic clang. A man stood in front of them. "Miss Ferguson, you wanted to see me?" Before Chloe could speak, he turned to Sue. "I'm DI Hunter. And you are?"

It was Chloe who answered first. "Mrs Wexford is a friend, and she has some information about my mum."

Sue said. "I have information about a crime committed against Mrs Ferguson."

He lifted his eyebrows but remained unsmiling. Detective inspector or not, with his sandy-coloured hair and splattering of freckles, Sue figured he should still be in school. Well, perhaps she could stretch it and give him twenty-five. What was it they said? You knew you were getting old when the police started getting younger. In that case, she must be ancient.

DI Hunter sat opposite her and said, "How can I help you?"

"I used to work with Anita Ferguson but hadn't seen her in years. I briefly met her again, about a week before her death."

His eyes sharpened. She had undoubtedly got his interest. "Do you have information about the embezzlement of funds from Mrs Ferguson's employer?"

"No, but I believe Anita was being scammed online in the same way as my late husband." She paused for a moment. "My Dave also took his own life."

"I'm sorry to hear that. But why you are telling me this."

Sue thought it was obvious. "I met Anita at a night class on cybersecurity. The attendees had all been conned."

He shook his head and shrugged his shoulders. "Again, I don't understand what this has got to do with me."

Was he deliberately being obtuse? "Well, it is obviously a clue. To help you catch these people."

"Mrs Wexford, I am sorry for your loss, but I am investigating the theft of a substantial amount of funds by Mrs Ferguson. That is the crime I am investigating. Did Mrs Ferguson willingly transfer money to a third party?"

Sue was flustered. "Well, yes, I assume so, but she thought it was a loan. She said that."

He leaned forward, elbows on the desk and his chin resting on his clasped hands. "But she still took money that wasn't hers and, without being coerced, paid it to someone else."

Chloe stiffened. "My mum was conned. Is there nothing you can do about it?"

He sighed, but Sue couldn't see much regret in his face—more like they were a waste of time to him. "I suggest you get in touch with a cybercrime officer, but to be honest, we don't have the resources to try and carry out this kind of investigation. I am sorry, but there is nothing we can do."

Sue stood, embarrassment mixed with anger. "It is outrageous that people are being victimised in this way and you do nothing. Come on, Chloe."

He walked them to the reception area, and his voice was smooth. "Call in and speak to Cybercrime Liaison." His smile was wide, but his eyes were dismissive. He had apparently already mentally moved on to whatever would be occupying him next. She doubted they'd hear from him again.

Once outside, she rummaged in her bag and pulled out her phone. "I'll see if Tom, the tutor from the class, can help us decide what to do next. One thing is for sure: we can't leave it here."

CHAPTER EIGHT

Marianne glanced around Tom's open-plan apartment. She had given the place a speculative once-over when they arrived. This was a high-tone area—all pastel-painted Georgian townhouses with shutters at the windows and fancy cars parked out front. She had met Sue, Emily and Chloe in the leafy square, and they had descended to Tom's basement flat together.

Tom had opened the door, ushered them in and immediately greeted Chloe. "Hi, I'm Tom. I met your mum in my evening class. I'm sorry to hear the sad news. Anita was a lovely lady."

Chloe's smile was brief. "Thank you for the kind words and also for agreeing to see us tonight. Sue says you're making us dinner. You didn't have to do that."

"It's no hassle. I couldn't meet earlier because I had some work to finish. And we all have to eat. However, I do have to confess I'm not making it, but dinner will be here soon."

Tom indicated the L-shaped sofa in front of a low coffee table, covered with opened bottles of red and white wine, a tray of glasses and some nibbles. "Okay, help yourselves to a drink."

They sat, and Sue said, "Thanks for agreeing to see us.

We're after some advice on what we can do."

Marianne interjected, "You said on the phone the police aren't interested, so I don't see what anyone can do."

Tom said, "The police don't have the manpower to look into every cybercrime they come across, no matter how serious. Crimes of this nature are increasing at an alarming rate. It's likely whoever is behind the scams won't even be in the UK."

Sue's heart was a lead weight pressing against her chest. "So that's it. We simply forget it?"

Tom shook his head. "Not necessarily. Let's have a chat over dinner and run through the exact scenarios."

There was a loud knock on the apartment door, and Tom loped across the room to answer it. From his rigid stance, he wasn't pleased with who had come visiting. "Christ, Adam. What the hell are you doing here?"

"Apparently, I'm helping my housekeeper deliver dinner to you and your friends. Get out of the way, then. Helena has cooked up a storm for you."

A tall man entered the room, followed by a curvy woman in her forties. Each carried a large tray filled with covered dishes. He had wavy fair hair, left slightly longer than the current fashion. His broad shoulders were matched with a slim build. His dark jeans were pristine, as if they had been ironed, and were paired with a classic white shirt, unbuttoned at the neck. His brown loafers and belt were of quality leather. Marianne could smell the money from where she was sitting.

***

Tom stood as his brother laid the tray on the counter. Helena followed suit and said, "Here you go, Tom. Spaghetti Bolognese, salad and fresh garlic bread—just how you like it."

"Thanks. You're a star."

He glanced at his brother's grim face. Adam hadn't changed much in the months since Tom had last seen him. Tom apparently wasn't forgiven yet.

"How are you?" The outstretched hand spoke of formality. If that's how Adam wanted to play it, then so be it. Things had been awkward at their last face-to-face.

He took his brother's hand. "I'm fine."

"Are you?"

"Yes, I am."

There was a heavy silence for a long moment. Adam glanced at the women and then looked back at Tom.

"Sorry. Sue, Marianne, Emily and Chloe, this is Adam, my brother. Adam, I am helping the ladies with some online stuff."

Adam's smile was a brief lift of his lips. He glanced at them. "Ladies, it's a pleasure." His eyes returned to Tom. "Online stuff? Sounds interesting. Anything I should know about?"

Tom wasn't smiling. "Nothing to be concerned about."

"Oh, I stopped being concerned about you a while back. I better leave you to it."

"Do you want to stay for a drink?" He hoped the offer sounded more sincere to the others than it did to him.

"No thanks, regrettably I'm on my way to a dinner meeting." Adam didn't sound sorry in the least.

Right, so his brother wasn't here to hang out. He had

officially moved his residence to Monaco and had been in England infrequently over the last months. What the hell was he doing here now?

***

Marianne watched as Adam and Helena left. She turned to Tom. "You seemed a bit surprised to see your brother."

Tom ran a hand through his hair, leaving him looking ruffled. "Adam is a few years older than me. He was into computers a little bit, but I far exceeded him in coding skills. However, he is an outstanding businessman. He sold his original software company a couple of years ago and grew his new one since then. Adam lives between Monaco and London now. I haven't seen him in almost a year. When we are in London at the same time, which isn't often, we live in different worlds. This is his building, but I've rented this flat from him for years. Mum wouldn't let him kick me out."

"The air seemed a bit frosty."

Tom laughed. "That's an understatement. Adam and I had a falling-out, and a few choice words were said to each other when we last met. Never mind that. Take a seat and help yourself."

They sat around the dining table as Tom passed the serving dishes.

They piled pasta and sauce onto their plates, added the obligatory salad and sipped from large glasses of wine.

Marianne reached out towards the garlic bread, but Sue grabbed her hand and held it, palm down. "Marianne, I haven't seen you wearing that whopper of a ring before. I assume congratulations are in order?"

"Yes. My boyfriend, Adrian, proposed last night."

Tom raised his glass. "Here's to a happy marriage." The air was filled with the clinking of glasses and congratulations that sounded sincere.

"Thank you." She looked at Chloe. "It sounds like the police aren't able to help. What happens now?"

Chloe was toying with her food, twirling spaghetti around the tines of her fork. Her face was pale with heavy shadows under her eyes. She would be extremely attractive under different circumstances. "They called me this afternoon. I've been back to the station to collect Mum's laptop. Apparently, they accessed her Facebook and emails. She was in touch with a man called Tony Anderson. The police concede she was conned, but they said they have no resources to do anything about it."

Sue snorted. "The bastard tricked her, and nothing is going to happen to him?"

"Yeah, Mum helped out, and then he said he needed more. But she'd given him all her savings over the last couple of months. So she took it from work. I know it was wrong, but she would have intended repaying every penny from the promised insurance money. I know it." She sighed and rubbed a hand across her brow. "I need to sell her flat to repay the mortgage. She's also used her overdraft limit and maxed out her credit cards for living expenses. I hope I can get it sorted quickly."

Emily put an arm around Chloe's shoulders. "This isn't right. Someone has stolen money from your mum. And it looks like they will simply get away with it."

"I wish we could do something," Sue said. "Right now they are doing the exact same thing to someone else. My husband, Chloe's mum—these people, they don't care how many lives they ruin."

Sue's words were slightly thickened, and Marianne didn't believe it was from the wine.

Marianne understood where they were coming from, but they were missing an important point. "That's all good and well, but let's not forget it was Anita who stole the money in the first place." She jumped at a loud noise. A startled Chloe's fork had clattered into her bowl. "I'm sorry, love. But we need to face the facts. Yes, your mum was victimised, but she used someone else's money. Two wrongs don't make a right."

Sue jumped to Chloe's defence. "We know what she did, and no, it wasn't right. It doesn't change the fact that Anita was scammed; she grew to trust someone who didn't even exist. The exact same thing happened to my Dave, and I'm bloody raging."

"If you don't mind Sue, what exactly did happen with your husband?" Tom asked. "You said it was similar to what happened to Anita."

Sue quickly summarised what had happened. "And it all came to light after he killed himself. It was the same crap. They lure someone in, make them feel special and create a bond of trust. Perhaps they ask for some money, a little bit to begin with, but then it's more and more. My husband fell in love with this girl. I hope she's ashamed of herself."

Chloe said, "I've looked through Mum's laptop myself. It was the exact same pattern with her. His photo was handsome, his words were beautiful, and he came across like a good guy. He said he was based in Texas. I've read their messages over and over. He said his kid was in the hospital and needed an operation, but he couldn't pay. The earlier requests were for money to buy medicine. This guy, Tony, said he was having trouble with his army insurance. He was a veteran and still had health coverage with the forces. But there was a delay in the paperwork being finalised. Apparently, his son's condition worsened. He needed emergency surgery."

Chloe's elbows were on the table, and her head sank into her hands. She released a deep, shuddering breath. "By that time, Mum must have already given him everything she had. And that's when she borrowed money from her office." She turned to Marianne, a raging fire in her eyes. "And she did mean to pay it back. The day she killed herself, she had an email from her bank. They had refused her request to refinance the flat. She was trying to get enough money to pay back what she took."

Chloe trembled and gulped as her eyes watered with tears. Sue put an arm around her shoulders. She sat still for a moment before sighing, and saying, "I'm okay. Honest."

"And there is no chance the bank could get the money back from the account your mum sent it to?" Emily asked.

Chloe shook her head. "No, it went to a company's account in Switzerland, which apparently has now been closed. I found that out today."

Marianne froze and quickly looked at Sue and Emily. She was sure their startled expressions would match her own.

Sue asked, "What was the name of the company?"

Chloe wrinkled her nose and thought for a moment before saying, "I can't remember. No, wait . . . It was like an animal, well, a bird . . . I know, Magpie Enterprises."

47

Sue was ashen. "You have got to be kidding. That is the name of the company account my late husband paid money to."

Tom leaned back in his chair, hands behind his head as he rocked on the back legs. "Whoa! We have a connection, ladies. It has to be the same people behind this scam. I need to see the computers. We may have an opening."

"Chloe, is this okay by you?" Sue asked. At the young girls' nod, Sue said to Tom, "I'll happily let you have a look at my husband's laptop, but what are you looking for?"

Tom smiled. "Given the millions of scam messages flying around, it is almost impossible to try and find connections, patterns or anything that links to the same scammers being responsible for multiple cyber-attacks. However, if you do have a definite connection," and here he grinned, "like money being transferred into the same bank account, then you have somewhere to start. All you need is a brilliant computer guy," and here he flicked a finger at his chest, "and you have a better chance than most of identifying who these people are. Are we on?"

Marianne considered the others. Sue, Emily and Chloe were nodding, eyes bright with excitement. Marianne poured herself another drink. Bad luck was bad luck. Someone had accessed her online banking and wiped out her account. It was a few thousand, and she could afford to lose it. She'd changed her passwords and stopped saving them in applications. She wasn't some vigilante. What the hell did they think they would achieve by this?

"Earth to Marianne."

She shook her thoughts away and turned to Sue. "Sorry, I was in a dream. What is it?"

"Are you up for this?"

Before she could reply, Tom said, "We could meet back here tomorrow night if you want."

All the replies were positive, and Marianne went along with them. "Yeah, sure. Tomorrow is fine."

CHAPTER NINE

Marianne had been in the office since 7 AM; it was now 1 PM, and all she had done was sort out other people's problems. Some days she thought being the boss was more trouble than it was worth. She had cancelled lunch with Adrian, she couldn't justify two hours at the local bistro when her inbox was overflowing, and the tasks were piling up.

She would have her PA, Sandy, run out and get her something quick to eat. There was a loud click as her office door opened. Adrian came in with a wicker basket from a fancy delicatessen over one arm. She glanced at her groaning to-do-list. There was a tiny flash of panic, but she pushed it aside as she rose, and moved out from behind her desk, arms outstretched.

Adrian put the basket on the low coffee table and, with a huge smile, gave her a hug, his mouth capturing hers in a perfectly passionate kiss. She opened her eyes and caught their reflection in the floor to ceiling window. They looked good together.

His voice was low, his breath a hot whisper on her face as he held her close. "I know you said not to bother you. Believe me; I had to wrestle my way past Sandy, but I managed." He pulled back, held her at arms-length and grinned. His perfect teeth dazzled, pristine white against his yacht-tanned skin. "I ordered a picnic."

She moved out of his arms. "I have a lot on at the moment. Honestly, problems are exploding all around me. I have Compliance and HR on my back. I don't have time to go out to the park."

He laughed and bent to rummage in the basket. Pulling out a soft woollen blanket, he unravelled it with a flourish and laid it on the floor. He said, "We aren't going anywhere." He grabbed her arm and pulled her down beside him, as he unpacked the basket.

"I've got Tuna Nicoise, salmon sandwiches, artichokes and strawberries, plus a nice Macon Lugne to wash it down."

He waggled the bottle of white wine, before opening it and pouring a glass for her.

She raised her hands as she shook her head. "Not for me. I've got work to do, remember."

"How could I forget? Come on, have a little one."

"No. I need a clear head."

He shrugged, grinned and handed her a chilled bottle of sparkling water and a glass before drinking the wine himself. Not for the first time she considered the different worlds they inhabited. Adrian was long-lunches and charity events; she worked. Perhaps she needed to loosen up a bit.

He had unpacked china plates, silver cutlery and proper glassware; she'd grown up with picnics off an old tartan blanket - cheese or ham sandwiches and orange squash - maybe some fruit if they were lucky. But they'd had fun. Why was she thinking like this? Her mind returning to a place and time she had left far behind.

"This is lovely. Thank you." She sipped at the water

and picked at the salad.

"I hope last night was fun, you said you were going to someone's place for supper. Who were they?"

"Just some people I met." She hadn't told him about going to the night classes. Shit, she hadn't even told him she'd been hacked. She had to think quick. "They're from a charity I support. Victims of cybercrime."

"I didn't know you had an interest in that."

"It's the business really. We are a tech-heavy industry; this is giving something back to the wider community." The lie made her pause. Perhaps she should do something like that?

"Well done. It does seem a bit above and beyond the call of duty. I mean, having to meet them socially. What kind of people were they?"

Certainly not his kind. They were far too ordinary for that. His crowd was made up of trust-fund babies and socialites. She considered his evident snobbery. If only he knew precisely how humble her own beginnings were.

She grinned in her brightest smile. "They're not really people we'd usually mix with, but it was a one-off. I doubt I'll see them again."

The words hung in the air as she bit into a delicate sandwich. She was enjoying an impromptu picnic in the office of a business she had built, sitting beside her fiancé, who was an educated, aristocratic and wealthy man. She had neither the time, the desire nor the inclination to get involved in some stupid wild goose chase. It was tough, but both Anita and Sue's late husband were simply scammed by someone who was smarter than them. It was shame how it had ended up. But it wasn't her problem.

They were due to meet at Tom's place that evening. She hadn't said she was going to go but then again nor had she said she wasn't. A little twinge of guilt burrowed deep inside. She ignored it.

***

Tom met Sue at his front door with a smile of welcome and words of regret. "Hi, Emily and Chloe are already here. I'm afraid I had a call from Marianne earlier. She said she couldn't make it and wished you all the best of luck."

Sue wasn't surprised. She shrugged and walked in to greet the others. "Well, good riddance to bad rubbish is all I can say. Madam Marianne strikes me as the kind who is only out for herself, and that's not what we need. Not now."

Emily's soft voice spoke harsh words, "We haven't known each other long at all, but we have a lot in common; either we or people who were close to us were victims of these same violations. She simply dropped us."

Chloe piped up, "Well, Marianne is nothing to me. And this doesn't change why we are here. Tom, what should we do?"

Tom cleared his throat. "Okay, let's get started. Let me see the laptops."

Chloe had put a large laptop on the coffee table in front of her, and Sue placed her husband's next to it.

Tom said, "Pop in the usernames and passwords and open up the emails and Facebook; plus any other messaging sites used."

Chloe quickly typed in the details, which she obviously knew by heart. Sue rummaged in her handbag and pulled out a cheap pair of reading spectacles and a tattered address book. She propped the glasses on the end of her nose and flicked through the address book until she got to the *L* section. She found the login details for Dave's laptop and quickly entered them into the computer. She heard a pained sigh, followed by a muffled curse.

"Tell me you don't have all of your login details and passwords written in your address book," Tom groaned. "The book lying unattended in your handbag; the handbag where you keep your smartphone too?"

"Of course. How else could I remember all these damn passwords and usernames?"

"You sure you even listened during lesson one?"

"Don't be cheeky."

"Sorry, I couldn't resist." His smile dropped. "The hackers need to have some skill to be able to access your computer. Don't make it easy for them. If anyone stole your handbag, they would own every part of your life."

Sue knew he was right, and knew she was more than a little foolish. Tom didn't say anything else. He was too busy concentrating on the laptops. His gaze flicked from one screen to the other, his fingers flying over each keyboard in turn.

He shuffled forward, his gaze intent. Sue was sure he wouldn't have heard any of the women even if they had screamed at him.

The laptop screens were filled with lines of text, random configurations of numbers and letters. Sue asked, "Is something wrong? Are they broken?"

Tom spoke without taking his eyes off the screen. "No, it's fine. I'm getting the IP addresses."

Emily asked, "What's that?"

"It's a unique point showing where the email messages originated from. Some people think it's the computer's address, but it isn't. And that is where it is helpful to hackers."

"But if we can tell whether the message originated from them, we know who sent it. Don't we? Why can't the police do the same?" Sue asked.

Tom slowly shook his head. "Unfortunately, it only points to the area where the physical machine the message was sent from is located. The hackers are able to piggyback off machines and Wi-Fi belonging to other people. IP address can make it look as if the message was sent from a smartphone in Munich when the actual signal had been infiltrated and diverted by a hacker in Bangalore."

Chloe stared at Tom as if he were speaking a different language. Sue rather thought he was. The younger woman said, "No wonder they rarely get caught. It's impossible."

"That's not the half of it. These guys hide their own IP address and process the messages through various different Wi-Fi systems, servers and configurations."

"So we're totally screwed," Emily said.

"Not necessarily. I need to do a little bit more digging, and, ideally, I'd like to have a look at your laptop as well, Emily. I want to check something."

"That's easy. My laptop is in my bag." Emily disappeared under the table, and when her head popped up again, she was brandishing a slimline laptop. She flipped it open and stared at the screen. The computer automatically turned on with a message reading, *Hello Emily.*

Sue glanced at Tom. As expected, he winced, and his words displayed his agitation. "For the love of God, don't ever use facial recognition. And on that topic, why do none of you have your cameras covered up?"

Sue waited for a beat. She knew she was going to irritate him with her question, but she had to ask. "What camera?"

Tom closed his eyes and sank back against the sofa. He took several deep inhalations, followed by slow exhalations. Perhaps it was a meditation technique. When he opened his eyes, he didn't look relaxed at all. "I gave each of you a handout when we first met, and all of this is contained in it. Did anyone read it?"

Sue's laugh was an unladylike snort. "You sound like a grumpy maths teacher. Will you smile if I promise we will all do better?"

"Yeah, I guess that will be okay. Let me get on with this."

He ran the same checks on Emily's computer, and the screen filled with unintelligible digits and numerals. He froze, and for a moment Sue thought he was holding his breath. He turned to the other two laptops and rechecked the screens. He jumped up and crossed to his desk, got some paper and a pen and quickly copied some of the text from each device. Seemingly satisfied, he sat in the swivel chair in front of two full-size monitors, tapping at the keyboard as his eyes raced across the screens. More clicking of keys.

He sat up straight and said, "Holy shit."

"What is it?" Sue asked.

"Bulgaria. All the devices, all the IP addresses relating

to the messages on each of these three computers, the scamming message—they all came from Bulgarian IP addresses."

"What does that mean?" Emily asked.

Tom smiled. "It's too coincidental. If these were all different scammers, different hackers, they would be using IP addresses in many different countries simply because they would be in different locations themselves. But that hasn't happened here. We could be looking at a massive hacking ring, and their base is in Bulgaria, even more specifically in the capital city of Sofia."

Sue said, "What now?"

"We have to dig a little deeper and find the administrator name. Then we have to try and identify them as a person, perhaps by trawling social media. I don't hold out much hope of success, but we have to try."

It was all sounding a bit like hard work to Sue. "So the administrator is a person. What then?"

"I have a contact who usually knows what is going on in this world. He hears the rumours and knows the players. We used to . . . Well, let's say we once had some interests in common. He would be in the know if anything big was going on."

"Well, that's good, isn't it? You can give him a call and see what he knows."

"It's not that simple. He won't say anything on the phone or via a computer. He would only talk in person, and he's a bit reclusive. I can try and meet up with him, but I can't guarantee he'll agree to that. After that, we would need to be on the ground in Bulgaria—and know who to talk to—to get any more info. These people are notoriously secretive."

Sue said, "And then what do we do?"

"Have you considered what you are trying to achieve here? If it's to find out exactly how the scammers got access, then we can try and do something, but if it's to collect sufficient evidence for the police to try and press charges, then I don't know if that is likely."

Sue looked at Emily and Chloe.

Chloe shook her head. "I didn't think too far ahead. All I know is that I want these people punished."

Emily said, "I just want my money back."

Sue covered her face with her hands. "I don't know what I want. I thought I wanted answers, but if I am honest, the only person who can give me those is dead."

Chloe slumped forward, her eyes bleak. Sue shared her fear. The scammers would get away with it again.

CHAPTER TEN

Marianne was working late. Her latest fund had launched six months previously and had been massively oversubscribed. Those investors would be ripe to invest in anything new she floated. However, she didn't have a strategy in place for a new fund, and she wouldn't put her name to something she didn't believe was a substantial opportunity.

She stretched her arms above her head and yawned as the tight, knotted muscles in her shoulders groaned. She was spending too much time in this office. She glanced at the clock on her desk. It was gone 9:00 p.m., and she fleetingly thought of Sue and the others. She brushed the thought aside, how they got on was none of her business.

She was about to switch off the computer when an email came in. The subject line caught her eye.

Read me, MJ. You will be sorry if you don't.

The sender's name was MJS, which were her own initials. Was this a joke email from one of Adrian's friends, or perhaps even her fiancé himself? His crowd loved some banter and practical jokes. She double-clicked on the email and opened it up. She read it once, shook her head as the words wouldn't process and reread them. She stared at the screen, her mind a chaotic mess, then said, loud and clear, "Fuck".

Attention of MJ Sinclair,

Thank you for the recent withdrawal we took from your bank account. You should know better than to open attachments from unknown sources.

You will receive instructions over the next few days. Your firm will be promoting a new bitcoin fund to its investor base. We will supply you with all the details, we will issue all communications and, for our efforts, collect all subscriptions. All you have to do is keep quiet. We will deal with any investor queries.

We'll disappear after closing, and you'll never hear from us again. Promise.

Stay tuned. We'll be in touch.

She grabbed her handbag, shoved her laptop into it and ran out the door.

***

Marianne rang the bell again. What the hell was keeping him? She tapped her feet, rang again—only this time she kept her finger on the buzzer. She could hear movement inside the flat followed by a terse, "Hold on. I'm coming."

The door was quickly pulled open, and the look on Tom's face changed from disgruntlement to surprise. "Ah, Marianne, better late than never."

"Are the others still here?"

"Yeah."

The three women sat around a low coffee table littered with laptops, empty coffee cups and bowls of crisps. All three seemed taken aback, but Sue recovered first. "Well, well, well, we thought you'd done a runner."

"Look, I'm sorry I couldn't make it. But I have other

matters that need my attention."

Emily asked, "Why are you here, then?" Her gaze was direct and her voice more than a little snippy.

Marianne was immediately on the defence. "I need to speak to Tom."

Chloe said, "And we need to let you know what's happened. There may be a connection between the scams." Her eyes sought Tom's. "You tell her."

"All the IP addresses lead back to Bulgaria, which makes me believe the scammers are physically present there. I have a contact who will know people in Sofia, but I would need to talk to him in person."

Sue said, "Tom rightfully pointed out that we need to know what we're trying to achieve, and I don't think any of us do. Looks like we'd be biting off a bit more than we could chew."

Marianne didn't have the luxury of time to be interested in their futile endeavours. "Well, probably all for the best." She looked at Tom. "I need to talk to you." She glanced at the other women. "In private, if you don't mind." She knew she was rude, but her heart thundered an erratic beat, and her head pounded.

Tom stared at her, then shook his head, as if brushing away her words. "You're a total piece of work, Marianne. You don't bother turning up with everyone else tonight, you couldn't care less about what we've discovered, and all you are apparently interested in is whatever is bothering you. If you have anything to say to me, then you have to do it in front of these ladies."

Marianne conceded she had asked for that. They all stared at her. She sighed, "Oh, very well. Here, look."

She opened up her laptop and pulled the email onto the screen. The women crowded around Tom as Marianne turned the laptop to face them. All four faces registered shock as the words made sense.

"What the hell is this all about?" Sue asked.

Marianne replied, "It's fairly obvious. I am being scammed again, or rather I am being used to con what could amount to millions from my investors."

"That is fabulous," Chloe said excitedly. "Well, I mean the police will have to act now, won't they? They can't ignore something this big."

Emily joined in, "That's an excellent point. The police won't simply ignore the warning that hundreds, perhaps thousands of investors could effectively have money stolen."

Marianne grimaced. "I was hoping Tom might have a better solution. I'd prefer not to go to the police. I'll be ruined if it gets out that someone has control of my systems." Not to mention the reaction of her backers who had loaned her the money to set up in the first place. They wouldn't be happy if she had a tarnished security reputation.

Sue said, "You don't think the breaking news that your investors had lost their money, your computer system had been hacked and communications from you falsified would ruin your business? Your investors would pull their money, and no one would touch your funds."

"Of course I know that. And that's why I have to stop these criminals." She turned to Tom and realised all her hopes were packaged in a youthful computer geek. "You have to help me, please."

Tom sighed, took her laptop and settled himself on the sofa, calling over his shoulder, "Can someone get me a black coffee?"

Chloe went to do Tom's bidding.

Sue stood next to Marianne. "Tom can help us all. I'm glad you are in this with us now."

"Well, I don't know about that. What happened to Anita and your late husband is in the past. Finding these guys isn't going to change anything for you. Whereas if I can stop them, I'll save all the investors."

Sue retorted, "What you want to save is your business."

"Of course I do. I don't want to see all I have worked for destroyed and broken because of some selfish scammer."

"But you're the selfish one." Sue grabbed Marianne's arm.

She didn't flinch, even when Sue's nails dug into the soft flesh of her forearm.

Sue continued, "Listen to me. You met Anita, you had drinks with her, and we were all starting to get to know each other. Have you got it into your thick head that she killed herself, took her own bloody life, because of some lowlife bastards who spend their lives lying to people and conning them? I'm determined to find out who is responsible and get enough evidence to make sure the police take action."

Marianne brushed her hand away. "Don't ever touch me again, or I'll knock you flat." She knew her accent had roughened with her temper, the Scots burr rolling her *r*'s, but hopefully, no one had noticed. She took a breath and modulated her diction. "What the hell is it to you? By your own admission, you hadn't seen or spoken to Anita in years. You barely knew the woman. None of us did."

She heard a shocked gasp and turned to see Chloe, eyes wide and mouth hanging open. Ah, that hadn't sounded right. "I'm sorry, Chloe. I know it's your mum, but I've nothing extra to give at the moment."

Tom's voice snapped them to attention. "I will only help you if I help them, Marianne. We need to investigate in more detail, and you need to go to the police. But it will be a small price for you to pay, don't you think?"

She knew when she was defeated. "Shit. You're right. I'll go to the police in the morning. I'll need to call a meeting at work and debrief the Chief Risk Officer and the head of Legal. See if you can find out anything about the email I received—"

Tom's voice broke across her, as he stared at the screen, "I don't believe it. It's the same IP addresses, the exact same. Unless Bulgaria has suddenly become a hotbed for individual hackers, then we are looking at one organised crime group who are hitting the UK big-time."

CHAPTER ELEVEN

Tom made them coffee, and Marianne sipped at hers, luxuriating in the aroma of expensive burnt beans. She was delaying the moment when she'd have to go home and be alone with her worries throughout what would undoubtedly be a sleepless night. She appraised Tom as he chatted to the others; his T-shirt was baggy and his jeans frayed. He had some designer stubble going on and seemed to be enjoying his older brother's largess. This coffee had to be seriously pricey.

A ringing noise interrupted the subdued chat. It was her personal mobile, and only a handful of people knew the number. The caller ID was blocked. She quickly answered; her senses on red alert.

"Hello?"

"Good evening MJ." The voice didn't sound human; it was tinny and robotic, like some kind of device was being used to disguise the caller. "I need you to listen carefully and not say anything unless I ask you to. Do you understand me?"

"Yes." Her heart thundered, and she could barely believe this was happening. She hadn't expected to hear from them so soon. But now she was talking directly to one of the scammers. She waved her hand in the air to get the others' attention and held an upright finger against her lips. They were still and quiet. She pressed the speakerphone button but still held the phone to her ear. She would speak directly into the microphone and hope they'd not realise the others were listening.

"We have created the Alpha Bitcoin Capital Protected Fund. A series of emails will be coming from your email account offering investors an opportunity to be part of the initial offering. The replies will be rerouted to our people. You don't need to do anything. Keep quiet and let us do what we need to."

"Don't be ridiculous. I can't do that. I won't. I'll go to the police. You won't get away with this." She hoped he couldn't hear the tremor in her voice. In her mind, she saw everything she had worked for disappearing into a black hole. Adrian would leave her. He'd never stand for his name being associated with the scandal. And what a scandal it would be. The FCA would get involved, and she didn't need the regulator looking too closely at some of her earlier deals. She'd grazed the wind on a few transactions, and her actions wouldn't bear too close a scrutiny. Shit, the press would be all over it. And her—they'd look into her past; no matter how well-buried she thought it was. But she had no choice. They couldn't get away with this.

The voice, still distorted, broke across her thoughts. "I thought you might say something like that, but you don't have a choice. I've sent you a video. Take your time looking at it. I'll be in touch."

The line went dead, and she stared at the mobile for a moment before placing it on the desk. Her hand was shaking as she crossed to where Tom sat with her laptop.

He pointed towards the screen, at an email that flashed

into her inbox, once again from "MJS."

"I guess I better open it." She was cold, and her palms were clammy as she tapped the screen. She opened the attachment without thinking. That's probably how the sneaking worm had got into her system in the first place; through an innocuous attachment. The video started playing as soon as the file opened.

She heard movement behind her, followed by Sue's quiet voice in her ear. "Take it easy. We're with you."

It took a moment for her mind to compute what she was seeing, so out of context was the image. Two pretty teenage girls lingered outside a high-street coffee shop, their hands filled with bulging bags that bore the logos of the trendiest stores for their age group. It took a moment for Marianne to appreciate what, and who, she was looking at. Her heart started to hammer in her chest. She took several deep breaths to calm herself. It didn't work.

They were talking to a youth who had his back turned to the camera. She could tell he was young by his slender build and dress, even the louche way he stood. His voice came through loud and clear.

"Thanks for the directions." He was talking to them both, but his body faced the taller of the two girls. She was also the prettiest, but then Marianne was biased. He made to walk away, stopped and spoke. "Look, I know this is a bit cheeky, but I'm only here for a few days. Do you fancy meeting up for a drink?"

She smiled, and it splintered Marianne's heart. "Yeah, sure. That would be cool. But both of us right?" She glanced at her friend, who already had a protective look on her face. Thank God.

He held up his hands, palms facing out in mock surrender. "That's fine. I only want some friendly company. I saw a bar earlier. The Feathered Goose, I think. You know it?"

The pretty smile was serene. "I've been a few times before. We could meet you there at seven. Okay?"

"It's a date. Well, kind of. See you both later." And with that he walked away, stopping to cross the road and looking back over his shoulder with a wave. He was a handsome devil, which made her stomach drop even farther. Her telephone rang.

The tinny voice mocked, "You should be careful with your emails. Maybe delete those you no longer need. Otherwise, someone looking for dirt is going to find a bucketful." Thank God she hadn't put it on speaker this time. The metallic voice was direct. "Did you see enough?"

"Yes. What the hell is going on? You better not touch her."

The caller laughed. "Oh, he'll do more than touch her given half a chance. Whether he has that chance is up to you. Are you going to play like a good girl or not?"

She wanted to curse, to scream—she wanted the prick to be man enough to stand in front of her—she'd give him what for. But all she could do was keep the rage at a simmer and ask, "What do you want me to do?"

"Nothing at all. Keep quiet and don't get in our way. I'll be in touch. And keep away from the police." The line went dead.

She was staring at her screen when the email with the video attachment disappeared.

Tom was at the keyboard in a second. "The email's

been deleted. The bastards are in your system right now." He quickly checked the trash. "They've emptied it already. Even if you wanted to go to the police, there is nothing to show them."

Her thoughts were tumbling over each other. How did they know? No one knew . . . Well, hardly anyone. And none of them was going to talk.

Her stomach somersaulted as nausea rose, and her heart beat faster. She'd hired a private investigator a few years back to see how the family was. She had never deleted their report. She'd ignore it for months on end before, driven by something indefinable, she'd torture herself by reading the PI's summary of his investigation. His words, her family. The hackers must have found it. The violation ripped at her insides.

She picked up her mobile and searched for a number. One she had never called before but had gained courtesy of the PI, and saved it in her contacts list. She called over her shoulder as she walked to the front door. "I need to make a call. I'll be back soon."

CHAPTER TWELVE

S he perched on the small, wooden summer seat outside Tom's front door. She was surrounded by wooden tubs filled with colourful geraniums, clumps of daisies and what she thought might be night scented stock. She gently rocked back and forth in time with the ringtone. Her heart pounded. It rang and rang until a breathless woman answered. "Hello? Jenny Galbraith speaking."

The voice hadn't changed in all these years, still sweet and calm.

"Hi, Jenny."

She heard the sharp huff followed by an eloquent silence that spoke volumes.

"It's me."

"Yes, I know. What do you want?"

The tone was wary, but what could she have expected? They'd made a pact, and Marianne was breaking it.

What to say? What to say? "How are you? Is Amelia okay?"

"My daughter is fine, Mhairi. I'll ask again. What is this about?"

"My name is Marianne now." She paused, torn. "Look, is she away from home at the moment? I mean, keep her safe."

"Where the hell do you get off?" Jenny hissed. "We agreed never to contact each other, which damn well suited you seventeen years ago. Stop this pretend concern and keep away from us."

The call disconnected. For the second time in as many minutes, someone had hung up on Marianne, and she didn't know which one bothered her the most.

***

The others were huddled together, talking in hushed tones when she walked in. Sue took one look at her face and said, "What the hell is going on? Who was the girl in the video?"

"Amelia is my sister's daughter."

"The bastards." Chloe's expletive was spat out and apt.

Emily asked, "Did you call your niece? Is she okay?"

Marianne paused for a moment. She could hardly explain that she had never spoken to Amelia and no doubt never would. "I spoke to my sister. Amelia is okay." At least she assumed she would be, for now.

"Are you okay, honey?" Sue's eyes were compassion-filled and touched a part of Marianne she had long thought frozen.

"I'm okay, I guess. Thank you."

Tom said, "There is another issue. You saw that they were in your system and deleted the video and the earlier email they sent. That means there is nothing for the police to go on. You did change all your passwords, didn't you?"

She counted to three. "Of course I did. What do you take me for?" *Actually,* she thought, *he probably thinks I'm an idiot.*

71

"If you changed your passwords, then they have compromised your entire system. Any you change in future, or security you engage will be visible to them. Be diligent how you use that system in the future. Make no mention of anything to do with any of us or what we've been doing. And don't use your applications for anything private you don't want them to know about."

"What the hell do I do? I need my system."

"You look like you've got enough money; go and buy a new laptop. I'll set you up with a different email address. Get a new phone while you're at it and use a pay-as-you-go card."

Sue said, "I'm maybe slow here, but what exactly are they going to do?"

"They're using my business name and my reputation to launch a fake bitcoin fund."

Sue grimaced. "That sounds dodgy. Isn't that some kind of new funny money? Why would people want to invest in that?"

"Yes, it is. Bitcoin, Ethereum, and a host of others are currencies that operate outside the traditional banking system and financial markets. There are no physical coins, no bank that you can walk into; the transactions and balances are self-regulated by the investors themselves."

"Okay, I get it . . . I think. People will believe they've made a legitimate investment, but there is no fund, and the money gets diverted to the bad guys."

"Exactly. The fund doesn't exist. It's purely fraudulent paperwork. Communications originate from my firm, and we are a professional, regulated organisation. The customers trust us, and they'll be desperate to get involved.

Prices in bitcoins are volatile, but there is money to be made there. Many people prefer the comfort of investing into a fund managed by professionals instead of buying bitcoins themselves. They trust us, they trust me."

Her heart pounded. All she had worked for was going to come crashing down. But she had to protect Amelia.

CHAPTER THIRTEEN

Tom slept poorly and woke up late. His furry tongue and thick head were a testament to the amount of red wine he had sunk. He'd ditched the coffee and shared a good few bottles of wine with the girls. He showered, dressed in his usual jeans and T-shirt and was heading to a job when a sharp knock preceded the opening of the interior door that connected his apartment to the main house. Adam stood there.

"Can we have a word?" Adam walked in and closed the door behind him.

Tom shrugged. "Well, I suppose so as you're in already. What is it? I don't have much time."

"I won't be long." Adam raked his hair up, and Tom recognised the gesture as one of his own. Adam was nervous. "Look, I've spoken to Mum."

"How are they?"

"They're fine. Enjoying the Tuscan weather and the renovations to the new villa are apparently going well. Once Mum knew I was in the UK, she was badgering me to speak to you, said it's time we cleared the air. And I guess she is right."

Tom sneered and mimicked a childish voice, "And you always do what Mummy tells you to?"

"Don't be a dick. I'm serious. We have barely

exchanged more than a dozen words in almost a year. Last Christmas was a nightmare for Mum and Dad."

"This place was packed with your bloody hangers-on, Mr Moneybags, us not talking to each other would hardly have been commented on."

"It was noticed by Mum. I have forgiven you for what you did. No harm was done to the business. But we need to get back on an even keel as brothers. We're family."

Tom knew Adam was talking sense. He also knew that Adam had had no option but to fire him; he had brought it all on himself. "Yeah, well, we said a few harsh words to each other, and that can't be easily forgotten."

"Perhaps not, but we have to start somewhere. I'm having a party tonight. I'd like you to be there."

"All you do is party. How can you be bothered? Most of the people you spend time with are barely acquaintances."

"It's how the people I mix with socialise and do business, and I enjoy it. You prefer chatting online with a takeaway and a six-pack. I doubt you've even met most of these guys in the flesh. As they say, each to their own." His brother's voice was an offended snap.

Mixing with Adam's top-drawer, moneyed friends wasn't high on Tom's list of how to spend an evening, but he realised his brother was making an effort, and the least he could do was expend the same amount of energy.

"Okay, what time?"

"Nine o'clock onwards. It'll be a late one as some guests are coming after other dinner commitments. I organised the whole thing last minute. Bring your friends."

"What friends?"

"Marianne and Sue, wasn't it, and the other two ladies."

"I don't think they'd be up for that." Why the hell would they? A dreary night of chitchat and small talk.

"Ask them anyway. I'd like you to be comfortable. I don't want you sulking in a corner on your own."

"Okay, fine."

They'd say no, he'd have done his bit by asking and would show his face at the swanky party for an hour max. Job done.

***

First thing in the morning Marianne picked up a new phone and laptop, upgraded versions of what she already had, and worked in her office for the rest of the afternoon. Her stomach was churning, and she didn't know which way to turn. She worked on a few deals she was heavily involved in, spinning plates and moving pieces on the corporate chessboard until her schedule was cleared for the next few days. She could take some time off; if she wanted to, that was.

She stared through the glass wall that separated her office from the main floor where her research analysts sat cheek by jowl with traders and market specialists. She had built a good team. But they wouldn't hang around long once the fraudulent fund was being investigated. It wouldn't matter that she, and her firm, had been the victim of a crime and had been unwittingly used to defraud the investors. They'd leave, and since her business was built on selling people's skills in the relevant markets, her company would fold with them. Oh, and what if the FCA scrutinised her past business practices? She'd never done anything illegal, but in the early days the sales team had sailed close to the wind and bigged up past performances.

She gagged as bile rose and a sour taste coated her tongue. She had to sort this out. She sent an email to her head of HR and her most senior colleague, one of her co-directors. She was taking some time off, would work from home if needed, but she had to see this through with these maniacs.

There was no point in trying to call Jenny again. She had to assume that Amelia would be safe while she played the game. A game she had to win—whatever winning meant.

Her new mobile rang. She had only texted the number to Tom and the girls so far. The caller ID announced it was Tom.

"Hey, did you get your work finished?" she said by way of greeting.

"Yeah, a small online business boasts greater security than it's ever had in the past."

"Good. Are you up for having a look at my situation tomorrow?"

"Yeah. Sorry I was tied up today. I can't guarantee I'll find anything, but there may be something that will mean the police could act quickly."

She knew she had no choice. She had to involve the police. No matter the threats.

"I'll catch up with you tomorrow."

"Wait! Look, you don't have to say yes to this. I mean, you won't want to go. I didn't think the others would, but they said yes. Anyway, no obligation—"

"Spit it out, Tom. I don't have all day."

77

"Oh, sorry. My brother is having some fancy party tonight and asked if we would all like to go, but I am sure you won't."

She laughed. "You're doing your best to give me a way out of it, but I'm afraid I can't come anyway. I have to meet my fiancé and his parents for the theatre and dinner. Otherwise, I would have loved to come. I could do with something different to take my mind off what is happening."

"Really? I certainly don't want to go, but I have to now. I was only going to show my face, but I'll have to hang around if the girls are there."

"Enjoy. I'll speak to you tomorrow when I bring my new laptop around, or earlier if I hear anything."

She went into her private bathroom and checked her appearance. She wore a plain black sheath dress and no jewellery. It had been perfect for the office. She rummaged in the wooden drawers to the side of the wash basin and pulled out fresh underwear, tights and a big, in-your-face costume jewellery necklace. She had some high-heeled black-and-silver sandals hidden somewhere in one of the filing cabinets, and that would have to do. She had to meet Adrian at the theatre. She had no idea how she would be able to concentrate. *Les Misérables* was precisely how she bloody felt.

***

Sue straightened her skirt and fluffed her curls. The front door had mirrored side panels, and she couldn't avoid her reflection. She twisted and turned and saw that the back of her hair was slightly out of control, and she self-consciously ran a smoothing hand over it. Her chin was getting a twin, and, in the neon overhead light, she didn't recognise herself. There were only odd glimpses of the girl she had once been. But that had undoubtedly been the case for some time. Was that why Dave had turned from her? She'd once been thin and pretty. She blocked the images and tucked hot shame away into the "do not open" box.

She flicked on the positive switch. She didn't have a bad figure, and it was shown to its best with a scoop-neck red floral maxi dress. Her curls were bohemian rather than bird's nest, and she was wearing more makeup than usual. She'd have to do.

She had barely rung the doorbell when it was opened by a young man in black trousers and shirt, a black apron around his waist.

"Hi, I'm Sue. I'm invited to the party. I'm a friend of Tom's."

He smiled and pressed something on the iPad he carried. "Welcome, Mrs Wexford. Please get some refreshment and go on through. Have a good evening."

He gestured towards two open doors, to the side of which was a long table covered in champagne and wine glasses and presided over by a pretty waitress. Sue accepted a glass of champagne and walked into a scene out of the society pages.

Handsome, sun-burnished men in posh-boy uniforms of coloured trousers, open-necked shirts and blazers were the norm, albeit they were interspersed with sharp suits and even jeans from those too precious to give a damn. The women . . . Well, if Sue hadn't been swamped by insecurity before, she certainly was now. Whip-thin, chic blondes and glossy brunettes were draped in shimmery, summery numbers. A stunning woman, with dark skin, dangerous curves and artful curls sashayed past. She simply didn't compare to these people. She couldn't see Tom, Emily or Chloe. She didn't belong here. Palms sweating and heart pounding, she turned to leave and bumped into a man who had apparently just arrived.

"Whoa, you're in a hurry. Is the party that bad?" The man was tall and well built, with a square-jawed, handsome face. His dark hair was flecked with silver at the temples, and Sue figured he must be in his fifties. A well-preserved, I-have-a-personal-trainer fifties.

Her face burned. "Oh no, not at all. I really should go."

His smile was kind. "Bit of stage fright, perhaps? Tell you what, I don't know anyone here much at all. Will you keep me company for a moment?"

He had a charming accent. Russian, perhaps? What harm would it do? "Yes, that would be nice."

"Good. Let me introduce myself. I'm Karl Radinsky. What do I call you?"

"Sue. My name is Sue Wexford."

"It is my pleasure to meet you, Sue." He raised his champagne flute and gently touched it against hers. "How do you know Adam Capelli?"

"I don't—not really. I know his brother, Tom."

"His brother? I didn't know he had one."

Sue asked, "Are you a friend of Adam's?"

"Yes, I am. Adam has been a good friend to me."

A deep voice returned the compliment. "No more than you have been to me, Karl."

Adam joined them with a smile. He was followed by Tom, who immediately greeted Sue. "Glad you could make it. Emily called to say she wouldn't be coming, but I'm still expecting Chloe."

Karl moved closer to Sue as a few guests squeezed past. "So what keeps you busy?"

"Oh, nothing much," she replied. "I do some volunteer charity work, and I paint."

Tom said, "I never knew you painted."

"You never asked."

Karl laughed. "Well, now we know. What do you paint?"

"I prefer abstracts, but painting children and dogs pays the bills. Well, some of them at least."

"Not cats?"

"They'd never stay still long enough." They laughed, and Sue thought she may actually enjoy the evening.

***

The lights dimmed, and the darkness cocooned Marianne in her own suffocating bubble. Her thoughts tortured her throughout the entire performance. She wasn't in the mood for more socialising, but she had no way of getting out of the night's full entertainment programme. Adrian had organised for his parents to join them at the charity performance of *Les Miserables*. It was followed by supper, which was how she found herself sitting opposite her future mother-in-law in Scott's.

No matter how much Adrian professed his mother's pleasure at their engagement, Marianne wasn't sure he was reading it right. Instead of the four of them for dinner, as she had expected, there was a fifth at the table. Lily Anstruther-Gough was twenty-eight, a former *Country Life* cover girl and an excellent horsewoman . . . and Adrian's ex-girlfriend.

His mother had been contrite. "I knew you wouldn't mind, darling. Poor Lily was let down at the last minute. We couldn't let her dine alone."

Let down, my ass, thought Marianne. This was a setup if ever she saw one. She had enough on her plate without battling Adrian's mother and fighting off the ex. So she merely smiled as she sipped her wine.

Lily said, "Congratulations on your engagement. Your family must be thrilled."

Why? Do I look like I'm totally marrying outside my class and comfort zone? She took another slug of her wine before replying. She'd be sozzled at this rate. "I don't have any family. They are all gone, unfortunately."

"Oh, I couldn't live without Muffy—that's my elder sister. We're terribly close. Don't you have any siblings?"

"No, like I said, no family." In some ways, that was the truth. She had been alone for almost two decades.

"I hear you're extremely successful and make lots of dosh. Well done you." Lily's voice was a loud whisper, and her gaze sly and conspiratorial.

Marianne shifted in her seat. "My business does okay. I can't complain." She paused for a moment, considered her words and went in anyway. "I'd imagine you were pretty comfortable. Your family are well-off, I believe."

Lily's laughter tinkled, there was no other word for it, and it grated on Marianne's nerves.

"Ah, we're asset rich and cash poor. That's the trouble

with us old money, I'm afraid."

Marianne guessed that meant she must be new-money, cash-rich trash. There wasn't much she could say to that. The conversation turned to other subjects, and Marianne smiled prettily and drank her wine. The meaningless discussion flowed around her, and she merely observed. Adrian was laughing, his teeth straight and white, perfect skin and carefully styled hair. He smiled across the table at her, his eyes held her gaze, and he blew her a kiss. He was handsome, successful, wealthy and connected.

He was everything she had ever wanted. She couldn't mess this up.

***

Sue laughed as Karl snagged them more champagne from a passing waiter. He gave one to her and passed the other to Chloe, who had arrived moments before.

The fizzing bubbles tickled Sue's nose as she sipped. "Oh, my nose is itchy. It's late," she said to Chloe. "Were you somewhere beforehand?"

"I had dinner with my dad. We try and catch up every few weeks. I thought I'd pop in and show my face as I had to pass near here anyway. I'm going to head home after this drink."

"It is nice to meet you, Chloe," Karl said. "You are also a friend of Tom's?"

"Yes, he's helping us with some computer stuff."

"And what would that be?"

Sue answered, "Tom is showing us proper security and things like that."

He smiled. "You can't be too careful these days."

Chloe asked, "Where is Tom?"

Sue replied, "He headed off with Adam to talk to some people he knew."

"Okay, I'll try and say hello before I leave."

A familiar voice came from behind them. "Thinking of leaving already? I'm glad I caught you, then."

Sue turned in surprise. "Marianne. Good to see you. I thought you weren't coming."

"The dinner I was at finished earlier than I thought."

CHAPTER FOURTEEN

"Tom, you remember Ryan, don't you?"

Tom froze before slowly turning to face his old friend, who was leaning against the outdoor bar. "Of course. How are you, Ryan? You look well." He meant it. He hadn't seen Ryan Williams in almost a year. His skinny frame had filled out a little, and his once-greasy hair had been chopped and styled. He had apparently learned the benefits of shampoo. He might still be wearing jeans, but they were expensive ones and paired with a designer T-shirt. More importantly to Tom, however, was what the hell his old school buddy was doing at a high-society party. And how did Adam even know him? He'd been at boarding school with Ryan and was sure his brother had never met him then, or after when he and Ryan been online buddies, midnight prowlers across the dark web.

Adam clasped a hand on each of their shoulders. "I'll leave you two guys to it. There are some people I should say hello to."

They stared at each other, and the silence between them pounded in Tom's head. Ryan pulled him into a bear hug. Tom stiffened. This wasn't the welcome he had expected. He relaxed and hugged him back. They parted with a manly pat on each other's back. The apology was filling Tom's headspace, the words clogging his throat. He had to speak. "I'm sorry, man. Sorry for disappearing offline like that and not contacting you or the other guys. I got my head down and my shit together."

"Forget it, all water under the bridge now."

"I'm surprised to see you here? How did you get to know Adam?"

"I knew he was your brother and got in touch to see what was going on. He said you'd gone travelling."

"Yeah, I bummed around Europe for a few months before coming home. Why are you here? I'm a bit confused."

"We got talking, and Adam offered me a job. I work in Cytech's operations department on the finance side. Actually, I run that area now. I've given up coding; it wasn't for me, and I was definitely on the wrong side of the law."

"I'm surprised I haven't seen you around. I mean, I live in Adam's basement."

"Adam mentioned in passing that you came back months ago. I've only been to the house a couple of times. I'm based at the Cytech offices in the City. I didn't like to make contact since you'd made it clear you wanted to be left alone."

"I needed some head space. Sounds like you got yourself together. Looks like life is going well for you."

"Yeah, it is. You won't believe it, but I bought Ardale."

Tom did a double take. "You bought our old school?"

"The college moved to larger premises a year or two after we left. The original place was empty for a long time, and I picked it up for a decent price. I've been doing it up a bit at a time. It'll take a while though."

The elegant Victorian manor was surrounded by agricultural land, bordered by its own woods and miles from civilisation. A fact they had bemoaned as bored teenagers. "What the hell are you going to do with the place?"

"I thought I could turn it into a spa retreat. You know, walks in the woods, yoga on the lawn. Townies with high-pressure jobs, busy lifestyles and the disposable income to buy relaxation and mindfulness. That's today's trend."

Tom didn't like to dwell on how much better his friend was doing than him. And he was completely legit.

"Adam must be paying you well, and he's invited you to his fancy party. You've landed on your feet."

Ryan laughed. "Apparently, some potential investor is going to be here, and Adam wants to make sure someone can talk the money. That'll be me."

Tom faced his inadequacy head-on. "For the longest time, I didn't think I'd have the strength to keep away from the dark side of computing. Yet you managed it with ease."

"The opportunity of a job with your brother wasn't going to come up twice. I jumped at it."

***

Adrian's mother and the simpering ex-girlfriend had royally pissed off Marianne, to the extent that she had declared, as soon as the meal was over, that she had to leave as she had a busy day ahead.

Adrian had, of course, offered to drive her home. She'd have been fuming if he had stayed. She'd pleaded a headache as they neared her place and suggested it would be better if he didn't stay the night. She was out of sorts and needed to collect her thoughts. He was charming and understanding, but hadn't seemed that disappointed, or was that her imagination? She'd roamed her flat for half an hour, unable to settle. She'd been on edge, and sleep was a long way off. She'd called a cab and headed to Mayfair.

She looked at the man standing next to Sue. "Hi, I'm Marianne."

"Pleased to meet you. I am Karl Radinsky. Sue has been kind enough to keep me company."

Sue was quick to comment. "It's Karl who has been keeping me company, and I am extremely grateful."

Marianne sipped her champagne. Bit of a mutual appreciation society going on there. Sue was a little flushed, perhaps from the alcohol or the heat of the crowded room, but Marianne would bet it was the handsome Karl that was firing her up.

Karl stared across the room. "I am sorry, please forgive me. There is someone I must say hello to. I will be back."

As he walked away, Sue's eyes tracked him across the room. Marianne couldn't resist her smirk. "He's a bit of all right. You're in there."

Sue blushed as crimson as her dress. "I don't know what you're talking about. Really, I don't."

"Yeah, sure."

Chloe said, "Well, Karl is talking to a pretty gorgeous couple. A fancy blonde in a slutty dress and her guy looks like a male model—the craggy, millionaire version."

Marianne smiled as she followed Chloe's gaze. "Ah, I see her. The dress is slutty but sexy as hell. I might wear it myself. Right, let's get another drink—" The man Karl was talking to turned around and placed his empty champagne glass on a nearby table. His face was clear, unmistakable, and her voice trailed off. Her mind stuttered, images breaking into a million pieces and coming back together to form a fractured picture that couldn't be true. It couldn't be him. Her mind went blank, her heart hammered, and everything turned dark as she slowly slid to the ground.

***

Marianne could hear a noise. It was an old-fashioned clock—*tick-tock, tick-tock*. She was warm and comfortable, relaxed and . . . Where the hell was she? Her eyes flew open. She was in a chic bedroom, lying on a large bed. She quickly checked under the sheet that covered her. Thank God for that.

"As you can see, I didn't undress you, if that's what you're thinking."

For a moment, she thought she had imagined it, that she had been mistaken and the recent stress and champagne had gone to her head, causing hallucinations. But the voice removed any doubt. It was deeper, more gravelled, but it was unmistakably his. She pushed up and into a seated position. She somehow found the words and forced them through a dry throat, "Well, Jamie MacLean, this is a surprise. What the hell are you doing here?"

"It's James Foster now. I had a little incident a while back, and a new name was the best option. I could ask the same of you. What are you doing here, Mhairi?"

"It's Marianne now."

"Oh, is it indeed, Marianne? How posh. Why did you

change your name? Maybe more to the point, why did you fucking disappear almost eighteen years ago?"

"I can't have this discussion."

A tic was working away at the side of his mouth, and his eyes were shadowed. He bent forward, his shirt straining across his muscled chest. Had he learnt how to manage his anger? She needed to get away. She instinctively moved to the bottom of the bed, farther away from him. His voice had risen.

"Well, I would bloody like to talk about it. We'd been together since we were fifteen, made every promise to each other known to man and you disappeared." He snapped his fingers. "Just like that. I found us a flat, you know. I came to tell you. That spiteful cow of a mother of yours took great pleasure in telling me you'd gone to visit your cousins in America. Would be studying there and wouldn't be back. I thought it was a joke. A bloody joke that never ended. Years later, I walk into a party in poncy Mayfair, and there you are, tarted up to the nines and as bold as brass. You owe me an explanation."

His voice had roughened, and she could hear the Scots burr. There was a time when those melodic tones had driven her wild. Now she couldn't wait to get away.

She pushed the sheet back and swung her legs to the floor. Her head was spinning. Her shoes were lying next to the bed, and she quickly put them on. She stood, and dizziness had her reaching out to clutch at the bedpost. She closed her eyes and was disappointed when she opened them, and he was still there.

"I owe you nothing, James. Same way you don't owe me anything. We're two people who knew each other as kids. It was all a long time ago. Please let me be. I don't have the strength for this." She hated the wobble in her voice.

He stood, nodded. "Very well, Marianne." He pronounced her name with a spiked edge. "But this isn't the end of it."

She tried for a natural smile but wasn't sure she pulled it off. "Of course it isn't. The end was almost two decades ago."

"Not of my choosing." The words haunted her as she opened the door and walked out. Her legs were shaking, but she held her head high. She turned a corner as a figure barrelled round it and almost crashed into her. She held them by the arms. It was Sue.

"Oh, thank God, Marianne. Are you all right? That man rushed over, picked you up without a by-your-leave and walked out with you. By the time I raced after you, he had disappeared. I've been in half the rooms in this bloody place."

"I'm fine. Nothing to tell—he's someone from a long time ago. Please give my good-byes to the others. I have to go now. I'll get a cab outside. Tell Tom I'll text him, but I'll come by tomorrow and drop my laptop off."

Sue bit her lip. "Are you sure you should be alone? Who the hell is he?"

"Yes, I'll be fine. Please leave it." She heard the snap in her voice and winced. She needed to be alone. "I'm sorry. My head is messed-up at the moment."

"Don't worry. Take care."

She decided to walk for a bit. She craved the cool, night air. She strolled through the polished streets of Mayfair. It was a long way from a Scottish coastal town and a seventeen-year-old girl who was mad for a boy with a handsome face, a motorbike and a dark edge. She had once thought he was everything to her and that he would remain so for all their lives. Then Jamie started drinking heavily. The new crowd he ran with was a bad influence. They were older, harder and immersed in lives of violence and crime. Jamie was changing in front of her eyes, and when the worst happened, she knew she wouldn't be safe if she stayed with him. So she left. He would never have let her go. She quietly disappeared. And now she had inadvertently walked back into his life. She shivered and hugged her arms across her chest. She had to keep away from him.

She dreamt of him that night. But it wasn't Jamie, the boy—it was James, the man.

***

Sue watched Marianne hurry away, head held high and body rigid. She exhaled, long and slow. Marianne was a tetchy nightmare and usually wound up like a clock, but this episode had shaken her. Whoever that guy was, he had undoubtedly made an impact.

She headed back into the party to get her bag and go home.

"Ah, there you are. Everything okay?"

Karl stood in the hallway, outside the entrance to the party room. Had he been waiting for her?

"Yes. Marianne has headed home."

He held two fresh glasses of champagne and handed one to her. "I have to say I am intrigued. What's her connection to James Foster?"

"Is that his name? He is someone from her past, I believe."

"Well, she certainly got spooked. I've never seen anyone faint before. Christ knows what Cathy will make of it."

"Sorry, who is Cathy?"

"The blonde with James. They're seeing each other. Ah, speak of the devil."

He pointed into the crowded room. Chloe, with Tom and some other guy in tow, was approaching who she now knew was James Foster and his equally stony-faced girlfriend, Cathy.

Sue sensed a scene on the way, so she quickly hurried over to join them.

Chloe was speaking, hands on her hips, jutting chin and belligerent eyes. "What the hell have you done with Marianne?"

Not a flicker of emotion was discernible as James replied, "Nothing. She's fine."

Chloe opened her mouth to speak, but Sue quickly stepped in. "Marianne is good. I've seen her. She has gone home, said she was overtired."

Chloe nodded, seemingly mollified.

Karl said, "Good to see you, James. You look lovely, Cathy."

Sue thought she also looked bloody furious.

Karl carried on, "These are my new friends, Sue and Chloe." He waved a hand towards Tom. "And this is Tom, Adam's brother. You know Ryan, of course."

Ryan smiled at Sue and Chloe. "Hi, I'm an old pal of

Tom's."

Sue inclined her head in a quick hello; she was more concerned with preventing any issues between Chloe and this Cathy.

Cathy barely acknowledged Sue or Chloe but smiled at Tom. "Pleasure to meet you. So what keeps you busy? Are you in IT like Adam?"

"I guess you could say that."

Sue was in the mood to be decidedly more direct. She locked her gaze onto James. "I hear you know Marianne from way back."

A muscle pulsed at the side of his mouth. "That's correct." His set mouth was a testament to his not being particularly willing to say any more.

Cathy flashed him a blazing look, and the air thrummed with tension, made worse by the lengthening silence.

Tom drained his glass and said, "Right, I'm off. Sue, Chloe, how are you getting home?"

Chloe hitched her bag higher on her shoulder. "Tube for me. It's two minutes away."

Sue gestured at her feet and lifted her heel. "In these shoes, I'll hail a cab. I'll be in touch, Tom."

She glanced at the pleasant-faced Ryan, an unsmiling Cathy and a granite-faced James. "Nice to have met you." Sue winced inside. Of course, it wasn't remotely pleasant to meet them at all, but that's the kind of rubbish you spouted in social situations.

Karl said, "I'll walk you outside."

Sue's heart fluttered, and she ignored a slight queasiness as they moved through the crowded room and into the cool hallway. The front door was immediately opened by the waiting staff. Karl followed her outside. She turned to face him.

"Thanks. It was good chatting. Bye."

"Wait, I'll get you a cab."

He raised his right arm, and within seconds a black cab rolled to a halt at the kerb. He spoke through the window to the driver. "The lady will tell you the destination."

He turned back to face her, his eyes intent and unblinking. "Sue, I'm glad we met tonight. May I be unforgivably forward and ask for your telephone number? I'd love to take you out for dinner one night."

She was glad that darkness had fallen as it hopefully hid her flaming cheeks. It took all her control to keep her mouth from falling open. He smiled, long, slow and sexy, and she had an awful feeling he knew how flustered she was.

"Yes, I'd like that." Had those words, spoken calmly and coolly, emanated from her? Apparently so, for she also dug deep into her handbag and pulled out one of the dog-eared contact cards she used for her art business. "My number's on here."

He took the card and caught her hand in his with a delicate caress. "Thank you. I'll be in touch soon. I promise."

The cab took her home, but she could almost have floated there herself.

CHAPTER FIFTEEN

Marianne showed up for work, but only her body was there; her mind was caught in the crossfire between worrying about Amelia, concern about the scammers and disbelieving dread that she had bumped into Jamie—no, he was James now.

She lasted until late afternoon, before leaving for the day. She had called earlier, and Tom said the others would be at his place by 4:00 p.m. They were all there when she arrived.

Tom got straight to the point. "Who the hell was that guy?"

Marianne knew they'd ask, but it wasn't any of their business. She didn't even know what she thought about the situation, she certainly couldn't speak to anyone about it. Her head was thumping, and a tension ache was creeping into her jaw. "Never mind him."

Sue sighed, placed her empty coffee cup on the table and said, "I'm not leaving the subject until you tell me who that guy is. We spoke to him after you left and he wasn't in a mood to discuss anything to do with you. You could have sliced the atmosphere with a machete."

She pursed her lips. How did you speak of someone you had left behind, who belonged to another time, another life? One you had abandoned because you had no choice. She sighed, ran a hand through her hair and shrugged. "We were teenage sweethearts. He was a bad boy and running with a worse crowd. I got cold feet and took off. He'd never have let me go. I moved to England and prayed he'd never catch up with me."

Tom instinctively rubbed his hand across his jaw, shaking his head. "I know it was a while ago, but do you need to be careful? If he was the possessive sort and you ran out on him, won't he be out for payback?"

Marianne laughed, the first bout of genuine mirth she had experienced in days. "It was eighteen years ago. I doubt it. It's all in the past." A little worm of fear burrowed into her mind. Was she sure?

She decided to turn the tables. "So, Sue, what happened with Karl after I left?"

Sue's face was aflame.

"Oh, like that was it?" Marianne sniggered.

"No, no. I mean, yes." Sue laughed. "He asked for my number and suggested we have dinner. That's all."

"And . . . ?"

"Yes, I gave it to him. God, I haven't been on a date in almost thirty years. I hope he doesn't phone."

Emily said, "He sounds great, and I bet you do want him to call."

"Well, maybe a little."

Marianne was glad one of them had a happy outcome from the party. She wished she had never gone.

***

Tom rubbed his hands together and crossed over to his desk. "Right, enough of that. I need to get on with looking at your laptops. Marianne, have you got your new one?"

"Yes, here it is." She pulled it from her bag and passed it across to him.

"Great." He set her laptop to the side. "I'll run through it later and set up your new email and security."

Tom sat at his desk, the laptops ranged around him in a neat semicircle. He checked each one individually. "We have an administrator name—Perev—and the IP addresses in Bulgaria."

Sue said, "You star! All we need to do is find this Perev. I didn't expect it to be this easy."

"It isn't," Tom said drily. "This Perev will simply be the muppet whose Wi-Fi and hardware they're piggybacking off."

He turned back to the laptops. He was only going to access Anita's, Emily's and Sue's late husband's. He was keeping well away from Marianne's old one at the moment. He didn't even want to look up any of Marianne's social media accounts. He needed to avoid leaving a trail that the hackers could follow.

He wanted to get a pattern of their social media activity and then look specifically at Dave's online girlfriend. None of them had Twitter accounts, Emily and Anita were both on Instagram and Pinterest, and all three had Facebook accounts. This could take a while.

Tom looked at the Instagram accounts first. Neither woman had a large number of followers, and the pictures they posted were of relatively mundane matters, and the posts they liked mostly consisted of food, fancy cocktails and cats.

Next up was Pinterest. He tutted when he realised that the accounts were completely unsecured. None of the privacy settings had been activated, and anyone could see what they had expressed an interest in. Emily's and Anita's pins were images of clothes, buildings and books. With some cats liberally sprinkled throughout the mix.

Nothing much to see here. He needed to find Dave's girlfriend. And that was who he was looking for next. On each laptop, he brought up the Facebook accounts of Emily, Anita and Dave. He started with Dave's first and reviewed his list of friends. One name jumped out at him. He turned to Sue.

"Anita was one of your husband's Facebook friends."

She shrugged. "I didn't know, but that makes sense. Dave often went into my Facebook account and sent people I knew Facebook friend requests from his own profile. He spent much more time on it than I did."

The girlfriend wasn't hard to find. Petra Medalov sounded more Russian than Bulgarian, not that it was likely to be her real name, and of Dave's two hundred and something friends, she stood out like an exotic flower in a bed of weeds. Amongst what appeared to be golfing buddies, work colleagues and old school friends, her youth and beauty marked her as different. As did the fact that she had never posted on Dave's timeline or commented on any of his posts. He turned to Sue. "Is that her?"

She stared for a moment. "Yes."

Tom moved across to his own computer, his private cloaked and hidden network, and pulled up Facebook and searched for her. When her page came up, he noted the photo was the same, and her profile picture had been changed three times. There were no other posts, no other comments and she only had a handful of friends. He checked each of them. A few women, a couple of men, all internationally located. Or were they? Tom knew that it was highly possible that none of these people existed. The names could have been made up, and someone's photo illegally copied from somewhere else. It could be one scammer who had set everything up. If it wasn't for the fact that Sue said Dave had video chatted with this woman, it could even have been a man hiding behind the online profile.

"You mentioned he had a video of her. Can I see it?"

Sue hesitated, then shrugged. "Sure, there are a couple saved in his downloads folder."

He found them quickly enough and clicked play on the first one. It took a moment for his eyes to adjust to the poor quality of the video. When they did, he clearly saw the girl sitting on a bed, leaning back against a wall. She was pretty with neat, smiling features. She had long dark hair, wide brown eyes and a full mouth that was moving, but there was no sound.

Tom tapped away at the keyboard. "Damn, I'll turn up the volume."

The sound boomed out of the laptop, and the girl's voice was clearly not British. He listened carefully. "She sounds Eastern European, but I can't make out what she is saying."

Sue said, "Find another video. He taped a few of their calls."

Tom tapped away and within moments brought up a

clearer image. He pressed play. The girl's voice was much clearer. They could also hear Sue's husband; his well-spoken tones seemed thickened with emotion as he whispered his affections. Tom tried to zone out the sweet nothings and instead concentrated on the surroundings. The girl was in a bedroom, unremarkable in its decor. The image went fuzzy and stalled.

No one spoke. What did you say to a woman who had lost her husband and, after his death, found out about his online affair and plans to leave her? Tom kept quiet, as did the others.

Next, he went into Dave's direct messages—private messages on Facebook that couldn't be seen by anyone else. And he read through the downfall of the man over a multitude of conversations. He didn't know what the state of Sue's marriage had been, but no wife should be grieving her husband and have to read how he fell in love with a girl less than half her age. Petra had made the first contact. The message was bright and breezy.

Thanks for connecting. We have a friend in common, Ali James. I play golf with him.

Dave had quickly replied, no doubt amazed that this young and beautiful woman was a keen golfer. Tom bet she'd never held a golf club in her life. It became apparent that Dave didn't know Ali James at all. He had merely accepted a Facebook friend request. Tom used his computer and checked out Mr Ali James. Or should that be handsome New York firefighter Alastair Gordon James?

"Shit." He pushed his chair back, the rollered feet skidding across the wooden floor.

Sue moved to his side, Emily and Chloe at her heels. "Have you found something?"

He ran a hand through his hair, yet again astonished at human naiveté. "No, I haven't found anything. I find it hard to believe how trusting people are when someone they have never met before approaches them on Facebook. They become a friend and believe they are exactly who the person says they are. All you need is an attractive profile picture, a good name and a uniform. Just like good old Alistair James, one of New York's finest firefighters." He laughed, although he knew this wasn't a humorous situation at all.

Emily spoke, her voice puzzled. "What does Ali James have to do with this? Do you know him?"

Tom slowly turned to face her, his mind whirling as his mouth dropped open. He snapped it shut as a thought— an incredulous thought—took hold. "No, I don't. But do you?"

"Sure, we are friends on Facebook. Oh God, has he been scammed as well?"

"I sincerely doubt it. How do you know him?"

"I don't, not really. He sent me a friend request. We had loads of friends in common. I only ever connect with people who know some of my friends."

But, thought Tom, *the majority aren't real friends. Not people you know in real life. They could be anyone hiding behind a fake profile.*

"Who is he?" Sue asked. "You were on Dave's laptop. Is it someone he knew?"

"I think it is someone he thought he knew."

He quickly brought up Anita's Facebook and searched

through her friend list. He already knew what he would find. He reviewed her messages as he asked Emily, "Did you get a message from Ali? Something with an attachment that you opened up?"

"No, not at all. I mean, we never corresponded. He just sent a Christmas wishes message."

He stilled. "Just Merry Christmas? No attachment?"

"Yes, I mean, no. I think there was a GIF I opened up. You know the type of thing. It was a little Santa doing a dance."

He opened up Anita's messages, and Dave's, and checked last December. He used both hands, one on each mousepad as he desperately scrolled back through the comment boxes, his eyes flicking between the screens. He stopped. December 23. Dave had a message from Ali James—*Merry Christmas*, and an image of a Santa holding a beribboned box, saying, *Open me*, and then, in fancy writing, *Forward me*. He didn't. He checked Anita's—her message came through on December 23 at the exact same time. The exact same message.

"Was this what you received?"

Emily peered over Tom's shoulder. "Yes, why?"

Chloe came up beside him. "What the hell is going on?"

"Ali James doesn't exist, at least not the one who befriended you. I will need to do some forensic analysis, but I sure we'll find that Ali befriended a whole load of people, probably thousands. Then, once connected, he sent friend requests to their friends and on and on until he built up a huge network. He could have started off by targeting people in the London area. That's a good tactic if you're going in as the front guy. The one who wants to make connections. Then he sent the message. I bet it has a Trojan horse inside it—a virus that, once opened, will allow the originator access to your entire system. At the least, they would have had access to your Facebook account. They'd see your pictures, posts and private messages. That's a helluva lot of information. I need to check Marianne's Facebook. I'll go in using an anonymous VPN so I can't be traced."

CHAPTER SIXTEEN

Marianne's legs gave way, and she thumped onto the sofa with a hard thud, grateful that she had already passed her brand new laptop to Tom.

"That must've hurt," Sue said. "You all right?"

"Yeah, yeah, I'm fine." Her coccyx ached, but she had more to concern her than the pain.

Her head was buzzing, and it took her a moment to process what Tom had said. "You're saying I opened a forwarded email from someone, who received it from a scammer, and a bloody dancing Santa unleashed a virus into my computer that gave these pigs access to everything?" She knew she sounded incredulous, and that her voice was shrill, but, Christ, this had to be a joke.

Tom replied, "Yes. But your Facebook friend may not even have forwarded the message. The hackers could have sent it from someone's system without them knowing."

Sue's weary voice came from behind, "It's so easy for them . . . so easy."

Marianne snorted a ragged sound that grated her nerves. "It is easy because I was stupid. If I got a work email, I would never dream of randomly opening an attachment from someone I didn't know. Yet I opened a dancing Santa wishing me a Merry Christmas from someone I have never met or properly communicated with. Shit! Shit! Shit!"

Tension weighed on her shoulders, and every part of her was tight, taut—her hands were curled into fists, and her nails dug into her palms. She half hoped she'd draw blood. It would serve her right for being stupid. She had brought the whole damn thing on herself. Her stomach somersaulted, and she rubbed a hand against her aching temple.

Emily sat beside her and put an arm around her shoulder, gently squeezing. "I did the same, but I may have been stupid enough to friend the original scammer."

Marianne froze. As a rule, she respected others' personal space and expected the same herself. She's been on her own for years. She didn't need anyone's support. But Emily was a sweet girl and meant well, so Marianne sat there, accepting the gentle touch until Emily patted her shoulder and withdrew her hand with a kind smile.

Marianne sighed. "We know how they got into the systems. What now? How do we find them, and, more importantly to me, how do we stop them from ripping off the investors and involving my business while keeping Amelia safe? Do we go to the police with what we know?"

Tom was direct. "Nope. These guys are too organised. I know that now. By the time the police got their act together, the scam would be over, and these guys will have disappeared into cyberspace. Pay them. This will be a huge scam, and the risks are high for the bad guys. It will cost you some money, but you may be able to buy them off. In return, they back off the business and your niece. This isn't a typical ransomware situation, but money always talks with this type."

Sue asked, "What's ransomware?"

"A way of making a quick buck, and is, effectively, cyber blackmail. The hackers lock you out of your account and threaten to delete everything unless you pay up. Most people do."

"Christ, isn't there anything else we can do?" She held up a hand to hush him. "Don't answer that. I guess paying them off is the only reasonable option. They get some money, my investors don't lose out, and the regulator won't be all over me." She paused. "And Amelia will be safe. Okay, how do I go about this?"

Before Tom could reply, Sue butted in. "And what about us? What about the fact that you believe it's the same people who indirectly, or even directly, caused the deaths of my husband and Anita? They conned Emily out of all the money she had. And you want to give them more?"

Tom held his arms wide in supplication. "I'm sorry, but this isn't your average hacker situation, someone working alone or on a small team, carrying out relatively low-value scams and cons here and there. This is organised. The attack via Marianne's business is big—it could bring in millions—and targeting individuals, like Anita and Dave, isn't a quick con. That takes resources—manpower, programmers, scam operators and even people to research the victims. And they would. Forgive me, but when your husband was approached, the scammers would have known if he was looking for something extra in his life and open to the honey-trap they set for him."

Sue opened her mouth to speak, but Marianne quickly cut her off. "Look, the most important thing is dealing with my business. We don't have the slightest idea how to go after these people. And why would we? We aren't bloody Charlie's Angels."

She was met by silence as a tight-lipped Sue, and a disgruntled looking Emily and Chloe stared at her. Sue puffed out a breath of apparent disdain and snapped, "You don't decide what's important. Not for us."

"I'm sorry, but there is nothing we can do. I am trying to prevent my clients, people who have invested with me, who have trusted me, from losing money. That has to be a priority. And once they have the money, they'll leave Amelia alone as well."

Sue laughed, and the mocking sound made her scream inside. "Marianne, you are a sanctimonious bitch. You don't fool me for one second. You couldn't care less about the investors. The only reason you don't want them scammed is that it would ruin your business, no one will invest with you in the future and by the sounds of it, the FCA would have a field day with how you've dealt with things in the past. It doesn't even seem you're that bothered about your niece either."

Sue grabbed her bag and stomped to the front door. "I am obviously not needed here. I would say I wish you well, Marianne, but I know you deserve everything you get. It's only the poor investors and that innocent young girl in the video I'm worried about." She yanked the door open and stormed out.

Emily and Chloe rose as one, got their stuff together and made to leave. As they reached the door, Emily spoke over her shoulder, "I guess we aren't needed either." With that, she walked out.

Chloe spoke to Tom, tears in her eyes. "You got my hopes up that we could do something about this. And now I'm worse off than before you interfered. Thanks for nothing, both of you."

Marianne and Tom were left alone in the room that resonated with the sound of the front door being slammed shut. She couldn't help these women right now, she just couldn't. She had to put Amelia first. However, she hadn't intended matters to blow up like that. Her stomach roiled and lurched. She was fierce in her business dealings but detested conflict in her personal life. "I'm not sure how we got to this, but it's probably for the best." She squared her jaw, ready for action. "Tell me what to say to those bastards to make this stop."

***

He looked over the balustraded terrace, his gaze ranging across the manicured gardens of the square, past the rooftops, towards the City and the lifeblood of London. His mind, for the first time in years, was drawn to the past. He had achieved a great deal and travelled a long road. In fact, it was difficult to believe that the boy he had once been shared the same skin as the man he was today. He contemplated the current project, the final pieces of which were slotting into place. At its conclusion, he would have had enough, enough to walk away from this life and take on the next challenge—whatever that might be.

He had walked a dangerous path for so long. Perhaps he would be unable to live any other way. But he had been lucky, and he couldn't push it too far. Maybe he was getting a little paranoid. Everything had to go well with this final job, and that meant he had to be on the ball, keep his wits and not trust anyone. Then again, he never did.

His memory corrected him. He had trusted someone once, and look what that got him. Acid burned in his stomach, and he marvelled that he could still experience physical pain at the mental recollection. He'd hoped never to see her again; even though all the while, he had yearned to do so.

CHAPTER SEVENTEEN

Marianne sent a message to the email address they had given her, a simple *please call me*, and waited not so patiently. Adrian called for a goodnight chat. He was busy socialising with potential customers, and Marianne was relieved that she didn't have to explain who she was spending time with, and why. She'd lain awake, her mobile clutched in her hand, until exhaustion pressed heavily on her aching limbs, forcing her deeper into the mattress until sleep claimed her.

A call came through a glimmer past dawn, and she sleepily contemplated if she could be bothered answering it. But she knew she had to face this head-on. There was no caller ID. Her heart was thudding in her chest, furiously pumping adrenalin, when she answered. "Hello?"

"What do you want?" The voice was distorted and robotic, and she had to strain to hear.

Her palms were sweating, but this was showtime, and she simply had to get on with it. She was used to tricky negotiations. "I want us to come to an arrangement."

"Really? About what?" She seethed at the robotic amusement that laced the voice.

"I want you to leave me and my business alone and keep away from the girl."

"And what would I get in return?" There was a

mocking tone from the tinny voice.

"I have cash and shares. I can liquidate my portfolio, and in all, I could get £200,000 to you by the end of this week."

"But we have the potential to get many multiples of that from the cryptocurrency fund. Why would we take that chicken-feed?"

"Because you are going to have to work for it. You need to send out a convincing prospectus, entice the investors in, and that will take time."

"Ah, no it won't. I've had my eye on you for some time. Everything is in place; in fact, the initial communication to investors is almost ready to go. Keep your money. You'll need it when your investors come after their lost funds, and your regulator takes an interest. Remember, keep your mouth shut and forward any emails to us that come directly from the subscribers. Any phone messages, you need to deal with in the same way. We've put an intercept on your main switchboard. All calls to your business will come through us first. If you don't do as I say, the girl will have a bad accident. Pretty little thing, isn't she? Someone could have a bit of fun with that cute piece of ass."

Ice rushed through her veins, and her hands were clammy. How dare they? How could they threaten someone's life like this? Bastards. Panic fluttered in her chest. "Please, I can maybe get some more money together. If you can wait a few weeks, I could get another £200,000."

The laugh was chilling. "Oh, Marianne, don't be such a fool. Do as you're told, like a good girl."

Rage erupted, and the words were out before she even knew what she was thinking. "Fuck off!" Her voice was a scream rarely heard in this type of Kensington apartment block. "You are getting nothing. I'm going to go to the police. Screw you!" She disconnected the call and hurled the phone across the room. Luckily, it landed on the rug.

Her breath came in massive, rasping gulps as her anger cleared and panic set in. She grabbed her phone and called Jenny. She had to warn her. There was no answer. This was the only number she had. She tried again. Nothing.

She curled up on the sofa and wept as she thought of her next step. She had to save Amelia. The police were the only option. She had to involve them and to hell with what happened to her. Her clients wouldn't care that she was the victim; their only concern would be that she, and their records, had been hacked. It would all be over once she involved the police. She had more to worry about than that right now.

CHAPTER EIGHTEEN

Tom was waiting at the chosen coffee shop by 8:00 a.m. He scraped the plastic chair across the linoleum floor and sat seconds before the door opened and Lou Spencer walked in. He hadn't seen Lou in almost a year, but he hadn't changed a bit, still carried the same weight, born of night-time takeaways and midnight snacking. His skin was a murky shade of grey from lack of vitamin D. They had first met online as young gamers, and a sort of friendship had grown.

"Hey, Lou, good to see you. How you doing?"

"Fine, fine." He wheezed as he hefted himself into the chair opposite Tom. There was a weary creak as the seat took his weight.

Tom had rarely met with Lou in person. Their conversations were usually conducted online via video platforms, like Zoom or Skype, in the hours before dawn. He had spent more days than he could remember locked into his PC for long stretches at a time, the world outside forgotten.

"Tom, long time no see. What you after?"

Lou's voice was a little rough as if he hadn't spoken in a while. The eyes staring into his were sharp, and Tom knew better than to pretend this was merely a social catch-up with an old friend.

"I wanted to know if there was anything profitable going on. I've heard some rumours."

"Not as far as I know." The reply had been quick and smooth. Not a ripple of emotion crossed his face, and that fact gave away more than Lou undoubtedly intended. He was hiding something.

"Come on, I know there's a lot of activity going on in cyberspace."

"Why do you care?" His look was sly. "I thought you got out. Life on the straight and narrow not so good?"

His life was his own damn business, but he needed to be convincing. "I need some quick cash. I thought I could use my skills."

"Why come to me? What have you heard?"

Lou was cagey, but his wariness alerted Tom to the fact that he was on the right track. "Just that there is an ongoing London attack using social media and that there is a Bulgarian connection."

Lou stilled. "Where did you hear that?"

He carefully maintained a smooth, even tone. "Here and there. You know I can't say."

Lou shifted slightly. "Shit! Best you keep your mouth shut and don't ask any questions."

"All you're doing is intriguing me. Come on, I need the money. Don't you think this gang would want me?"

"It's not that. You'd be in demand; of course you would. It's just . . ."

Lou rubbed his eyes with a podgy hand, and when he sighed and slumped forward, Tom knew he had an in. "These guys are seriously bad. I've heard some stuff about people who pissed them off. I've sent a few contacts to them in the past, but I try to keep out their way these days."

Tom leaned over the table, his eyes locked on Lou's. "Please, I can take care of myself. I just want to do what I'm told and get paid. I need cash, and I need it quickly."

Tom knew Lou would never probe about his situation. When you moved in their circles, you learned to be circumspect and keep your own counsel.

"Okay, fine, but this is on your own head. I take no responsibility for what happens."

"So who should I talk to?"

"The guy goes by the name of Petyr."

If that was his real name. It seldom was. The only reason Tom and Lou knew each other's own identities was because they had met when they were each too young to know any better.

"Will you set up a meet?" He may as well talk to this Petyr guy and see if he could find out a little more.

"Sure, but you're going to have to travel. It isn't only the hackers who are in Bulgaria, that's where the entire operation is run from. Petyr will only meet potential recruits in person."

Damn. That was a sight more inconvenient. Marianne was going to pay off the guys attacking her, and he couldn't see her being interested in trying to get some justice for the others. She would want to walk away and forget all about it.

Chloe was grieving, Emily would go along with the herd and Sue may not have the appetite to take this forward with him alone. At the end of the day, this wasn't his problem.

***

Marianne reapplied her makeup and caught a cab to the London Met offices—New Scotland Yard by the Victoria Embankment. This matter wasn't something to dial 999 for, and she had no idea if there was a local police station in Kensington. Anyway, she wasn't talking peanuts here; therefore the Metropolitan it was.

Her phone buzzed in her handbag. Repeatedly. She pulled it out, the incessant noise becoming louder, and saw text message after message. All saying the same thing: *URGENT! Check your emails NOW!*

She spied an empty bench across the road on the Victoria Embankment walkway. The lights were about to turn green, and she quickly dodged across the street. As she sat, she flicked through her phone and opened up her inbox. She saw it immediately. They had sent her an email.

The message said: *Watch the video before you go to the police. We're not joking around. Next time it will be worse.*

She'd heard people talk of being paralysed by fear and had thought it a load of emotive nonsense, but now she knew it wasn't. She merely stared at her phone as a multitude of scenarios ran through her mind, but one thing was certain. She knew the video would be of Amelia.

She scrolled to the video attachment, exhaled deeply and pressed play. Amelia was walking through a park. Marianne had no idea where it was, but that was irrelevant. The park wasn't particularly busy; a few dog-walkers and harassed-looking mothers circled the lawns and pond with prams and toddlers. A pretty, everyday scene.

The noise level increased as running footsteps came

nearer and nearer to Amelia. A jogger was coming from behind. He ran close to Amelia, shoved her hard and, as she landed in a heap, he kicked out, landing vicious blows on her torso.

Marianne was rooted, barely breathing and the world around her—the noise, the people—receded.

Amelia curled up in a ball, one arm across her stomach, the other trying to protect her head. The attacker stopped and simply jogged away. Marianne dragged her eyes from Amelia and took in the nearby surroundings. People had seen the attack and were running towards her; a man had dialled a number and was talking into his phone. The screen went black as the video finished.

Her phone pinged. The text message was brief but said it all. *Behave. NO police. Or next time she is dead.*

Marianne was nauseous and closed her eyes as hot tears escaped. She held her hands across her stomach and silently wept. She obviously couldn't go to the police now. The message was clear—she had to do whatever they wanted. If she didn't, Amelia would be killed.

CHAPTER NINETEEN

Marianne went straight to the airport and caught the next flight to Edinburgh. She'd stay overnight and be back in London the following morning.

Marianne would describe herself as organised, practical and logical, but her nerves were on high alert as she descended the stairs and stood on Scottish soil for the first time in over seventeen years.

While waiting at the departure gate, she had phoned the Edinburgh hospitals. She got lucky on the second call. People were stressed and busy the world over, and with a little cajoling, she soon knew that Amelia had been taken there, was in Robin Ward, and visiting was 3:30 to 4:30 p.m.

Not that she had any intention of visiting Amelia. No, it was one of Amelia's visitors that she hoped to talk to. She checked the time. It was past lunchtime, but she couldn't eat. She'd never keep anything down. She would get a taxi straight to the hospital.

She only had to wait around thirty minutes until visiting time was over. The entrance foyer had a small cafe, and she sat there unobtrusively. By 4:45 p.m., she questioned if she had missed Jenny. Perhaps there was another exit?

The elevator doors pinged open, and Jenny came out

with several others. Marianne hadn't expected the physical pain that coursed through her when she saw her. Seventeen years had added a few lines to her elder sister's face and several pounds to her figure, but it was the apparent tension that held her tightly together that pained Marianne the most.

Jenny walked alone and stared straight ahead as she strode to the front door. Marianne followed her. The hospital was flanked by two large car parks, and Jenny was heading towards one of them, keys in hand. Marianne quickened her steps, and called out, "Jenny! Jenny! Stop."

Jenny stopped but didn't turn around. Marianne touched her shoulder.

Jenny faced her, and Marianne could see strain and worry taking their toll in her drawn complexion and shadowed eyes. But concern for her daughter was gradually being replaced by what was undoubtedly displeasure at Marianne's appearance. And her words gave truth to that as, with eyes narrowed into slits, she demanded, "What the hell do you want?"

"I want to know how she is. Is she okay? Did he hurt her badly?"

Jenny had stilled, and her voice was a hiss. "How did you know about this? What the fuck has this got to do with you?"

The swear word shocked Marianne, and she knew it gave truth to her sister's state of mind.

"Look, that isn't important right now. How is Amelia?"

"Don't say her name. We had a deal. I clear up your mess, and you get a new life. And you never come back. That was the deal, Mhairi. What the hell have you got to do with this?"

"I told you, my name is Marianne." She winced at Jenny's snipe of a laugh.

"I have other names I could call you, especially for appearing here like this. Now answer my question: How do you know something happened to Amelia?" She drew back, a suspicious look on her face. "Did you organise this? Was it some twisted ploy to give you a reason to make contact? You bitch."

Marianne shook her head, but her "no" was cut off as Jenny grabbed her by the shoulders and shook her hard, again and again. Marianne let her; she deserved it. Sharp nails dug into her flesh, Jenny's face was contorted and tears coursed down her face. Marianne took the pain as her due. Suddenly, she was free, and Jenny leaned against the bonnet of a car, sobbing as Marianne told her the events of the last few days.

"So that's why you called. You should have told me Amelia was in danger. Shit, we need to tell the police."

"No, we can't. This all happened because I said I wasn't going to play along, that I would involve the police. That's when they attacked Amelia and . . ." She couldn't help it, her voice broke. She steadied herself. "They said they would kill her if I don't cooperate."

Jenny was pale, paler than Marianne would have thought humanly possible. Her hissed words coiled around Marianne's heart. "You destroy everything you touch. You screwed up your life, and Mum and Dad's. How do you think they've coped with not seeing you for almost two decades?"

"That's a bit rich! The deal was I stayed away."

"Yes, from me, but not from Mum and Dad. They could visit you in London."

"I send Christmas cards."

"Whoopie-doo, that's big of you."

"Don't get sanctimonious with me. I stayed away, as agreed."

Jenny threw out an arm as if to brush away Marianne's words. "My daughter is in danger, and it's all your fault." She leaned in closer, her face red and contorted, inches from Marianne's. "You sort this out. You fucking stop this. You almost ended her life once before. Get this sorted."

With that, she walked away, her shoulders rigid, her gait uneven. Marianne stood there for the longest time. What the hell could she do now? She knew one thing. Tom was still the only option she had.

CHAPTER TWENTY

Marianne rang Tom from Heathrow before getting the express to Paddington Station. She'd be at his place by 10:00 a.m. He agreed on the condition that she brought strong coffee and hot croissants. The cab had dropped her at a deli near his home, and, bearing gifts, she arrived at the appointed time.

A bleary-eyed Tom, dressed in his usual uniform of jeans and a rumpled T-shirt, ushered her into the messy apartment. The remains of a takeaway littered the island that separated the living and kitchen areas, and numerous empty coffee mugs covered the coffee table, as did piles of notebooks and computer printouts.

"Sorry, the place is a tip."

She shook her head to brush away his words. "I've more important shit than that to worry about."

When she told him about Amelia, her voice broke. "So I flew to Edinburgh straightaway. I hadn't seen my sister for a long time, and she didn't take it too well that this is down to me."

Tom didn't say anything for a moment. "This is serious." He raked a hand through his hair, and brown tufts stood on end, making him look like a twelve-year-old. "These guys are villains. The real deal. Shit."

"I can't go to the police now. Can you help me? There

must be some way we can stop this." She had a cheek to ask the question, she knew that. She was asking him to become involved in something where violence was casually meted out. If she could walk away and let them have whatever they wanted, then she would save Amelia—but at the cost of her business being front-page news and therefore destroyed. Marianne knew her nature. She wanted it all.

She looked around the apartment—the paintings, the furniture—and thought of something. "I'd offer you money, and I am happy to pay you, but it doesn't look like you need it." He could be living off Adam, but that didn't tie in with them having had a falling-out. "What is it you actually do?" She heard the suspicion in her voice. She had trusted him with so much yet didn't know him at all. Through narrowed eyes, she saw him tense before giving her a long stare.

He sighed. "You know a charity I work with supports victims of online crime. I do the night classes on the side, but I am on the trustee board, and we do educational work with schools and colleges."

She recognised some of the art on the walls. "I didn't know philanthropy paid that well."

"It doesn't. And I don't ponce off Adam either. I've got savings. Not that it's any business of yours or anyone else's."

"I'm sorry. I'm placing my entire future—and Amelia's life—in your hands. And I don't know that much about you. How do I even know you will be able to help me? I mean, what are we going to do now? They won't make a deal."

"Yes, that's obvious. These guys are vicious. After their reaction this morning, they aren't willing to compromise in any way. The only option is to wallop them, no mistakes or half measures. We would need to take them down completely."

"Now you're scaring me. How do we do this?"

"By threatening them with the ultimate cyber weapon. Something that, if activated, will destroy everything: files, emails, social media profiles, lists of potential victims and their details—all the intelligence they have managed to get. Even access to their bank accounts will disappear online. I'll corrupt every item of data they possess. We tell them to back off, or I activate."

"You can do something like that?"

"Absolutely."

This was undoubtedly hard-core hacking. She didn't think any of her IT guys would have a clue how to do this. "An interesting skill set you've got there."

"Yeah, I guess."

He didn't say anything else, meaning her curiosity was going to remain unsatisfied. "Surely they'll find it. Have some super IT security that protects them."

"Oh yes, they'll have that. But I'm better."

"Well, you are a bit full of yourself, aren't you?"

"Trust me." He glanced at his watch. "They should be here soon."

"Who?" She was in no mood for an interruption.

"Sue and the girls. After you called, I asked them to meet us here."

"Why would you do that? We don't need them for this." Tension needled across her brow. This was her

125

concern—her business, her sister's child.

"Yes, we do. I need to understand how big their organisation is if I'm to have a chance of inserting the corruptor into the areas it will do the most harm. We need support."

"What? From a fifty-year-old widow, a shrinking violet and a girl still at college?"

"I know you're wound up, but don't be a bitch. Apart from anything else, I need the data that is on their laptops. I need to see if these guys made a mistake somewhere that we can use to try and pinpoint who they are."

"I know I'm a cow but why would they even want to help? This is my problem, not theirs.

Before Tom could reply, the doorbell rang. This was a *fait accompli*, and she'd need to go along with it.

The three women walked into the room, Sue in the lead. Her smile turned to a frown when she saw Marianne. "What is she doing here? When you called, you said there had been developments. You didn't mention she was involved."

Tom held out his hands in supplication. "I'm sorry, but something has happened, something terrible."

Marianne heard the words as if they were talking about someone else as Tom filled them in on what had happened to Amelia and what the new plan was.

She saw the horror in Sue's eyes. "I'm sorry about what happened to your niece. Look, I overreacted the other night. I've slept on it, and I get where you're coming from. The best solution would have been for these monsters to take the money and walk away. They're obviously after the bigger prize of the investors' money. But are you sure these are the kind of people you should be tangling with?"

Emily spoke, her voice soft, and Marianne had to strain to hear the words. "We should go to the police. We can't beat people like this. I'm sure they can protect your niece."

Marianne vigorously shook her head. They hadn't seen the video. "No, they can't. These guys got to Amelia immediately after I told them I wasn't going to play ball and I was going to the police. They have people near Amelia at all times. I can't risk this. Taking the fight to them is the only option."

"I agree." Chloe marched forward, her eyes on fire and her mouth a tight line. "They are directly responsible for my mother's death. I don't want to see anyone else hurt. We have no other option. I want to help. Sad to say, but I want revenge."

Sue's shoulders were set and tense as she glanced at each of them in turn, then relaxed, shook her head and sighed. "You're right." She turned to Emily. "Are you in?"

Emily wavered for a moment and then shrugged as she sat on the sofa. "It isn't like I'm going to get my money back. But I'll help."

Marianne stared at them, one by one. "This isn't your problem. I'm grateful but why would you help me."

Sue's gaze was steady, unwavering. "Because we want to hurt these people, we want revenge, and we want to help save a young girl. You have your moments, Marianne, but I like you. That's enough for me to need to be a part of this. I want to see it through."

Marianne swallowed, hard. "Thank you."

Tom beamed. "Great. The only lead we have so far is Bulgaria. But the guy I need to speak with will only talk in person."

"Then we go and speak to him," Marianne said.

Tom looked askance.

"Yes, I'm coming with you. I've got too much to lose."
She considered the others. "Anyone else want to come?"

Emily wrinkled her nose. "Afraid not, I'm committed
to several hours part-time accounting work this week."

Chloe piped up, "I've got a few college lectures that I
can't miss."

"I'll join you," Sue said. "You could do with some
support."

Tom turned to Emily and Chloe. "I have some research
work for you two if that is okay?"

Chloe glanced at Emily and, at the latter's shrug,
answered for both. "Sure, let us know what you need us to
do."

They looked at each other, one by one, and Marianne
was consumed by rising excitement. They were going to do
this. They had to.

CHAPTER TWENTY-ONE

Marianne packed an overnight bag for Bulgaria and set her alarm for early in the morning—very early. She needed to get to bed soon.

Her phone rang. She smiled at the caller ID and answered quickly. "Hey Adrian. I called for a chat earlier, but the gallery said you were at the auction house."

"I was. Sorry, I couldn't see you the last couple of nights, but I couldn't get out of these work dinners."

"Don't worry. I know this is a busy time for you. I don't mind." And she didn't, for she had far too much on her mind right now.

"I've got some amazing news. David Bolton has chosen my gallery for his next exhibition."

"Wow. Everyone's talking about him at the moment. What a coup."

"I know. Now for the bad news. David is leaving in a week or so for a long break, and wants our contract terms finalised before he goes."

"Well that's good, isn't it? That way you'll have the deal all squared up."

"Yes, but he wants me to go and stay at his place in Norfolk. He has a studio there where he houses his latest paintings. It will give me a fabulous opportunity to agree on what we want to show. His agent will be there as well."

"So when do you go?"

"That's the bad news. I need to drive up there tomorrow morning. I'll be gone for at least a week."

He often travelled on gallery business, but usually there was some advance warning. The news should have upset her. Instead, she was relieved. She could get on with what she had to do without worrying about Adrian.

"I'll miss you, but I understand that you have to go."

"Will I come over now? We can spend the night together."

Shit! She was on the red-eye flight. "Oh honey, I'm shattered, and need to get some sleep. I'm sorry."

He sighed. "Never mind. I'll miss you, too. Call me."

"I will."

As the line disconnected, she had to admit that Adrian being away suited her just fine. With any luck, this would all be over by the time he got back.

For the first time in forever, she appraised her surroundings. She'd built a home, a life even, that was elegant and rich and classy. But was it her? Who the hell knew? She'd been turned upside down recently. It had started with meeting Sue and the others and had been exacerbated by seeing James after all these years, compounded by the ever-present fear for Amelia.

Her doorbell rang. It was almost ten o'clock. Who the hell could that be? It better not be Adrian. He'd called on his mobile. What if he was hanging about outside? She checked the intercom and froze. Speak of the devil, and he shall appear. Her hand hovered over the intercom. She hesitated, then pressed the button to unlock the main door and spoke, "Come on up. Top floor."

James faced the camera, unsmiling, and pushed the door open, disappearing from view. She hated herself for doing so, but she ran into the bathroom and examined herself in the mirror. She fluffed her hair and applied a little more eyeliner, wet her lips and sprayed some perfume. Chanel No 5. Heart thudding, she waited, her mind a jumbled mass of thoughts, one shouting louder than the others. She was going to be alone with him. She held her hand to her throat; her throat was constricted, and her heart raced.

There was a knock on the door, and she let out a long, low, shuddering breath. She let him in. "What are you doing here? How did you know I'd be alone? I could be married with kids."

He stared, his eyes eating into the heart of her. "But you're not." He glanced around the open-plan living area. "Nice place you got. Is it yours, or does it belong to the guy who gave you the ring?"

It took her a moment to realise what he meant. She looked at her left hand. "It's mine. I worked hard to buy it."

"Oh, you're financing him?"

His words were taunting. She rose to the bait. "No. My fiancé is the son of Viscount Shoreham." For Christ's sake, why didn't she just go the whole hog and add on the *nah nah nah nah nah*?

James smirked, and she wanted to hit him. Instead, she turned away. "I ask you again, what are you doing here? And how did you get my address?" The latter frightened her because her property was owned in the name of a company for privacy. The only way he could have got her address would be if he had access to her private records.

"I wanted to see you. As for your second question, well, I have my ways of getting information."

That wasn't a comfort. "Well, you've seen me. You can go now." Her heart thudded. She wanted him out of here. She didn't want him to go.

"Why did you leave me, Mhairi? Where did you go?"

The question smashed into her solar plexus like an angry fist, and she was breathless for a moment, unable to think, let alone formulate an answer. "You were headed down a bad path. Nothing more than a petty criminal. I didn't want that life."

He leaned against the kitchen counter, long legs crossed at the ankles, a million years away from the boy he had been. He was polished, urbane and prosperous. He ran a hand through his hair. "The funny thing is that you leaving was the making of me. I tried to find you. I eventually found your sister, Jenny, months and months later."

She stilled. "Jenny never mentioned it." Mind you, they hadn't spoken after she'd moved to London. They'd made a deal.

"I went to her house in Edinburgh and waited all morning until she came out. She'd not long had a baby, and I could see I was upsetting her. She said you'd gone to America and you'd stopped calling. She didn't even have your address." That was true, apart from the America part.

She couldn't help herself. She had to know. "What did you do next?"

"I left your sister, and Edinburgh, and headed to the army recruitment office in Glasgow. My gran died not long after you'd gone. As my parents had been dead for years and I didn't even know my mum's family in England, I figured it was the only way I could get away from the crowd I ran with. Even I could see they were no good. Nothing made sense with you gone. Anyway, I did my time. Army life suited me, and I took advantage of the opportunities. The discipline set me on the right path. I got out a few years back and started my own business. I've made a bit of money, and life is good."

"What about Cathy?"

"Ah, Mhairi, my girl, that's not a conversation we need to have."

She drew back, affronted. "Very well. And I am Marianne now. She's a different kettle of fish than Mhairi."

"Oh really? I suppose you think Marianne would never have fallen for me. But you did, no matter what you try and tell yourself now."

"I was a stupid girl, the first one naive enough to be flattered by your attention. I didn't realise that you needed more in a relationship than a handsome boy who flashed his tan and muscles, who thought a look from his big blue eyes was all it took to get you into his bed."

He laughed. "Ah, but that is exactly how it was. We were lucky my gran was virtually deaf and went to bed early. Your mum and dad thought you were at your mate's studying every night. You were so clever you passed your exams anyway."

She gritted her teeth. She needed him to shut up. She didn't want to remember. She had spent eighteen years forgetting. And she had been good at it. But his words, even his accent, opened a door long closed. He'd been born in England to a Scottish father and English mother. They died in a road traffic accident when he was ten. He'd gone to live with his father's mother. A little English boy learning to talk with a Scottish accent to avoid getting beaten up for being different. When she had met him, his words had been spoken in an English estuary accent, now they were tinged with Scotland.

"Just go, James, please. Despite long odds, we have bumped into each other. But we each have built our own lives. Let us get on with them."

He pushed back from the counter, and she turned, expecting him to follow her to the front door. But before she could take more than a step, she was pulled back and drawn tight against him. She trembled a little, struggled even less. She tensed. He bent his head and placed one soft, sweet kiss against her hair, whispering, "I missed you so much. I never thought I'd see you again. Christ, you hurt me."

She looked at his mouth, which was inches from her eyes and, without thinking, rose to her tiptoes and pressed her lips against his, just for a moment, a gentle caress to say she was sorry. She sighed and drew back, but he pulled her close and kissed her properly, his lips teasing and coaxing her into submission. She raised her arms and pressed one hand against the nape of his neck, drawing him closer. Desire consumed her, and she pushed her body against his, aching, longing, needing. He returned the fire. The years faded, melted away. There was no Marianne, no James. Just Mhairi and her Jamie. Young and hot and fired up for life—and each other.

His hand cupped her breast, and she sank against him.

He drew back, his voice husky. "Where's the bedroom, darling? Let me love you."

His words were like a slap. He wouldn't want to be near her if he knew what she had done. He'd been a bad boy then, and he could be a worse man now. She couldn't be drawn into something for old times' sake. It would break her.

She was engaged, and shame suffused her. She pushed him away, trying to ignore his bewildered eyes. "No, go, this can't happen."

"Marianne . . ."

"No, please go. Please."

He let her go. "You're right. I'm sorry. I truly didn't mean for that to happen. I'm sorry. I'm sorry."

He left, taking the last pieces of Mhairi with him.

CHAPTER TWENTY-TWO

The plane journey to Sofia took a little over three hours. One hundred and eighty minutes where she stared out the window at fluffy cloud formations, interspersed with monotone grey coverage, and thought of the night before. And James.

The mind could play some pretty powerful tricks. She honestly hadn't thought of him in years, which was amazing when she considered what they had once meant to each other. Their teenage love had been unhindered by adult inhibitions, no holding back for fear of being hurt, no thought that it would ever end. Then something had changed. As usual, this was the point her mind truly closed down, refusing to open that Pandora's box of tricks.

They settled into their respective hotel rooms and met in the bar for a drink. It was 4:00 p.m. and Tom had arranged to meet his new contact at five thirty.

Marianne and Sue sipped glasses of white wine while Tom toyed with a Coke. She looked at him carefully. "You okay? Are you nervous?"

"A little, I guess, but you need an adrenalin shot to give your best performance, and I need to hit the mark on this. There won't be a second chance."

Sue asked, "How exactly are you going to play this?"

"The guy who has introduced me, Lou, is solid, so I'm

hoping I won't be met with any suspicion. Apparently, he has sent a number of people to them for jobs over the years. There will be some talk about my history and background. I expect to be offered a job or at the least to know more about what they are doing."

"I don't get it," Sue said. "How would it work if you work for them? Would you need to be here?"

"No. I would be providing coding, ideas for how to deal with what they do in a better way. And you can do that from anywhere. I need to see their setup, understand how it all works. That way I can determine the best way to attack their systems."

"What should we do?" Marianne asked.

Tom laughed. "Just stay out of trouble. Seriously, you have to be careful in a place like this. The beggars crowd around the hotel entrances. It's like an invisible barrier is in place and a handshake agreement that says they won't crowd in front of the hotel and restaurants areas, but they will surround them. They will hound you, shouting at you to get your attention, trying to get money, desperate to get you to buy something. Keep away from them. Most are pickpockets or maybe worse."

Marianne rolled her eyes and couldn't help the snap in her voice. "We aren't children, you know. We'll be absolutely fine."

***

Emily and Chloe had been left with the login details for all the relevant social media accounts, together with Dave's laptop, and it was the latter that Emily had been looking at while Chloe flicked through Facebook posts.

Emily pushed back her chair and moved across to the window. Her spacious, rented flat overlooked a pretty green square. The apartment she had been about to buy was a little smaller but in an even better area, and there was a tiny, private rooftop garden. It was going to be the beginning of a new life. One without a cheating, lying bastard husband, but the money from the divorce was gone, and she didn't know what to do. She'd been working part-time while she decided what she wanted to do with her life, but now she needed any job that paid well. The reminder of her ex-husband's infidelity triggered a thought. "It's a crying shame that Sue had to see these messages between Dave and that girl. They were pretty deep."

"Yeah, if she had found when he was alive I bet she'd have kicked him into touch the moment she discovered he was sexting and Skyping some slag."

And there spoke the voice of youth. Emily was only forty-one, but it had taken her two years to kick her own lying scumbag into touch. She regretted the wasted time but couldn't help the rush of defensiveness. "It's not always that easy. You've got time and emotions invested, and we all are hopeful. Wishing it turns out right, that they'll change."

Chloe snorted, her pretty face wrinkling in distaste. "Not likely. My dad was back and forward between my mum and his second wife for years. Leopards and all that."

Was Chloe more mature than she was herself? What a thought.

"You could be right. Poor Sue, to see he's involved with a girl years younger than her."

"Yeah, Tom said to see what else we can find out about

that girl. I've googled her name and tried to find her on sites like Instagram and Snapchat, but she doesn't have a profile. I guess we should have another look at the videos."

Emily shoved the laptop across the table. "You better do that. I wouldn't know where to start."

Chloe hunched over the keyboard and started clicking away. "Right, there are several video files. Well, it's not that one. That's a bit sad."

Emily peered over her shoulder. The video was of a party. The camera was directly on Sue. She seemed a little younger and much happier. A man stood next to her. He was slightly greying, his laughing eyes crinkling as he smiled. It must be Dave. A candlelit cake came out to cheers and cries of good wishes. The cameras zoomed in on it. It wished Dave and Sue a happy anniversary for twenty-five years of marriage. "It's a shame. It can't be long after this that he killed himself."

Chloe huffed. "Which means he was getting hot and heavy online with that girl right about this time."

"You're right. But it isn't our business. And not our place to judge. Let's get on with this."

Emily watched as Chloe opened the grainy video of Petra they had seen before. She leaned forward and peered at the screen. "That's crap. I can hardly see a thing."

"I'll open the other video."

These videos had to have been made days apart. Petra was wearing jeans and a T-shirt again, this one white instead of blue.

Emily stared. "Wait, can you pull up the other video but do a split screen?"

"Yeah, sure."

They examined the two videos side by side. Emily pointed. "Look at the girl; just behind her is a bundle of clothes in both videos. I can see a logo T-shirt. Can you zoom in?"

"Yeah." Chloe zoomed in and locked on to the clothing. "It says *Folie's Cafe Bar*, and there's an image of a cocktail glass."

"Yeah, I see. It's one of those martini glasses with an olive on a stick. I'm googling it."

Emily quickly punched the details into her tablet and waited a few moments. "Yes, this looks like it. The logo is the same. Oh shit!"

Chloe spun around. "What's wrong?"

"We have to call Sue. The bar is in Bulgaria—in Sofia."

CHAPTER TWENTY-THREE

Marianne and Sue freshened up and settled themselves at the hotel bar. Marianne laid the drinks menu on the table, beckoned the waiter over and said, "Right, I'll have a mojito. What about you?"

Sue shook her head. "I don't fancy any of these concoctions. I'll have a gin and slimline tonic."

The waiter was young and impossibly handsome. Apparently, it was true the world over: the trendier the bar, the more attractive the staff. "What flavour, please?"

Sue looked puzzled. "What flavour what?"

"Gin. We have raspberry, rhubarb or elderflower and blueberry."

Sue blinked a few times, and Marianne laughed as her nose wrinkled.

"I'll have plain gin, the old-fashioned kind. You got any of that?"

When the waiter came back, he smiled as he delivered their drinks.

Marianne picked up her glass. "I'll raise my mojito to your gin and tonic. Here's to Tom having a successful evening."

Sue clinked her glass against Marianne's. "And here's to us having the patience to wait until he gets back." She laughed.

Before they could say any more, they were interrupted by the ringing of Sue's mobile. She checked out the caller ID and answered with a smile. "Hi, Emily, how is it going?"

She listened carefully, and the smile slowly faded from her face. "What? I don't believe that. Hold on, let me get a pen." The waiter had left the drinks bill inside a leather folder. Sue opened it and grabbed the pen. Marianne drew her brows together as Sue quickly scribbled something. Sue had gone pale, and her voice shook a little as she spoke. "Thank you, Emily. Well done. Tell the same to Chloe. We'll go there immediately and let you know how we get on later. Bye."

As soon as Sue disconnected the call, Marianne asked, "What did she want?"

Sue took a breath and sighed deeply on the exhalation. "They looked through the videos of Dave with that girl. They noticed something in the background. It was piles of clothing, and at least a couple of the items had a logo for a bar. It's here. In Sofia."

"Shit! Let's go." Marianne downed the rest of her drink, signed the bill and, jumping to her feet, headed towards the foyer. She didn't look back, but from the mumbled mutterings she knew Sue was following her.

As soon as they exited the hotel, the reality of Sofia hit them. There was an empty area six feet on either side of the hotel doorway, and the way was clear to the pavement. However, bordering the empty space stood crowds of street-hawkers. Or at least that is what Marianne thought they must be. They were not as poorly dressed as beggars, and many of them held baskets filled with flowers or cheap trinkets. They kept to the invisible perimeter but started shouting, "Pretty lady, buy a rose", "Buy my wares, very cheap." And those were the most direct ones. Elderly women, teenagers and young children stood at the front of the crowd, their hands outstretched and their beseeching eyes boring into Marianne's very being. Their request was simple: "A little money, lady, a few coins. I haven't eaten today."

Marianne grabbed a gawking Sue by the arm and hissed, "Don't look at them. Don't make eye contact. Just walk straight ahead. Come on."

They jumped into a waiting taxi, and Sue handed the driver a piece of paper. "Take us here, please."

The taxi driver was in his fifties with wiry grey hair, a missing tooth and a cigarette hanging from the side of his mouth. "Are you sure? Not good place, ladies." His voice was rough, the English broken, but the meaning was unmistakable. They had no choice. She answered, "Yes, take us to Folie's."

***

Tom was on his second beer, but his new friend, Petyr, was on his fourth whisky and Coke and becoming more ebullient by the second. Tom zoned back into what would no doubt be the punchline to yet another anecdote.

". . . and so Lou—oh God, our shared friend is a clever guy—anyway, this little gangster who employed us to train his operators, design the software and release the bugs, he refused to pay us our final commission. It was sixty per cent of our agreed-upon fee. We couldn't just take that. Anyway . . ." He started laughing, but it quickly turned into a cough that became a wheeze.

Tom's impatience was rising. All he had found out so far was that the guy's name was Petyr Rabovsky, and he had worked with Lou a few years back. "And?"

Petyr's wheezing subsided, and a sly look skittered across his face. "And we took his money. Not all, but more than enough. We scammed the scammer." His voice had dropped to a whisper.

Interesting though his anecdotes were what he needed to do was find out more about the operation. "Anyway, I told you I saw Lou recently, and he made this introduction. I need a few readies to get back in the game. Lou said there was a big operation going on here, and you would be the guy I should talk to about getting into a piece of the action."

Petyr smiled, tight-lipped, before shrugging. "Yes, I forgot to tell Lou that I am not the person you need to speak to about that. My boss is here for a visit and will want to be involved."

Tom kept a slight smile on his face and his eyes bright and interested, but all he wanted to do was scream. "So who would this person be, and how can I get in touch with him?"

"I'm a her, and all you have to do is turn around." The husky, feminine voice had his senses on full alert. He did as he was told—and froze. Her heavily made-up eyes and scarlet-tinged mouth had fooled him for a second. Instead of a fancy cocktail dress, she wore tight jeans, a figure-hugging top and a black leather bomber jacket, but it was Cathy—the woman from Adam's party.

It took her a second longer, but her eyes widened and

her smile faded. "Hello, Tom."

He jumped to his feet and pulled out a chair for her. "I'd say it's nice to see you again, but I'm still in shock."

Her eyes crinkled and her mouth curled as she sat. Christ, was she laughing at him? She raised her hand, clicked her fingers at a passing waiter, and within moments an ice-cold bottle of lager was placed in front of her. She sipped, licked her lips and regarded him from beneath lowered lids. "So, this is a surprise."

Petyr said, "Wait. You know each other?" He was anxiously looking at each of them in turn.

Cathy answered, "We have mutual friends. Petyr, give us some space." She jerked her head in the direction of the bar. Petyr dutifully acceded to her demand and left them alone.

Cathy was unsmiling. "What are you doing here? Who sent you?"

He shook his head, confused. "No one. I need to earn some cash. Look, my brother can't know about this."

"I'm with you on that one." Her tone was dry. "I would prefer you forget it was me you saw here today."

"Sure, sure." Of course, he would tell Marianne and the others. "I still need that money though."

"Surely your brother is wealthy enough to give you what you need?"

He went rigid. "I pay my own way. I live in my brother's home; that is enough largesse to dispense, don't you think?"

"It's your life, not mine. Tell me why I should give you money? What can you give me in return?"

"I've been introduced by Lou, who I believe you've

dealt with previously. He knows my work. I've been coding since I was ten and on the wrong side of legal for almost all the time since. I've never been caught, and I deliver. I can write the code to get you into just about anything."

She leaned back in her chair, rocking on its hind legs as she maintained eye contact. Her gaze was direct and not entirely comfortable. Eventually, she spoke. "Okay, finish your drink and come with me. Let's see what you're made of."

CHAPTER TWENTY-FOUR

The bar didn't seem to be in a dangerous area—there were a few smart restaurants and coffee shops—but Marianne couldn't see a taxi rank as they drew up nearby. She paid their driver and asked, "Will it be easy for us to get a cab later on?"

The driver shrugged. "You will have to hail one that is passing. Maybe there won't be too many around until much later."

Marianne calculated a sum in her head. "Look, I've got two hundred and fifty Bulgarian Lev in cash. I'll give you a hundred up front if you wait for us, and I'll give you the rest when we come back. We shouldn't be long. Half an hour maximum."

He had turned off the car engine before she had finished speaking. "Yes, yes. I will wait there." He pointed to some parking spaces outside a closed shopping mall.

Marianne handed over the cash, and Sue followed her along the street. They were about twenty yards from the bar when three people came out and got into a car parked in front. Marianne threw her arm in front of Sue to halt her and quickly pulled her into the nearest doorway.

"Whoa, what was that all about?"

Marianne said, "Keep back. Don't look out. That was Tom; he was with a man and a woman. I couldn't see them clearly, but they must be his contacts."

Sue froze. "Tom never mentioned where he was meeting them. When you add in that this is where we suspect Petra works, then that means the bar is connected to all of this."

"At the least, it's the meeting point."

Two burly doormen flanked the entrance. They said nothing but looked them both up and down, and the taller of the two pushed open the door, indicating they enter. They were hit by a blast of noise, and the thunderous, pounding music drowned out their thank-yous.

The place was dark, the lighting coming from pulsing strobe lamps. A long bar ran along one wall, and the customers were three deep. The seating areas were dotted around, and to their left three shallow steps led to a dance floor. Marianne had never heard this music before, but the thoughts that came to mind were of Euro-trash techno. A pounding, thumping cacophony that matched the strobing lights. There was a raised platform at the far end, cordoned off by a rope barrier and protected by two unsmiling bouncers. A swarthy, portly man sauntered up to the steps, giggling, an almost naked girl on each arm. You could see their high buttocks beneath the short skirts, and their perfect breasts were barely covered by scraps of leather and lace. The undoubtedly VIP dais had its own small bar area, and waiters milled around with bottles of champagne, filling the glasses of the chosen.

A barely legal waitress squeezed past them. Marianne looked at Sue and raised her eyebrows. The girl was dressed the same as all the other bar staff. The guys wore black trousers, the girls short skirts, but all of them wore cotton polo tops in a variety of different colours, all bearing the Folie's logo. It was the same top the girls had seen in the video.

There was no point in trying to be heard over the music. Marianne touched Sue on the arm and indicated that they move to the bar. With a few sharp moves, Marianne managed to squeeze her way to the counter and pulled out her phone. She found the text from Chloe and opened the attached photo. Because it was a video-to-still transfer, the photo quality wasn't great, but the girl's features were clear enough. She kept her eye on the bartenders, and as soon as one finished serving the guy next to her, she grabbed his arm.

"Do you know this girl?" She shoved the screen in front of the barman's face. He glanced at the picture and shook his head. "Nope."

"Are you sure? Please look again."

"No need. I don't know her. Look, lady, I'm busy. You want a drink or what?"

She wouldn't get anything else here. When she turned around, she couldn't see Sue anywhere. More than a little anxious, she scanned the crowd. The place was packed, and she could barely see two feet in front of her. She moved towards the VIP area and stood on the bottom step, ignoring the look from the bouncers. She could see over the top of the crowd, and to the far left by the edge of the dance floor, she saw Sue talking to two waitresses. She was showing them her phone, but the girls shook their heads and backed away. Sue's shoulders sagged, and Marianne could see the disappointment in her defeated posture. They had been sure it would be easy to find this

Petra—if that was even her real name.

Marianne raised her hand and waved, and when Sue saw her, she smiled and moved across the room. There was a small clearing near the gents beside the VIP area, and it gave them a brief respite from the jostling, drunken crowd.

Sue moved close and, cupping her hand, spoke into Marianne's ear, "Any luck?"

Marianne shook her head. "No, the barman said he didn't know her."

"Same with the two waitresses I spoke to. Mind you, they did look a little taken aback. I think they did recognise her. Wait, that's one of them, and she's in a hurry."

The waitress was moving quickly through the crowd, and she was headed in the direction of the VIP area. She climbed the steps and whispered something to one of the bouncers, who immediately removed the rope barrier. The VIP area was surrounded with a wooden slatted screen, but they could clearly see through the spaces. The waitress approached another member of the serving staff, who had their back to them. She put an arm around the girl's shoulder and whispered something in her ear. The girl dropped the tray of drinks she was carrying, stepped back and spun around, giving them a clear view of her face. It was Petra. She ran out of the VIP area, down the steps and towards the exit. She didn't once look behind her. Sue was quicker than Marianne would have thought. She was on the girl's heels straightaway, and Marianne rushed after her, mindful of her stilettos. They barrelled after her as she escaped through a side door, onto the poorly-lit street.

On another day, the girl would have been much faster.

But she seemed panicked, and her shoes had a platform—
the heel was a good six inches. Although Sue was wearing
sandals with a wedge heel, she had also slowed. The three
of them were contending with the same problem. The
pavements and roads of Sofia were littered with potholes
and broken slabbing. Marianne stumbled and fell against a
low wall; her heel had got caught in the uneven paving.
Sue halted, hesitated. Marianne called out, "Don't wait for
me. Keep going."

The girl had also turned around at the sound of
Marianne's voice and looked behind her but kept on
running. And that was a mistake, for she suddenly crashed
to the ground, and Sue was beside her in a second.

***

Sue stood over Petra, who was trying to get to her feet,
and said, "I don't want to hurt you, but I need answers
from you."

The girl looked at her in confusion. "You think I'm
someone else, lady. I didn't even know you."

"Oh, you're the bitch I'm after all right. Your name is
Petra, or at least that's what you told my husband. I'm sure
it's not your real name." The girl's eyes widened, and she
tensed.

Sue continued. "My husband was Dave Wexford. And
you scammed him out of almost £100,000. It was
everything we had."

Petra opened her mouth "I don't—"

"Shut up. Don't even try to deny it. He recorded your
Skype calls. I've seen the videos. I know it was you. Don't
give me any of your crap. I also know that you are working

for someone, and that's what I need to know."

The girl closed her eyes and slowly shook her head. She shakily got to her feet and leaned against the wall. "You must go away and leave me alone. There is nothing for you here—no answers."

"He killed himself, you know?"

Petra's mouth dropped open, and from the shock in her eyes, Sue knew she wasn't without compassion. "I am sorry. So sorry. I—I don't know what to say."

"Don't give me your false pity. Dave believed you. The bloody fool thought he'd leave me and start this wonderful new life with you. He didn't know you were only after a payout and that you'd disappear into thin air like the treacherous, lying little bitch you are."

Petra's face was devoid of colour apart from two pink spots on her cheeks. "You can't blame me for what your husband did." Her voice shook. No doubt more playacting.

"Actually, I can. But you're nothing to me. I want the puppet-master. I know you are working for someone. Tell me who they are. You didn't kill my husband, they did, as sure as if they put a gun in his hand."

"Forgive me. But I can't say anything. You don't know what they're capable of." And with that, she pushed away from the wall and ran across the street. Sue chased after her, but then Petra stopped, kicked off her shoes and, carrying them in one hand, ran faster than Sue could contend with. She called after her. "We're staying at the Belgrave Plaza, and my name is Sue Wexford. Help us."

CHAPTER TWENTY-FIVE

Cathy sat in the back of the car with Tom while Petyr sat in front with the driver. "Two very different brothers, eh? Does Adam know what you do?"

"No, he doesn't, and I would like to keep it that way. Does your boyfriend know what you do?"

She flashed him an icy look. "What James does or doesn't know is no concern of yours. And remember, you won't be speaking of this meeting to anyone."

She didn't talk to him after that. Just stared out the window, and he did the same, although he was conscious of her presence. They left the central city area, and the car climbed away from the brightly lit streets. They drove for no more than thirty minutes before stopping in an estate of residential apartments. The Communist-era blocks were cheerfully painted a dull grey and looked unlived in, uninviting and desolate. Cathy jumped out of the car, as did Petyr. Tom followed suit. It seemed like this was their final destination, which didn't fill him with confidence.

Cathy glanced over her shoulder as they entered the foyer and walked past the lift. "It never works. We'll take the stairs. Come on, hurry."

The stairs were narrow and lit by a single bulb on each landing. Tom almost gagged at the acrid smell of urine that assaulted his nostrils and clouded his throat but managed to force back the bile that rose. Cathy stopped dead on the first landing; Tom almost crashed into her. Hard hands grabbed him from behind and spun him around. Petyr pushed against his shoulders and pinned him to the wall.

Tom pushed back, struggled. "What the fuck . . . "

"Stop it. I want a word with you." Cathy's voice was a harsh command. He stilled.

She moved closer until she was a whisper from his face. She smelled of peppermint and expensive perfume, but her eyes were cold. "Who sent you? Come on, who put you up to this?"

He shook his head as much as he could. Petyr's arm was across his throat and pressing against this windpipe. "No-one. I don't have a clue what you're talking about." He tensed. Did she know about the girls and their plans?

"So, you want me to believe that you accidentally stumbled into my operation? That you had no idea I was involved?"

At least he could answer that truthfully. "Not a clue. Look, I need some money. Lou wouldn't recommend me if he didn't rate me."

She stared at him; something in her eyes chilled him. Finally, she moved back and turned to Petyr. "Let him go. He's okay."

Petyr stood back, and his look was apologetic. "Sorry. The boss needed to be sure of you."

Cathy said, "Not that I am entirely comfortable having you involved, but I will give you a chance. If you screw with me, there will be repercussions."

She turned away and, to his shame, his eyes followed

her jeans-clad ass. His libido had no self-preservation mechanism. They climbed four flights of stairs to the top floor. At least half a dozen apartment doors were set into one wall of the long corridor. The other wall was interspersed with windows at regular intervals overlooking the road below.

Petyr opened one of the doors and motioned for Tom to enter ahead of him. He did and stopped in surprise the moment he saw what was inside. The space was huge. All of the apartment doors led into this one long room, which mirrored any office the world over with rows of desks, most of which were currently occupied by a ragtag group of people. The ages ranged from teenagers to perhaps mid-fifties, some were smartly turned out, but most wore jeans and T-shirts.

Cathy said, "Six apartments have been knocked into one. It gives us a good space close to town, and yet we have privacy. There is an accounting firm two floors below, but most of the block is empty."

"Why is that?"

"We pay for it to be that way. Let's go somewhere we can speak in private."

She headed to one of the doors at the far end of the room. It led to a fancy office space, metal and chrome and a large window overlooking the city. "Wow, what a view. You would never believe this building housed a space like this."

"That's the whole idea. It doesn't pay to advertise." She sat at her desk, and he took the opposite seat. "So tell me about yourself. How did you get started?"

He figured honesty was the best policy. "I've been

coding since primary school. Adam did computer sciences at MIT, then he set up his first software development firm. I learnt loads from him, and it got me hooked."

"You took a different path."

"Yep. Like many a bored computer geek kid, I got a thrill from seeing what I could get into and where it would take me. I'd been in government agencies—you name it, I've been there, done it—and never had an issue. One day I got into a businessman's computer and rummaged around. I was at college at the time. His men came for me at 2:00 a.m. They were serious criminals, and I thought I was a goner. But instead of giving me a beating, they offered me a job. They were getting into cybercrime, and I could do the odd job for them here and there. I made the transition from a grey-hat hacker, nosing around for the thrill, to the illegal world of a black-hat with ease. It paid well, and I made some similar-minded and equally talented friends, which wasn't the best thing that could have happened."

"They led you astray?"

"You could say that."

"What are you doing now?"

"I got into trouble recently. I've been laying low for a while. It's nothing to be concerned about. I had a disagreement with the guy I was working for." Well, that was the truth, only it happened months ago. And it wasn't just some guy, it had been his brother.

She pushed back from the desk, stood and motioned for him to do the same. "I spoke to your friend, Lou, isn't it? Petyr speaks highly of him, and apparently, he thinks you're the dog's bollocks. I'll give you a chance. Come back tomorrow, and you can see what everyone is doing. When you get back home, you can start thinking of ways for us to do it better, faster and, of course, undetected. We'll talk money when you come up with something. And remember, I'll be exceptionally pissed off if you let anyone know you saw me here."

***

After closing her office door, Cathy sat behind her desk and pulled a mobile phone out of her bag. It was unregistered and didn't leave a trace. She only ever used it to dial one number. The telephone rang ten times, long beeps that tracked the same rhythm as her thudding heart. Finally, he answered.

"Hi. Sorry, I was in a meeting. Is something wrong?"

"You could say that. A guy came here tonight. He was a coder, good credentials and references. He is after some ready cash."

"That seems to be business as usual, Cathy. Why tell me?" He didn't say as much, but she could sense his impatience.

"Because it was Tom."

The silence lengthened until he expelled a long, slow breath. "What did you tell him?"

"Firstly, that he better keep quiet about me being involved in all this; and that he should look around tomorrow and see how he could help us."

"Good. You did the right thing. Let's keep him close."

CHAPTER TWENTY-SIX

Tom had tossed and turned most of the previous night and was in danger of falling asleep in the car. Petyr was driving him to the operation headquarters and the rhythmic noise of the engine, and blasting hot air of the heater was making him drowsy.

He'd called Marianne as soon as he got back to the hotel the night before. He was ticked off that they'd gone to the bar on their own. Christ, anything could have happened to them, but at least they had found Petra.

He'd told Marianne about Cathy and wished he'd been there to see her reaction. This was all getting close to home, but at least they did have some leads.

Petyr's voice interrupted his thoughts. "Here we are. You're daydreaming." If Tom thought the place looked rough the night before, then he was forced to admit it was a whole lot worse in the daylight. The outside of the building was made of concrete slabs, the surrounding area was potholed, and the gardens were overgrown with weeds among patches of long grass.

Once inside the office, he took a better look around and noticed several doors leading into what he supposed were smaller meeting rooms. One opened, and a skinny blonde came out. She wore a tight T-shirt and faded denim shorts. Among catcalls, she high-fived the guy closest to her and said, "My man is sending another five thousand USD for my college fees." Her voice was heavily accented.

A guy at one of the desk units called out, "Hey, Freya, you must be a genius given the number of people who have paid for you to take college courses." Wild clapping accompanied laughter and shouted congratulations. They spoke in English, with a variety of accents. This was a multi-cultural group.

Petyr said, "Those are the quiet rooms where we have video equipment for the honeytrappers to get to know their marks better. They can work from their own places as well, but we don't encourage that."

"She seemed pretty excited."

"Yeah, we work on a commission basis. She will get five hundred once the full amount hits our accounts."

"That's generous."

"We are paid well, and the boss man gets even more."

"Isn't Cathy the boss?" Tom asked innocently.

"No way. She took over here about eight months ago. I used to report to another guy before that. She is a real MIT whizz kid and oversees all of the European operations."

"I like to know who I am getting into bed with. Who is the boss?"

Petyr laughed. "I bet you'd like to share that bed with Cathy. As for who the boss is, it is way above my pay grade to give out that information. Come on, let's show you what we're about."

Tom left it there for the moment. He doubted Petyr even knew who the boss was. But it seemed this operation was much bigger than they first thought. He needed to try and figure out how they could possibly threaten to do enough damage to make these people leave them alone. Or if it was even a possibility now he knew the size of the organisation. Was it too much for them?

***

Marianne had lain awake for most of the night. She'd called Sue as soon as she'd disconnected the call with Tom. Sue was as dumbfounded as she was. Knowing that this Cathy was involved wielded a double-edge. It gave them an in, something to go on, but it also meant something that impacted her personally. Was James part of this? Had he sunk that low? And, dear God, was he behind Amelia being threatened and attacked? Her stomach churned, and she rolled over onto her side and hugged her knees to her chest. She couldn't face the day.

The pinging of a text shattered the quiet. She quickly grabbed her phone. The message was brief. *You have mail.* She opened her email app and scanned her inbox, and there it was, among special offers from department stores, LinkedIn, Facebook notifications and the usual clutter of modern online life.

It was brief and to the point:

We have sent out the initial offer. The email address and telephone number we gave for questions or subscriptions will come directly to us. No communications should go via your offices. This will soon be over. And the girl stays alive.

She sat on the bed, thoughts furiously rushing through her mind. They were running out of time. She called Sue. She answered almost immediately.

"Good morning, Marianne."

"Same to you. I've received an email. They sent out the prospectus."

"What does that mean?"

"It is the offer documentation. It will give details about the fund, where it invests, expected rates of return and yield and, of course, where to send your money if you want to subscribe."

"And so it begins. How long will we have?"

"I would imagine at least a couple of weeks until they close the subscriptions. But it could be any time they decide. I imagine they will create some hype in the offer emails. They will want people to believe they're getting in early on the next big thing, so the subscription period won't run for long."

"Well, I guess we can't do anything until we meet with Tom tonight and see how his day has gone."

Marianne thought for a moment. "Let's go back to the bar, and try to see Petra again."

A heavy sigh came through the telephone line. "Are you sure that's a good idea? She may not go back there. Plus, if the bar is connected to all of this, we could be walking into danger."

"We have to give it a go. We're running out of time." She hated that her voice shook.

"Okay, Marianne, okay."

***

They were good; Tom gave them that. There were some seriously talented people working here. The actual scam operators took over once initial contact was made or access obtained.

He asked Petyr, "How many of these social media workers do you have?"

"It varies from time to time. It is the same core group of people who we have trained in exploitation and taught the appropriate language to use to build trust. We build up a file on the mark and provide information and background history to enable them to build relationships by telling people what they want to hear."

"Smart." It sickened Tom that people's vulnerabilities and loneliness were being exploited in this way.

"Yeah, the initial line of threat was ransomware. Most people pay, terrified they're going to lose all their applications and saved files. We started analysing the data in their systems and on social media. That led all the way to online honeytraps and sweet, unassuming messages that, when opened, possessed the power to infect your entire system and forward the virus to everyone in your address book."

"That's a lot of data to sift through."

"Indeed. We look for anything that helps us build a picture of that individual, then we can determine the edge that will allow us the opportunity to extract money—by whatever means necessary."

"Looks like you've got all this sussed."

Hacking was a game to him in the past, but Marianne and the others had shown him the brutal effect on real people, yet it was merely a business model to Petyr and his ilk.

Petyr walked across to a bank of desks and indicated that Tom sit and look at the monitors.

"What do you want to show me?"

"This." Petyr pointed to one of the screens. "This is the coding that we are about to use en masse. We have trialled it in the UK over the last six months, and it works well. We are seeing big results. The code, which we call a virus for ease, is attached to something that can be opened on Facebook or email, something that you have to click. On Facebook, it will typically be a funny picture or video and by email perhaps the video of what looks like a news story. As soon as you open it, the virus is in. Initially, it creates a pathway into your system and will infiltrate your address book and send a similar message to all your email contacts or your Facebook friends. They click, and it happens again and again and again, giving us remote access into all of those users' systems. The beauty is that it is completely undetectable, and, if need to be, the virus also has a self-destruct element that allows us to destroy a particular user's accounts if they don't pay."

Tom kept his mouth shut. He'd seen one of these viruses before. He hadn't expected anyone else to duplicate it this soon.

Petyr prodded, "What do you think?"

"Very clever. I can see that it will be useful." He took a closer look at the coding on the screen and froze. Coders were like graffiti artists. They didn't want anyone to know who they were, but they did want people to recognise their work. Like the graffiti artist signed his nickname to his work, so did a coder. But they didn't use a signature. The used a symbol. A symbol that wouldn't change the coding, that wouldn't mean anything to anyone looking at it except for those in the know, who would recognise their handicraft. Tom saw the symbol, blinked and reread it. He knew that symbol. And he knew it belonged to the originator of the code. For he was the coder, and that was the symbol he used when he developed it.

CHAPTER TWENTY-SEVEN

The same taxi driver was in front of the rank outside the hotel, and Marianne directed him to take them back to Folies. "You like the bar, ladies?" Marianne stared at him. He'd seen them chasing the girl. "Yes, that's right."

"You go there to meet someone?"

"No, we like it. The place is filled with local colour."

"Ah, you think it a fun place?"

Marianne and Sue kept quiet, and after a few more of the driver's inane comments, they were met with silence until he stopped outside the bar. Marianne jumped out first. "Wait here, please. We won't be long."

As they walked in, Sue indicated the bouncers at the door. "Those two guys are different from the ones last night. Hopefully there won't be any bother."

"There's only one way to find out." Marianne sailed on ahead, remembering the old adage that said you could get in anywhere by simply acting as if you belonged. She swept up the shallow steps that led to the entrance, and a bored-looking bouncer pushed the door open.

The bar was relatively empty. Only a few tables were occupied, and the VIP area was deserted. Food was being served, and she guessed the place doubled as a restaurant during the lunch hour.

Sue grabbed Marianne's arm. "Look, that's the girl I spoke to last night. The one who tipped Petra off."

Marianne approached the waitress, Sue trailing behind. "Can I have a word?"

The girl stopped, a polite smile on her face. "Of course, what can I do for you?"

"You can tell us where your little friend is—the waitress my friend spoke to you about last night." She waved a hand in Sue's direction.

The girl's smile disappeared, and the shutters came down. "I am sorry. I don't know anything."

"Okay, play it that way if you want. But we don't want to harm your friend or cause her any problems."

The girl rolled her eyes.

"No, we genuinely don't. I know you have to do what is needed to get by, and it may not always be palatable. We need some information, and we're willing to pay for it."

"This is nothing to me. I cannot help."

Marianne pleaded. "We don't want the girl. We want to know who is in charge. Look. Just tell us. Please."

"I can't help. I am sorry."

A harsh voice interrupted them. "Natalia, get on with your work. I don't pay you to stand around chatting."

Natalia slowly backed away, as all colour leached from her face. "Sorry, Anna." Her tone was deferential and, if Marianne wasn't mistaken, a little afraid.

The woman turned to Marianne. She was of average height with a muscular physique, her long dark hair scraped back into a ponytail. Her makeup was heavy, her dress provocative. Her face, however, was unsmiling and her eyes hostile.

166

"What do you want here? I saw you last night, and here you are again today. This is not the place for people like you."

Her voice was laced with attitude, and Marianne sensed a threat in her words. She nudged Sue. "We're going. Don't worry."

The woman, Anna, stepped in front of them, effectively blocking their exit. "What do you want with Irina? I saw you follow her when she left last night."

Ah, Irina was her name, not Petra. Marianne babbled, "We got the wrong girl. Sorry to have been a nuisance. We won't be back."

She grabbed Sue's arm and brushed past Anna, who reluctantly moved out the way, throwing her arms in the air. "Go, go, but be careful. I wouldn't like to see you get hurt over mistaken identity."

Marianne didn't break her stride as she headed to the exit. Outside, her eyes strained as they adjusted to daylight after the unnatural darkness of the club. They hurried along the street, and it was with sighs of relief that they sank into the seats as the cab quickly took off.

"Jeez, that woman freaked me out," Sue said.

"Yep, a bit of a scary bitch. We can't come back here even if we wanted to. All in all, it's been a disappointment. Petra, or should I say, Irina, is a dead end. We'll not catch sight of that one again." To her shame, her voice caught on the words.

Sue laid a comforting hand on hers. Marianne's instinctive reaction would once have been to pull away, but she didn't. "I am sorry, Marianne. Let's hope Tom has better luck."

Marianne's phone vibrated, and she quickly answered, putting the call on speaker.

"Hi, it's Tom. Let's meet for dinner. I've been recommended a place called Nero's, which apparently has good food that isn't overpriced. I'll meet you there. Shall we say six-thirty, and we can have a drink first?"

***

They were leaving the next day and were no farther forward. Marianne's mind whirled as she waited for Sue in the hotel foyer. She spent the afternoon trying to ignore their current predicament and catching up on work emails. None of her colleagues mentioned anything about the new fund, which meant they hadn't taken any direct enquiries about it. At least that was what she hoped.

"You look like you are deep in thought. You okay?"

Marianne shrugged at Sue. "My mind is jumbled. I don't know what to think. I hope Tom has found a way forward."

"He strikes me as resourceful. But we don't know a great deal about him, do we? Actually, none of us truly know each other."

"You are right. But we're all each other has at the moment." Marianne started walking towards the door. "Come on, let's grab a taxi and go meet Tom. Hopefully, he did better than us today."

***

Sue stood in line beside Marianne as the concierge hailed a taxi. The usual crowd of beggars stood on either side of the hotel entrance. The cries for money were accompanied by gestures showing all the goods they were supposedly selling. The temperature was pleasant, and Sue shrugged her arms out of her coat. She noticed that someone in the crowd was staring at her intently. The figure was slight and wore jeans and a baggy sweatshirt with a hood obscuring their face. They clutched several roses in one hand.

Marianne's voice drew her attention. "Come on, here's a cab."

As Sue walked past the beggars, she heard: "Sue Wexford, come buy my roses."

Her head jerked around. A part of her was not surprised to discover that it was the hoodie-clad beggar. They raised their hand and drew the hood back until their face was clearly visible. It was Irina, formerly known as Petra. Sue immediately moved towards her. She could hear Marianne in the background. "Come on, Sue, what are you doing?"

Sue stood in front of the girl, ignoring all the other hands reaching out to her. "Why are you here?"

"Here, take my roses." The girl bent closer and whispered in Sue's ear, "Please give me some money. Make it look real."

Sue scrambled in her purse and pulled out some lev, which she pushed towards the girl. She was so close her breath feathered Sue's ear as she whispered, "I can't be long. Meet me tonight. The address is in with the roses. Bring more money." And with that, she turned and disappeared into the crowd.

CHAPTER TWENTY-EIGHT

Marianne rolled her eyes and kept her voice low as they settled themselves at the table where Tom was waiting for them. "Just open the bloody note, will you?"

She explained to Tom, "She was too nervous to open the damn thing in front of the taxi driver. I don't know what you were thinking. Did you wonder if he was working for the scamming gang? Hmmm, maybe the waiter over there is as well."

Sue's retort was quick. "You can mock me all you want, but that girl was scared, and the woman at the bar frightened me."

"I know, I know, I'm on edge too. Please open the note."

The roses were wrapped in cellophane, and they could all clearly see the note sticking out the top. Sue pulled it out and read, "9:00 p.m. 8 Avenue Vladimir Outside the blue building."

Tom took his phone out and tapped away. "Right, got it on google maps. It seems to be about fifteen minutes from here by taxi."

They ordered food and drinks, and Marianne waited until the bottle of red wine was opened and poured and the waiter left them alone before saying, "How did you get on, Tom? Are you any closer to finding out who is behind this?"

Tom didn't answer straight away. He sipped his wine, and Marianne saw a dark flush spread across his neck. He seemed decidedly uncomfortable.

Sue cocked her head to one side. "Are you okay, Tom? Because you don't look it."

Tom sighed and fiddled with the cutlery at his place setting. He let out a deep breath, his gaze direct. "It was interesting today. These guys are carrying out all the scams we have seen plus many others. They are closely managed though, and I couldn't find anything about who is behind it."

Marianne's heart sank as her stomach tumbled. "This means our only option is for Irina to be able to tell us something, isn't it?"

Sue said, "At least we still have that option." She looked at Tom. "You've done all you could. It isn't your fault."

"It might be."

"What do you mean?" Marianne asked.

He sighed and ran a hand through his hair. His Adam's apple was working furiously. What the hell did he have to say?

"I saw something. It was a piece of code that lies hidden on a system and opens a doorway. A hacker can enter and access your entire computer network, but there is no digital footprint. They are like a ghost."

"Is that what happened with ours?"

"Yes, they root around your system and build up a picture. They want to know your worries, fears, hopes and dreams so they can play on them and manipulate you."

"And this code would have got into the system with the Christmas message?" Sue asked.

"Absolutely. Christmases, holidays and special events are great for getting access. People are naive and are enjoying the holiday spirit. They'll happily click on something when they don't even know who the sender is."

Marianne had the clear impression she wouldn't like what she was going to hear next. "So why is this your fault, Tom?

"You can leave a signature in the coding. It could be a symbol or a line of code that is meaningless. One that doesn't do anything at all and doesn't impact any software applications. If someone copies your code, there is a good chance they will copy the entire thing. That way you will know if they are using your code. You could tell if someone else obtained access to it. It often happens with companies who have their own coders and therefore have proprietary material that is unique to their business."

"And . . . ?" Marianne held her breath.

"I always used the exact same stream of signature code. I invented the virus. The virus that the scammers are using."

Marianne heard the words, but they didn't make sense. "You little snake. Are you part of this? Are you?" Her voice rose, and she slammed her fist on the table, causing the bottle of wine to fall onto its side. The contents spilt out and slithered across the white tablecloth like a river of blood. The waiter came rushing over and hurriedly cleared the table. The three of them sat in silence while the table was readied. Marianne turned to the waiter. "Thank you.

We will have another bottle of red wine, please."

Tom opened his mouth to speak, but Marianne held up a hand to silence him. "Not yet. I imagine Sue and I will both need a drink while we hear your story."

Another bottle was deposited on the table, and Marianne poured a glass for each of them. She sat back, sipped at the drink and said, "Okay, the floor is yours. You tell us how this happened and what you are going to do about it."

"I don't know how it happened. I worked for Adam's software company but got kicked out a year ago. I'd been in a bad crowd for a while, and he found out I'd been hacking. He didn't want it to spill over into his own company—which is completely legit, by the way. Adam was enraged I'd been using his computer system, and he wouldn't let me take anything I had been working on. He said it would be safer that way and temptation would be out of reach."

"So your brother could be behind this?"

"Marianne, you've met the guy. He's a schmoozing fancy-pants. This isn't his style. The most likely explanation is that someone got access to those computer files. There was a lot of work I left behind, not only Dolus."

Marianne had to ask. "What is Dolus?"

He blushed. "Ah, I name my code. Dolus was the Greek god of trickery and guile."

Marianne stared. He really was just a kid at heart.

Sue said, "So what are we going to do?"

"I have to talk to Adam. He needs to know that someone has accessed those files."

The food arrived, and Marianne slowly started to eat the steaming plate of pasta. How could she trust him? But then she remembered he was her only hope. Unless the girl, Irina, knew something that could help.

They ate quickly, conscious of the time, but also, Marianne reflected, what was there to talk about? Sue was lost in her thoughts and picked at her meal. Tom took a few mouthfuls and pushed his plate to the side. Marianne picked at half her meal but drank more than her share of the wine. Sue drank the remainder, and the alcohol seemingly made her brave.

"You're a dark horse, aren't you, Tom?" There was a hard edge to her usually soft voice.

Tom flushed a deep, dark red. "It's in my past. I'm different now."

Marianne said, "So we're to believe you realised the error of your ways?"

"Yes, and I feel guilty."

Marianne signalled for the bill. "I find myself completely unconcerned by your motives or your supposed guilt. You said you will continue to help us, and that's all I need to know. I'm keeping an eye on you, a close eye. Come on, let's go and see what this girl has to say."

CHAPTER TWENTY-NINE

The taxi driver stopped at the address they had given him and asked, "Are you sure this is the place?"

Sue checked the paper in her hand. "It must be."

Tom handed several notes to the driver. "There you go. That should be enough." He opened the car door, jumped out and held the door open for first Sue and then Marianne. The driver called after them, "Do you want me to wait?"

Tom shook his head. "No thanks, mate. We'll be fine."

"But we will need a taxi to get back." Sue considered the deserted street. "And it doesn't look like we'll get one that quickly here."

Tom waved the taxi on its way. "We're sticking our noses into some nasty people's business. You never know who anyone is working for or even if they have a general arrangement where they provide information. You don't want the same taxi driver taking you all over the place. Especially if you're doing something you don't want the bad people to know about."

Sue glanced at Marianne, who shook her head. They were obviously keeping quiet about their earlier travels with the same cab driver, then.

The street was wide and dark, and the solitary lamppost

flickered in a desultory manner. There were a few cars parked along the road, but there were no pedestrians. The buildings huddled close together, their shabby doors matched by the peeling and faded paintwork on the window ledges. Few windows were lit apart from slivers of light poking through the gaps in drawn curtains.

The blue building across the street was apparently in darkness, but if you stared hard, you could see a glimmer of light escaping heavy drapes.

Sue turned to Marianne. "Should we knock on the door?"

Marianne shook her head. "I'm not too sure. Let's wait here for a moment. It's only just nine o'clock."

The silence lengthened, and they exchanged glances. None of them knew what to expect. A creak of an opening door was like a cannon blast in the quiet street. Their eyes fixed on the blue house. Irina came out, wearing jeans and a baggy sweatshirt, and carefully closed the door behind her. Looking around the street, she crossed over towards them. As she drew closer, Sue could see the drawn face clearly illuminated by the pale moonlight.

Hurrying past, she stared straight ahead and said, "Follow me but stay back."

They kept close behind as they shadowed her. Sue looked around as if they were searching for a particular address. She was worried at the girl's obvious distress that they would be seen together. Was she being watched? She glanced at Marianne and Tom and could almost touch the vibrations of tension.

They headed towards a crossroads. Irina turned swiftly to the right, and they followed suit. They entered a narrow alleyway no more than two feet wide. It was a passageway between two tall buildings. As Irina receded farther into the dark, her voice quietly beckoned them. "Please, come closer."

They did, and Sue advanced in front until she was close enough that she could easily have reached out and touched her. "You wanted to see me. Why?"

The alley was relatively dark except for the muted light from small round windows set into the roof space of the buildings on either side. Irina's face was concealed, but her eyes were visible. And at this moment she seemed pained and unless Sue was mistaken, ashamed.

"I am twenty-two years old. I have a son. He is five, and he lives with my parents. This is their street. I work at the bar at night. During the day, I work in a shop. And I am paid little. And to earn enough money to look after my son, I sometimes work for some people who will pay me well if I read a script and talk to people online. That's all I have to do."

Irina's voice broke, but Sue wasn't moved.

Tom said, "Who are these people? Do you work for Petyr?"

Irina's eyes widened, and she took an involuntary step backwards.

"I know Petyr," Tom continued. "I know Cathy. I know if you are working for them, there is someone else behind this. Do you know who it is?"

She shook her head. "I am sorry. I cannot help."

Sue grabbed her wrist and held tight. Irina's eyes flashed, but she didn't move away. "You needn't worry. You won't be connected to this. Not by us, at any rate. We didn't even know Irina was your real name. We only want to know who is behind this. I lost my husband, and a girl not much older than you lost her mother. My friend's business and her family are in danger. And another friend lost her one chance for a new life. You're involved in a dirty business. Do the decent thing."

"Shit!" Marianne hissed. "Look who's here."

Sue turned and looked back along the alley. It was Anna, the woman from the club. She was accompanied by two heavyset men, and all three were advancing towards them. The woman called out, "Well done, Irina. You can go now. We'll deal with this."

Sue kept a tight grip as she pushed Irina against the wall. "You treacherous little bitch. My husband is dead— fucking dead—all because of you. Don't you get it? Whoever is behind these scams caused a woman I have known for years to kill herself because she couldn't face what she'd done and couldn't see a way out. That's what you're involved in, love. You're a dirty little piece of trash."

Irina's face was set, unsmiling, but there was something in her eyes that Sue could almost believe was regret. "What did you expect? They own me." Her words were a pained whisper.

The trio reached Tom, who stood protectively in front of Sue and Marianne. One of the heavies pushed him against the wall and held him by the throat.

Anna hissed at them, "You better be gone from Sofia by tomorrow, or the boys will come to visit you. It is not our fault that some stupid people killed themselves. There is nothing good for you here, only bad." She pointed at the man holding Tom. "Ivan will release him, and then you must leave immediately."

Ivan didn't let go. He squeezed his hands tight around Tom's neck. Sue froze; Tom was going purple.

Anna laughed. "Ivan, I spoil your fun. Let him go." There was steel in her voice.

Ivan stepped back and loosened his grip as Tom straightened, kicked out and launched a low blow to his shin. This threw Ivan off balance, and he stumbled to the side. Tom followed with a strong punch to the heavy's chin. He fell against the wall.

"Georgi, do something!" Anna's command to her second heavy was answered immediately as the Frankenstein-like character that was Georgi lumbered forward, and jammed his massive fist into Tom's stomach. Tom folded over, and Georgi grabbed him by the shoulder, pulled him upright and, with a vicious thrust, kneed Tom between his legs.

"Fuck." Tom doubled over and collapsed to the ground, groaning.

Anna looked at Sue, still holding on to Irina. "Let her go."

Sue did, and Irina ran, barely looking at Anna as she left the alley.

Anna hissed, "I meant what I said. Next time, we come after all three of you."

She turned and walked away, her heavies following her out of the alley.

CHAPTER THIRTY

Emily invited Chloe for dinner. It was chilli con carne and a bottle of cheap wine, but the food was delicious, even if she did say so herself, and the wine not too bad. They'd moved onto a second bottle that Chloe brought with her.

Emily sat on the sofa, her feet tucked to the side; Chloe sat on the floor, her back against one of the chairs, her legs stretched out in front as she scrolled through her mum's laptop.

Emily savoured the blackberry tones. Since her divorce, she'd been on an economy drive. She usually bought wine that was as cheap as possible without actually being vinegar. "This is nice. Where did you get it?"

"It was one of Mum's. I thought that was fitting. It wouldn't have cost a lot of money, but it's certainly drinkable."

Emily took another sip and appraised Chloe as she peeked over the rim of her glass. "How you doing?"

Chloe's smile wobbled, and she briefly closed her eyes. She exhaled, long and low. "I don't know. I'm busy trying to sort out the finances and hoping and praying that someone pays for what they've done that I haven't processed that Mum is gone forever."

Emily sipped her wine, unsure of how to reply when

suddenly there was a loud pinging noise. It was coming from the laptop. Chloe clicked on the keyboard. She froze. "It's a notification from Mum's Facebook page. It's from Tony Anderson."

Emily stared. "Shit. That's the guy who scammed her." She quickly sat beside Chloe on the floor. "Open it, then."

Chloe did, and Emily leaned over her shoulder as they both read the message at the same time. They looked at each other, then back at the screen.

I am so sorry I haven't been in touch, Anita. I've been so worried that I haven't been able to concentrate on anything or speak to anyone. My son's operation went well overall, but there has been a complication. The insurance is still tied up and will be for another few weeks, and the bills are mounting. I hate to ask. Could you help? I will pay you back as soon as the insurance pays out. You know, I've been thinking. I'd love to speak to you properly. Maybe we could Skype. We have a real connection, and I need you so much right now. Shall we meet in person when all this is over?

"The utter bastard." Chloe shoved the laptop to the side and jumped up. She started pacing in front of the fireplace. "I can't believe this. I've got a right mind to reply, telling them exactly what they've done and what happened to my mum. They killed her." Chloe fell to her knees and started to weep. Emily crouched, put her arms around her and held her close. She made shushing noises as she stroked the younger girl's hair. "I know it's difficult. But we can't be hasty. Maybe we shouldn't reply until we speak to the others?"

"Why the hell not? It isn't all about Marianne, you know. Crap happened to others as well. Yet all we're doing is trying to make it right for her."

She sobbed, and Emily's heart ached. Her mother wasn't even cold yet, and she was having to contend with the person who had been instrumental in Anita taking her own life. Or was she? "Sweetheart, none of these people are who they say they are. There is no Tony Anderson. He is a fictitious character; a made-up person who the scammers thought would be most appealing to your mum. Any number of people could be behind the communications, not just one person."

"What difference does that make? They have to pay for this."

"And they will. We may be working on a deadline to help Marianne right now, but in helping her, we hurt these people, and isn't that what we all want?"

"Yes, I guess. But what should we do? Should we ask the others?"

Emily bit her lip, thought about it. "Yes, of course. We can ask Marianne or maybe Sue or even Tom what we should do."

Chloe started to speak, but Emily didn't hear what she was saying. What she heard was ex-husband's voice telling her, as usual, that she was insipid and listless and never made a decision for herself. She relied on other people too much. His voice berated her for leaving her well-paid, but stressful, job. It was a familiar argument they had encountered many times before. She tried to tell him, attempted to make him understand that the loss of her baby was too big, too all-encompassing. She would never get over it, and only desired to live in her quiet bubble.

But for once in her life, she wanted to answer the voice back. She could look after herself. Hadn't she been doing that for the last couple of years, maybe longer? Her husband emotionally left long before he physically moved out.

Chloe was staring at her. "Have you heard a word I've been saying?"

"No, I haven't. Sorry. Let's think about how we should reply." She had a thought. "Let me see your mum's Facebook profile pic. Did she post lots of pictures of herself?"

Chloe laughed. "No way. Mum's Facebook picture was one of me when I was about four years old. She didn't think she was photogenic and would always destroy any pictures she was in. Since everything went digital, she'd either avoid the camera or ask someone to delete it." She stopped, stricken. "Oh God, I hardly have any photos of her."

"I'm sorry about that, but it is a positive in this situation. Even if the hackers went through your mum's computer system, it's unlikely they would know what she looked like?"

"Yeah, I guess that's right. Why?"

"I'm about to make a new friend."

***

Marianne exited the taxi first, before turning to help Tom. He brushed her hand away. "I'm fine." His voice was techy.

Marianne rolled her eyes and blew out a huff of air. "There's no need to be all macho. You got kneed in your balls. It's bound to hurt."

"Thanks for reminding me." His teeth were gritted, and

there was a bite to his tone. Marianne decided silence was best.

She marched ahead, ignoring the beggars, as Tom and Sue followed her into the deserted hotel foyer. It was that time of night where guests were either fast asleep in bed or out at the late-night bars. They headed straight for the elevators. Their flight was early in the morning, and there was a lot to process. None of them would sleep much tonight.

A voice called out from the reception desk. "Mrs Wexford, I have a message for you."

Sue halted and shot them a quick look before going to the reception desk, where the smiling night clerk handed her an envelope. "You have a telephone message, madam."

Sue took the envelope and ripped it open. Head bent, she read as she walked back to them.

Marianne asked. "What is it?"

"It must be from Irina. Listen."

Monaco and London. That is where Cathy goes from here. It is all I know. I'm sorry.

Marianne made the connection immediately and looked at Tom. "Didn't you say your brother has a place in Monaco?"

***

Emily finished reading the messages between Anita and Tony. It broke her heart.

Anita had been sweet, lovely and flirtatious. She'd shown great care and sympathy with the predicament of Tony's son, the one supposedly undergoing treatment for a life-threatening disease. And Tony, the former US Army veteran now running his own garage in Pennsylvania, seemed lovely, a man you could love, a man you could trust.

"What a crock of shit this is. You can see the bloody con taking shape, drawing your mum in bit by bit. And all these excuses about the insurance."

It was to have carried on for a period of time after he left the army, but he was having trouble with the paperwork. The insurers were trying to say they would only cover a certain amount. But the army lawyer confirmed that it was okay. He was covered. He had it in writing. They hadn't paid the hospital and wouldn't be able to for some time, and that meant they might stop treatment.

Chloe said, "He had her at hello and all the way through. I have to admit that I would have believed him."

Emily knew she would have done the same. She would have wanted to buy into the image of a handsome, silver-haired army veteran, a widower trying to look after his family as best he could. From his raw, bare comments, one would surmise that his son's illness ripped him open, and left a gaping, emotional wound. Anita would have been compelled to help him.

"Pity the bastard doesn't exist." With a new determination, Emily logged into Facebook messenger and typed a message to Tony-the-imposter. Simple and to the point. She asked Chloe to read it. She nodded her confirmation, and Emily pressed send.

Tony, I have been worried about you. I will need to wait a few days to get some extra money, but I would love to speak to you by video. How do I do that? I'm not that technical.

Chloe said, "I guess we wait now."

"Yes, we do. But we also need to get a plan in action. We need to talk to the others."

CHAPTER THIRTY-ONE

The three of them headed straight from Heathrow to Tom's apartment. Tom's plan was simple. He would access his brother's business computer system and get to his old files with the coding details.

Marianne sat on the battered sofa and asked, "Why do you need the files?"

"I don't need the actual files as such. I need to identify who has accessed them since I left."

"Wow, you can tell that?"

"Everything leaves a trail, but sometimes you can only find a pattern in the dust if you put the right detectors in place. A background program ran behind all my files, telling me if anyone accessed my data."

"Well, we're racing against the clock here. Let's hope you find it sooner rather than later."

She didn't regret the rebuke in her voice. She'd received a simple, one-line text from Jenny. *Is it over yet?* She replied that she was working on it. She hadn't heard anything else since. And she hadn't dared to ask how Amelia was.

Sue said, "This could be someone who works in your brother's company or, I do hate to say this, but we have to be realistic, your brother himself."

Tom laughed. "Adam? No way, he is too uptight for any of this. No, Adam plays inside the rules. Always."

His smile was tight, and Marianne figured he was a little offended. The truth was they had to look at this as an option. "Your coding was taken from files belonging to your brother's company, and Monaco, where your brother lives, is implicated through that Cathy woman. Who, lest you forget, we met at your brother's party."

"I hear you. Really, I do, but I know Adam. This isn't his style. And Cathy is hooked up with your old boyfriend. What does he have to do with all this?"

She'd asked for that. "Okay, let's leave it there."

"Nothing would please me more." He settled himself at his desk and, stretching out, cracked his knuckles before tapping away at the keyboard.

Marianne peered over his shoulder. "So what are you doing?"

"I'm cloaking my IP address and using my old credentials to get into the back end of Adam's business systems."

He swore, sat up straight, and then hunched over the keyboard, furiously typing.

"Shit!" Tom pushed back from his desk. "I can't get in. The security has been massively upgraded."

"What does that mean?" Sue asked. "That it will take you longer?"

"It means that every time I try and find a new way in, I come across another trap. A little beast of coding waiting to set off an alarm and alert whoever is monitoring it that the system has been breached. It means I can't get in. My IP address is hidden, but they will know someone tried to access that area and will immediately erect additional barriers. I can't get through the security." He finished with a frustrated snarl.

Marianne didn't want to hear this. "So what the hell are we going to do now?"

He shrugged. "Now I have no choice but to speak to Adam and ask him to give me access to my old files. The only problem is that he isn't in London. He has gone back to Monaco. This isn't a subject I can raise over the phone, not with our past history. I'll need to wait until he is back, but I don't have any idea when that will be."

Marianne's voice was a cold bite, and it surprised even her. Time was running out. "You get one chance to do things right in life. You'll go to Monaco to see him in person. And Sue and I will come with you."

***

Cathy's heart raced faster as the dial tone beeped once, twice, three times.

He answered with a curt, "Yes?"

For all her experience, for all she'd done in the past, giving this man lousy news was not something she relished. "An unauthorised user was snooping around the system."

There was silence for a moment. No words were spoken, but she knew his anger from the laboured breaths that flowed through the receiver. They said it was often the most charming who could suddenly flip to a darker side, and that was true here.

"Have we been compromised?"

She was quick to reassure him. "No, no—absolutely not. The new firewall and added security levels would have thwarted them."

"Either that or they knew they were walking into a trap. If that was the case, then we are dealing with someone who knows their way around secured access points. And that level of experience wouldn't be innocently strolling through our files."

"You know kids play around all the time. It's a badge of honour to see which companies they can get access to. Some even go after government records. I am sure it was nothing."

"Oh, you're sure, are you? Well, that does give me comfort."

His voice was cold, and she winced. She sounded like an optimistic Girl Scout. "I will keep an eye on it."

"Do that. But, if this is deliberate, why target this particular system? There are bigger fish to fry elsewhere. Just as long as no one tries to access any other areas. Make sure of it."

"Yes, yes, I will. I'll see you tonight."

CHAPTER THIRTY-TWO

Adam's villa sat high above the bay of Monaco, and it reminded Marianne of something out of a Bond movie. Pale cream walls were covered in scarlet and white bougainvillaea; the green-painted shutters gave the house a sleepy look. They strolled through a courtyard bathed in sunlight and circled a central fountain. There were no neighbouring properties in sight, and the vista was of the bay of Monte-Carlo and the turquoise sea beyond. This was a house built for pleasure and dipped in decadence. The heavy wooden door swung open, and Adam came out, a smile on his face.

"Welcome back, Tom. Ladies, you look lovely. It is a pleasure to see you here in Monaco, albeit a surprise. Sorry, I couldn't see you alone, but this drinks evening was planned some time ago. I have a pretty packed schedule."

Marianne figured Adam's upcoming appointments would be more fancy parties and events. Adam was undoubtedly the sociable type. The glance he gave her was appreciative, and she supposed they brushed up okay. She wore a simple black dress that stopped just above the knee. Spaghetti straps crisscrossed in the back, and silver sandals and a matching clutch completed the look. She'd swept her hair up and gone heavy on the eye makeup. Her uniform was in place, and she was ready to face the world. She had to admit that Sue surprised her. Her unexpectedly good figure was shown to advantage in a fitted raspberry off-the-shoulder number. Tom was in dark trousers and a crisp white shirt, mirroring his elder brother's choice of clothing.

They followed Adam inside and walked through the cool, tiled hallway, which opened onto a vast living area, furnished with cream sofas and royal-blue accents. The look was eclectic and inviting. The wall facing them was made of open French windows leading onto a balustraded terrace. A waiter offered them a selection of drinks. Marianne and Tom chose champagne. A clearly delighted Sue picked a glass of pale pink rosé, and Marianne suffered a pang of—what? Surely it couldn't be envy. She was perfectly happy with herself exactly how she was. Marianne didn't particularly like champagne but chose it as she considered it the done thing. Sue happily grabbed the rosé simply because she wanted it. Marianne was very different from the girl she had been. But that was a good thing, surely?

Adam swept his arm across the room. "Please enjoy yourselves while Tom and I have a chat."

Tom touched her arm. "You and Sue have a mingle. I won't be long. Don't do anything I wouldn't."

Well, that surely gave them plenty of scope.

***

Tom had been to the villa less than a handful of times. Adam bought it just before they argued and a relationship of cool hellos and quick goodbyes became the norm. He didn't have a clue where he was going as Adam led him through wide corridors, the walls adorned with expensive artwork. Business must be exceptionally profitable.

"You said on the phone you needed some security codes you'd been working on, and it was to do with Marianne and Sue. What's going on?"

The suspicion in his brother's voice irked him. He recited the pre-prepared fabrication. "Marianne and Sue initially hired me to run a security check on their business applications. They are expanding into an online sales storefront and want me to re-design their website, along with creating protocols for security and management. It's an area I'd like to get into."

"I told you on the phone that I'd be back in the UK soon. It couldn't wait until then?"

"No, the girls are desperate to get their site live, and they offered to pay me more if I could get it finished in the next week."

His brother appraised him in silence for a long moment before shrugging. "I hope they paid for your flight."

Tom laughed. "Of course. I'm billing plenty for this."

"Good, it's profitable work if you do it well. Perhaps you're finally growing up."

Tom didn't answer as he knew this wasn't a question and Adam wasn't inviting comments.

Adam stopped before an open door and said, "I've organised for access to be set up in here for you."

The small sitting room faced the side gardens. The French doors were closed, and an electric fan whirred away the stifling heat. For a weird moment Tom wondered if the doors were locked. Did Adam want to prevent him from leaving? He must stop thinking like this. Adam was his brother and wouldn't do him any harm.

Adam's voice came from behind him. "There's a laptop there. A user ID has already been created and entered. Someone will log you in and watch while you access the correct file area.

"Christ, Adam, what's with the Fort Knox security? What the hell do you expect me to do?" Tom was, of course, lying to his brother about his motives, but there was no need for this cloak-and-dagger stuff.

Adam flashed a tight smile. "It's sensible to take precautions." He turned and looked over Tom's shoulder as the French doors opened from the outside and Ryan stepped in. "Ah, there you are. Let Tom have the access as agreed so he can source the files he needs."

Ryan smiled. "Sure, come on, let's get you logged on."

The door closed behind Adam. Tom shook his head. "I guess you're my minder. Funny job for the finance guy."

"I'm here for some business meetings, and Adam thought it would be better if I gave you access since we know each other."

Tom shrugged and waited as Ryan tapped away and entered the passcode.

"Okay, I assume the files are under whatever was your username. What was it?"

"Just my initials. THC."

Ryan smirked. "I won't ask what the H stands for."

"Yeah, best not to."

"Anyway, here you go. You're in. What are you looking for again?"

He sat in front of the monitor and said, "Just some security code I wrote for websites that have a lot of client sign-ups and payments online. I need it for the work I'm doing for Marianne and Sue. It will save me ages if I don't have to develop it all over again."

"Hey, whatever pays the bills."

Tom scanned the screen. He'd been given access to his old directory. This would be a piece of cake—as long as Ryan left him alone. "Hey, bud, you couldn't grab me some of that water could you?" A bottle of Perrier rested in an ice bucket, surrounded by tall tumblers.

"Sure, I'll get some myself as well."

As soon as Ryan turned his back, Tom was in. He clicked on the personal directory. Nothing was there. Nothing. Every subdirectory was completely empty. He accessed the archives and trash. Nothing. It was all gone.

***

"Marianne." She turned at the sound of her name. An unsmiling Tom motioned for them to join him at the end of the terrace.

Marianne feared the worst. "What's happened?"

"The files are gone. Everything has been deleted."

Sue asked, "What does that mean?"

"We're screwed."

Marianne's stomach lurched. "Shit! This is not good. Not at all. What do we do now?"

"I don't know. I need to think . . . Oh no!" The colour bleached from Tom's face.

"What is it?"

"Cathy just walked in. She's over there. She's with a guy. It's your old flame."

Marianne couldn't resist. Before she could stop herself,

her gaze found them in the crowd. James was handsome and at ease in his surroundings. Cathy wore a tight dress and a bright smile. Marianne stilled. Her heart was beating a furious tattoo. "Yes, that's them. She can't see you from where she is."

"I have to go. I don't want to face her right now. I'll head out to the grounds and wait for you. Adam has laid on drivers for tonight to ferry people to their hotels or homes. Meet me, and we'll get one of the cars."

He disappeared into the gardens before Marianne could say anything.

Sue said, "I guess we all need to get out of here."

A deep voice, the foreign accent pronounced, broke into their conversation. "You can't be going already, Sue. I just got here."

Sue turned around first, and her face flamed as a broad smile lit her eyes at the sight of Karl. Marianne looked between the two of them. There was a definite spark here—yet another complication for them to deal with.

"Karl, what a surprise to see you here."

"That makes two of us. I couldn't believe my eyes when I walked in and saw you. What are you doing here?"

"Tom, Adam's brother, is working on our website and needed some information from his brother. We decided to make a fun trip of it."

"What is your website about?"

"We sell stuff that is made by small businesses. I sell my art through the site and source the other suppliers. Marianne runs the business side of things."

They chatted away, oblivious to Marianne's presence. She was relieved that Sue wasn't so googly-eyed that she'd forgotten their cover story. It actually sounded like a good idea for a business. Perhaps one day she'd do something different with her own life.

She quietly moved off to the side. She'd keep Sue in view but give her a little privacy. The timing was the worst, but the woman had been through hell with the fall-out from her late husband's devious actions. Who was Marianne to deny her a few minutes of flirtatious talk to boost her confidence? She'd give them five minutes before she'd grab Sue, and they could find Tom. She jumped as a large hand caressed her shoulder, and hot breath whispered across her skin.

"You keep turning up. Every time I turn round, there you are. Perhaps fate is trying to tell us something."

James's voice was low, and his eyes were burning pits that seemed to bore into her soul. The intensity caused her to rear back. She stumbled as her heel caught on the top step that led to the lawns. He grabbed her; pulling her close until not a puff of air separated them. Her breasts were pressed against his chest, and her overly sensitised skin ached. Neither of them spoke. His eyes held hers and spoke volumes. He was as affected as she was.

"Oh, Mhairi, you make me ache, the exact bloody same as when I was a randy teenager finding my way around your body." He let out a shaky breath, placed his hands on her upper arms and, holding tight, carefully stepped away from her. His arms fell to his sides, and the desire slipped from his eyes.

"What are you doing here?" He was apparently now in full control of himself and his voice bit with an authoritative edge that she did not like, not one bit.

"That's none of your damn business. I could ask the same. You're quite the party boy these days, aren't you?"

A pulse worked at the side of his mouth. "And, to follow your lead, that is my business. You gave up any right to know what's going on in my life when you disappeared. What's your relationship with Adam's brother?"

His change of direction startled her for a moment. Then she laughed. "Jesus, Tom must be about twenty-five, which is a decade younger than me. You think I'm seeing him? What's it to you?"

His gaze flicked to the side and he shook his head. "Nothing, nothing at all. I merely wondered what the connection was."

She opened her mouth to speak, snapped it shut as a female voice called out, "James darling, there you are. I've been looking for you."

Cathy was walking towards them, her smile fixed. She hooked her arm through James's and snuggled in tight. Was this show for her benefit? The satisfied smirk Cathy shot her way was confirmation enough.

"Hi, I'm Marianne." She held out her hand, and Cathy briefly took it.

"I know that. I'm Cathy Sutton. James, you need to come with me. There is someone I want you to meet."

James's gaze trapped hers for a moment before he acceded to his girlfriend's command. "Good-bye, Marianne. Take care."

As he walked away, she realised she may never see him again. And that was for the best. When you're hiding a secret from someone, it's best you keep as far away from them as possible.

***

Marianne's suite was furnished with a spacious seating area. None of them was in the mood for more alcohol or food, so she ordered coffee from room service.

"What about the deleted files?"

Tom slumped in his seat and covered his eyes with a hand before rubbing it along his jawline. "It's all gone. Every bloody thing I ever saved. I couldn't even recover the deleted records. It's as if the files never existed."

"What do we do now?" Sue asked. "We're at a dead end. We don't have a clue what to do next."

Marianne's heart was thundering. Was it over? Would these bastards get away with ruining her?

Tom swung his feet to the floor and leaned forward. "It's not over yet. We know Cathy is involved in all of this and that Monaco has something to do with her. We need to follow her."

Marianne shook her head. "But she's seen us all."

Sue said, "No way she won't remember you. That look she threw your way was a stinker."

Tom said, "But she hasn't seen Emily."

CHAPTER THIRTY-THREE

Marianne bolted upright as her mobile rang. They'd arrived back in London late the night before, and she was shattered—more from tension than anything else. The Caller ID announced it was Gavin, her Chief Risk Officer.

"Hi, Gav, is everything okay?"

"I'm not too sure. One of the sales team took a call they didn't understand and reported it to me. The caller is an existing client who was under the impression we're launching a new fund."

Damn. She sat still, her brain furiously working. It was too soon for this to get out.

"That's odd. What exactly did they want?" She was amazed at her cool, even tone.

"They said they were investing £150,000 and wanted to know if their brother could do a similar amount, perhaps more, as apparently, the fund is only open to existing clients. Thing is, I wanted to let you know that I'll be reporting this to the FCA as this is a regulatory matter. Someone is impersonating us."

"Perhaps I should give this client a call?" She was clutching at straws as she didn't want to be seen as being involved in this scheme.

"I think it's best we inform the regulator, and they can

direct us on the investigation. I've got a hospital appointment this morning but will draft an email notification after that. It should be ready to go out by mid-afternoon."

"Okay, thanks for letting me know."

She disconnected the call and chewed at a hangnail while she thought. Gavin had recently been diagnosed with depression and was undergoing treatment. His wife had left him, and the hope was that he just needed a little extra support at this time. His appointment usually took several hours for him to get there and back. The wrath of the regulator would be unleashed once there was a suspicion that a fake fund was being promoted, and they would be all over the systems. An announcement would also have to be made to all existing clients.

She would get in touch with the scammers; surely they would have to back away now. But would they do it without extracting retribution?

***

They met at Tom's; Chloe and Emily eager to hear their news.

"Well, we can safely say you had an eventful trip."

Marianne huffed out a puff of air as she looked at Chloe. "Indeed, except we are no closer to finding out who is behind this."

Emily flashed a look at Chloe. "A Facebook message came in last night for Anita. It was from Tony Anderson. He's back for more money."

Sue hissed, "Bastard! I could smack him. Pity he's not a real person."

Chloe said, "Tony is playing a game, but then so can we. We messaged him back."

Marianne was surprised. She hadn't expected them to have the courage to act on their own. "Well done. What happened?"

"I said I needed time to get money. That gives us an opportunity to decide how we deal with him."

"So our only option is to try and find out more from him," Sue said. "That'll be challenging. He's playing a game, so he's hardly going to give anything away."

Tom said, "We do have some other paths. We know Cathy was involved in the whole mess from the time I spent with her in Bulgaria. She is connected to Monaco. That is where my brother is based part of the year. And, finally, the coding used in Bulgaria, which Cathy is involved with, was invented by me, the details of which were stored in my brother's company's computer system. Cathy's boyfriend was in Monaco as well. What's the betting he knows what his girlfriend is into? My brother's name crops up too often for my liking, but everything leads back to and circles around Cathy."

"So we need to keep an eye on her," Sue said. "But first of all, we have to find out where she is."

Tom said, "Adam called me. He wanted to know why I disappeared from the party. His plans have changed as his potential investor wants a follow-up meeting in London. He is coming back tomorrow and has asked me to join him and some friends for dinner. He mentioned that Cathy and James Foster would be there."

Marianne's stomach tumbled. James was none of her concern, and she didn't want to see him, but an ache lingered. "But what if she says something about seeing you in Bulgaria, Tom? You can't meet with her."

"I've been thinking about this. All Cathy is aware of is that I have talent in coding and I need money. I can handle this. I'm going to go to dinner with them, then we need to have Cathy followed. She is the key to the whole situation."

Emily said, "I've got nothing better to do. And she has never seen me. I'm happy to wait outside where you're having dinner and follow her from there."

Chloe piped up, "Me too. I know she has seen me, but I was done up to the nines with a full face of makeup on. I'll scruff myself up, and we'll keep well back. If we know where she is staying, we at least have a base to work from."

Marianne turned as Tom gently touched her shoulder. "My brother asked if I wanted to bring someone. I'd like you to join us."

Marianne's already uneasy stomach twisted, and dread constricted her throat at the thought of being at the same table as James after having spent the last eighteen years hiding from him. She had no option. He was somehow involved in this. Him and his girlfriend. "Sure, that will be fine. We are running out of time now. Gavin will have communicated with the regulator by this afternoon. After that, we would potentially only have days before the law is brought in."

Sue asked, "What did you tell our scamming friends about this? You said you emailed them?"

"Yes, I explained the position and said they had to walk away as the regulator would know we there was an issue by this afternoon. I reiterated that I couldn't stop this. It was out of my hands."

"Will they leave you alone?" Sue's worried eyes were locked on to her face.

"I don't know. I simply don't know what to think anymore."

But one thought kept needling. Was it a coincidence that James was back in her life just as she was being targeted? The one person she had most harmed, even if he didn't know the half of it. Was this some kind of payback?

CHAPTER THIRTY-FOUR

Marianne dressed to impress. She chose her outfit with care, but, she told herself, it was because she needed a confidence boost; a shield to protect her from the current situation and the coils of the past. She picked a red dress, her go-to colour when she needed that extra boost.

The neckline was high but dipped past her shoulder bones at the back, the hemline an inch above her knees. Her hair was loose, her makeup elegant and she strode into the restaurant on nude high-heeled suede sandals. Tom said he would meet her there, and, true to his word, was waiting by the entrance. He wore smart trousers, an open-necked blue shirt and a blazer-style jacket.

He whistled appreciatively. "You scrub up all right."

"Thank you. I could say the same about you."

He tugged at his collar. It seemed a reflexive action as the top-button was already undone. "Are you nervous?"

"Yeah, a bit. I just have to remember that I am helping you and Sue with your business's online security. Mind you, Cathy will see right through that."

"She probably suspects you're scamming us. Good on her. Let her think what she wants."

Marianne berated herself for the acidic tone. She had nothing against this Cathy person. Nothing at all.

"Anyway, we're off the hook for the moment. I called Gavin this afternoon at the office. His secretary said he hadn't come back after his doctor's appointment. He's got a bit of depression. He'll have sloped off home to lock the world out. It's been happening more and more. I'll call again tomorrow and see if he is in. But this could buy us some time."

She followed Tom into the restaurant, her heart beating an erratic tattoo. She scanned the room. The popular and trendy eatery was full. It was an expensive place with a great menu, but none of that gave her any pleasure tonight. The dining area seemed to contract, the walls closing in as her eyes were drawn to a table in the middle of the room. A prime see-and-be-seen spot. Three people were already seated. Adam and James rose to their feet as they approached.

Jamie, the tearaway, had learnt his manners. He stood in front of her, a man now, handsome and polished. His dark hair was neatly trimmed, and some designer stubble grazed his jaw. He enjoyed exercising and working out as a teenager and apparently still did, although he now had a more athletic build. In his face, she could see the remnants of the boy he'd once been. The boy with tousled hair, a handsome face and a whole heap of attitude. But he'd loved her, shown her what desire was and she continued to yearn for his touch for years after she left him. But that was the past.

Adam kissed her on each cheek, the cosmopolitan greeting she was accustomed to. He was charming, welcoming, and polished. Was he also a devious, vicious criminal? Was he the creep behind the attacks on Amelia?

She was cold and clammy, and her senses were on full alert.

"I am glad you could make it, Marianne. Of course, you've met Cathy and James before." His voice was smooth.

Cathy's inclined her head, her face unsmiling as James came forward. His lips were a silken caress against the flesh of her cheeks, and a bolt of longing spread through her belly.

"Yes, Marianne and I go way back. We knew each other as children."

He made it sound as if they had been playmates. She guessed that was true, but you played different games when you were seventeen than when you were seven.

Adam's voice came from behind. "And I believe you've met my brother, Tom."

Marianne bit her lip. Cathy accepted a welcome kiss from Tom and when he said, "Nice to see you again," she murmured, "Same here." Tom shook James's hand.

Marianne sat, relieved. Cathy was thankfully up for playing the game of make-believe.

Without any preamble, Cathy said to Marianne, "I do hope you have recovered from your dizzy spell. Something must have upset you for you to faint. What brought it on?"

There was a sly intonation that Marianne did not like. Not at all. "It was the heat, I expect. Thankfully, James got me into a cool room, and I was better almost immediately."

Tom was seated next to Cathy, and he asked her, presumably as a diversion tactic, "Are you in London for long?"

She toyed with the stem of her wine glass. "Just for a week or so. Then I shall be going abroad."

No doubt she would be heading back to Bulgaria. "What do you do, Cathy?" That was a natural question to ask.

"I'm in IT security. Pretty similar to what I hear Tom is doing for you. I analyse business vulnerability and suggest how they can strengthen their overall security."

"Who do you work for?"

"It's a small company. You won't have heard of them."

Adam asked Cathy, "How do you know what Tom does? I didn't realise you'd spoken before."

James interjected, "I believe I may have mentioned it. Marianne told me she knew Tom through his work with her business."

Cathy stood. "Excuse me for a moment, please." As she sashayed towards the loos, Marianne noticed a few males among the other diners whose eyes tracked her progress. She wore a tight dress and high heeled boots. Marianne couldn't help the bitter twist of her heart as she thought of James and Cathy together.

James was sitting next to her, and she'd done her best to ignore him this far. Mentally, that was. Physically, he caused an ever-present throb. She heard a movement to her side, and he bent closer, the crisp cotton of his shirt brushing against her bare arm. She tensed.

"Are you all right?"

"Yes, why wouldn't I be?" Her voice was low but sharp.

"Don't get your knickers in a twist, Mhairi. I only asked how you were."

She glanced at Tom and Adam, who appeared engrossed in conversation. She pressed a little closer, and he stiffened. Her voice was a whisper. "I am fine, and my name is Marianne."

"Of course it is. Forgive me."

"I hope I haven't missed anything interesting?" Cathy settled back into her chair and idly caressed James's arm, a flirtatious look on her face.

Marianne was sure the food she picked at was delicious, the wine she barely sipped superb, and the conversation that floated around her scintillating, but all she could focus on were the inches that separated her from James. The minuscule amount of space seemed to be a yawning canyon.

"It's late. We should be going." Cathy's voice brought her back to the moment.

James sat back in his chair and called out, "Adam, thank you for a delicious meal, and . . ." He paused and smiled at Marianne. "Interesting company. I'll see you at your offices tomorrow at eleven."

Adam beckoned for the waiter and mimed the age-old signing of the cheque. "I'll stay back and settle the bill. It's my pleasure you could join me tonight. Marianne, we'll make sure you get a cab. Tom and I can share one home."

***

Emily's heart was pounding so loud she could hear a drumbeat in her head. She and Chloe had huddled in a shop doorway for almost an hour, Chloe's moped parked by the kerb in front of them.

A dark-haired guy who was a bit of all right and a

woman who looked like she belonged by his side came out of the restaurant. The woman's choppy blonde hair swung around her strong face. She wore a black fitted dress, teamed with a black leather jacket and high-heeled ankle boots. Even without Chloe's persistent nudging, Emily would have guessed this was Cathy from the descriptions.

Cathy and the guy, who she assumed was James, got into a cab and headed west.

Chloe whispered, "Come on. That's her."

They rushed to Chloe's moped, and Emily grimaced, hitched up her trousers and cocked her leg over the saddle. She bemoaned her lack of height as she pushed her bottom against the seat so that her feet could at least touch the ground.

Chloe started the engine, and everything else was drowned out by the revs. She shouted, "Feet up and hold on tight, Em. Here we go."

"I can't believe you talked me into this." Emily clutched Chloe's jacket as the moped sped away from the restaurant in pursuit of the taxi, staying far enough back so as not to attract attention.

Chloe's next words were a ragged shout in the wind, "It's the fastest way to stay behind them, not be seen and yet be nippy enough to slip through other traffic."

The cab indicated left and headed deeper into Kensington, travelling the quiet roads with the usually bustling coffee shops, restaurants, antique shops and boutiques closed for the night. The cab stopped in front of a narrow townhouse, its pale painted walls almost luminous in the moonlight. Chloe turned into an alley that faced the house and killed the engine. Her voice was a husky whisper, "They won't see us here. What's going on?"

James stepped out, pausing for a moment to look around, before leaning in the open car window. James walked away, but Cathy remained inside. A moment later the car slowly moved to the end of the street, parked and dimmed its lights. James climbed the steps to the front door, opened it with a key and quickly stepped inside. A light flicked on in a downstairs window, and a shadow passed behind the curtains.

Emily kept her voice low. "How odd is that? Wait, look. He's coming back out."

The house was in darkness again, and James locked the front door, glancing along the street before walking briskly to the waiting cab. He carried some paper files.

Emily said, "We keep following. We want to know more about Cathy, and where she's staying is a good start. They haven't done anything suspicious so far though."

"No, I guess not." There was a strange edge to Chloe's voice.

"What is it?"

"Probably nothing. But see that blue car over there?" She pointed down the street, the opposite direction to where the cab was parked.

"Yeah, what about it?"

"It, or one like it, was a few cars behind us when we drove away from the restaurant. It's just parked there, and no one has got out." She shook her head. "Sorry, I'm getting paranoid. Come on, the cab's on the move."

Chloe fired up the bike, and they took off after them. Emily glanced over the shoulder. The driver of the blue car switched on their lights and slowly moved into the traffic flow a few cars behind them. She held on tight.

CHAPTER THIRTY-FIVE

"**S**o they went to the Regent Hotel, and both of them got out there. We didn't dare follow them inside."

Marianne brushed aside the implication of James and Cathy as an item. "That's fine. But what about the house?"

Tom asked, "Do you know the address?"

Emily nodded. "16 Beaufort Gardens."

Tom whistled. "That's a high-tone area. It's probably James's home, and he needed to grab something before he went to the hotel with his girlfriend. Cathy could be staying there, or perhaps they book into a hotel every now and again to add some spice to their sex life." He chuckled.

Marianne gritted her teeth. "Well, that's supposition, isn't it? Anyway, that is none of our concern."

Tom conceded. "You're right. What is our business is that Cathy is up to her neck in the scamming ring that is using my old code, and she knows both James and Adam. She said she reported in to someone. It could easily be one of them."

Emily pushed herself to her feet, a hand pressed against her lower back. "I'm catching the tube home." She held up a hand towards Chloe. "No arguments. My back is killing me. I've had enough of riding pillion for the night, especially as I'll be on it again tomorrow. I'll see you at the hotel at around 8:00 a.m.? There's a coffee shop across the way, and you can park the bike outside."

"Okay, let's see what we can find out tomorrow."

Marianne glanced at the TV. Sky News was on silent. "I better go too." Her eyes caught the breaking news banner. "Shit. Turn up the volume. Quick." The words written on the banner were repeated by the newsreader. "Earlier today there was a fatal road traffic accident at Piccadilly Circus. Gavin O'Hare, a compliance director at a city firm, is reported to have been waiting at a crossing from Piccadilly onto Regent Street when he fell into the oncoming traffic and was hit by a bus. Mr O'Hare suffered severe head wounds and was pronounced dead at the scene. It is thought that Mr O'Hare suffered from depression. And in other news . . ."

Sue said, "Oh my God, is that your compliance guy?"

Marianne was shaking. "Yes, yes it is—was, I mean. I had no idea he was so ill, no idea."

Marianne grabbed her handbag and fumbled around until she found her work phone. "I put it on silent in the restaurant. Oh shit!" There were numerous missed calls from her Human Resources directors. "Our HR people must have been trying to contact me."

Emily said, "The report was obviously alluding to it being suicide and not an accident."

Tom cleared his throat. "I hate to be indelicate, but the report says this happened midmorning, which means he wouldn't have had time to contact the regulator. We're off the hook."

His words hung in the air, heavy and tainted, but no one could doubt their truth.

CHAPTER THIRTY-SIX

Early the next morning Emily had an inspired idea. She found a pay phone, a rarity of beasts, near the coffee place and called the hotel.

"Hello, I'd like to speak to one of your guests please: Cathy Sutton."

The singsong voice of a receptionist assured her that she would be put straight through. Within seconds, the phone rang and was answered almost immediately. "Yes?"

Emily slowly replaced the receiver. Good, she hadn't left for the day yet. She rounded the corner and saw Chloe in a prime position at the tables and chairs outside the coffee place. She waved at Emily.

"I got you a latte and a muffin. It's blueberry."

"Great, thanks. I called the hotel and got put through to Cathy's room. She answered."

"At least we don't have to worry if she is there or not. It also tells us that the room is booked in her name and not James's."

They fell into a companionable silence, looking like nothing more than two women taking an early break and watching the passing crowds. Emily looked at Chloe. There were dark shadows under her eyes, visible beneath heavy concealer. "How you doing?"

She smiled, a brief quirk of lips. "I'm fine."

"No, darling, how are you really?"

Chloe's lips quivered. Pretence fell away, and her eyes were bleak. "I am trying not to dwell on Mum not being here. I'm focussing on giving these bastards a bit of what for. That's how I'm getting through each day. The nights are a different matter. Then it all comes slamming back, and in the dark, I can't summon the defences. She's gone, and I have to find a way to deal with that." She sat straight, her jaw firm and mouth set. "But first I'm going to screw these pigs over in any way I can."

Emily raised her latte in a toast. "Here's to revenge."

Chloe returned the gesture, and then said, "Look! It's Cathy. She isn't stopping for a cab though. She is on foot."

Emily thought. "Okay, we need to go after her. So on foot it is. Come on."

Cathy was dressed in jeans and a T-shirt, a slouchy bag over one shoulder and a thin sweater tied around her waist. She navigated the roads that crisscrossed this part of London with ease. Emily figured she was either from here or spent a great deal of time in the city. The streets were busy enough that Emily was sure that she and Chloe were well concealed. Or rather, that was what she hoped. She had a vision in her mind of being a stealth-like glamorous super-agent but knew she was more a downtrodden abandoned wife. Or was she? That's who she had been, but maybe she could turn that around. She stopped and pushed her arm to the side to keep Chloe from moving forward. "Wait."

A man came out of one of the expensive townhouses and walked towards Cathy, gesturing to the manicured gardens of the communal square. He held out his hand, revealing a cigarette and lighter. Cathy smiled, shrugged and waited by the closed gates to the garden oasis. The man greeted her with welcome kisses and, using a heavy key, opened the gate. He gestured for her to enter, followed and then shut the gate. He lit his cigarette, and they disappeared beneath the canopy of trees.

Chloe gasped. "That's Karl, the bloke Sue met at Adam's party in London."

Emily's heart was racing. "Shit! He seemed decidedly friendly with Cathy. We can't get into the square. What should we do?"

"We wait for her to come out. There's a bus stop across the road. Let's sit in the shelter. That way they won't spot us, but we can see who comes out of the square gardens."

They crossed the road and walked past a line of parked cars. Suddenly, a car door opened, halting their passage. The driver, a tall, muscular type with a handsome face, exited the vehicle. He was blocking their way.

Emily smiled. "Sorry, can we get past?"

"Not until we have a little chat." His voice was heavily accented, and it took a moment for the words to register. She took a step back, and Chloe did the same.

"I don't know what you're after, mate, but we're not interested."

A voice came from behind them. "But we're interested in you."

Emily swung round and faced another man, shorter than the first but equally as muscled. He looked meaner and not someone to mess with.

Chloe said, "What the hell is going on?"

The first man said, "Why are you following Cathy? What is she to you?"

Emily froze, her mind blank. Something flickered in a recess of her memory. The car door was blue. It was the car from the previous night. It had been following them. She shouted at Chloe. "Run."

They moved to either side of the shorter guy. Chloe made it straight past him, her young legs carrying her at speed along the road. Not so Emily. He grabbed her the second she moved and pushed her to the ground with force. Her head jerked to the side, and she saw the driver chase after Chloe.

The man pushed his face against hers. His breath stank, and she gagged. "Who are you? And what do you want with Cathy?"

She couldn't speak, just shook her head. He raised his arm and brought it down, smashing his fist against her jaw. She howled in pain. He lifted it again, ready to strike, and paused as the air was split into a million pieces, a loud, wailing siren-like noise blotting out any other sounds.

He let her go and jumped to his feet. The wailing noise continued; doors opened as people came out of their homes. Emily struggled to her feet and ran across the road. He didn't stop her. The second heavy ran back to the car, and the men jumped in and sped off.

Chloe stopped running and was maybe thirty yards away. She tossed something into the bushes and jogged back to Emily, grabbing her arm. "Come on, let's get out of here."

"What the hell was that noise?"

"My rape alarm. Mum bought me one and insisted I

carry it with me all the time. Shit, that was loud."

"Thank God for that."

They ran out of the square before Cathy exited the gardens.

CHAPTER THIRTY-SEVEN

Marianne arrived on Tom's doorstep in a state. Her face was pale, she was shaking, and her eyes were red-rimmed. Her voice was accusing. "I've been calling you nonstop. Where the bloody hell have you been?"

He stepped back at the fierceness of her words. "Whoa! I've been working online, had my headphones on."

She brushed past him. "This is getting out of control."

He followed her. "What do you mean?"

She shoved her phone at him. She stared at her trembling hand. "Read that."

Before he could, the doorbell rang. He opened the door to reveal Emily and Chloe. They were flushed and on edge. Before either could speak, he said, "Marianne wants me to read this email. I'll read it out loud. *Problem solved yesterday at 11:42 a.m. Let us know if you need any more assistance.*"

He looked at Marianne, puzzled. "I don't get it."

She snatched the phone out of his hand. "Well, I do." Her voice was a broken sob. "They killed him. They murdered Gavin O'Hare."

***

They'd called Sue, and she arrived shortly after Emily and Chloe. The five of them sat around Tom's dining table. Sue didn't know about the others, but she was numb.

"I knew Karl was too good to be true. Is he having an affair with Cathy?"

Marianne shrugged. "Who knows, but they are obviously more than acquaintances, which puts him in the frame for being involved in her dirty business."

"I can see that. This has massively stepped up a gear. Whoever is behind all this is claiming responsibility for a man's death, and they've attacked Emily."

Marianne's voice was calm and her words considered. "Yes, this is bloody serious now. We need to back off. I hate to say it, but they have won."

Chloe slowly shook her head. "I guess so, although it kills me to say it. It's not worth anyone else getting hurt over this. Mum wouldn't have wanted that."

Emily said, "I lost money. That is nothing compared to a life. Nothing, but I was terrified today. I can't go on with this."

Emily sobbed, and Chloe pulled her into a hug. "We're all scared now."

Tom said, "These guys are the real deal. It's like the Mafia or something. I'm sorry we couldn't stop them though."

Sue tried to put her thoughts into words and then realised she couldn't hold back. "They are evil, and what they did to Amelia was a vicious warning. A warning you have taken to heed. I don't even want to think what would have happened to Emily if Chloe hadn't set off the alarm. We don't know if those guys were tailing Cathy because they were her protection or if they had some other motive."

Marianne said, "What? Like a rival gang?"

"Maybe. Look, I hate to say this, but if they killed this guy, it was because you let them know there was an obstacle. They may not have been responsible for his death. I mean they could be taking credit for an accident. Making themselves look good by taking advantage of the circumstances."

Marianne flushed, an unbecoming redness creeping across her throat. "I realise that, Sue. Thanks for the reminder. If I hadn't contacted them, there is every chance that Gavin would still be alive."

"So what now?"

Marianne narrowed her eyes. "I told you what now. We back off. They take their money, and I have to hope I'll be seen as the innocent party when everyone realises they have been scammed. I'm sure I'll be fine."

Sue's stomach clenched. She hated confrontation, but she was burning inside. They had come too far to back off now. "Of course you will, but this isn't just about you. Or Amelia. Or any one of us. It's about every poor bastard whose life has been ruined by these shits. It's about people who believe in your business, and who will sign up to anything you say because they trust you—and who are about to lose big-time. It's not about you, Marianne. Get your ass in gear, and we all work together to do something about this and get proper evidence to give the police, or I'm going to them anyway, and I will make them listen to me. What do you say to that, then?"

***

Marianne couldn't believe how dense Sue was being. "Don't be stupid. They killed someone. We need to back off. My decision is final. They can run with their fake fund, take what they want and then safely disappear, as long as Amelia is safe." She stood, ready to leave.

Sue looked at Tom. "I want to carry on with this. Will you help? You can do this; I know you can."

Marianne waited for Tom to refuse, but he didn't say anything at first. When he spoke, his eyes avoided Marianne. "My coding started this off. Truth is that was the simplest bug I developed. There are details, workings and notes in my files for more. A lot more. I can't live with the fact that I am the root cause of all this destruction."

"I said my mum wouldn't want anyone to be hurt trying to avenge her, especially me. But I don't care," Chloe said. "We can't go to the police. For if we do, they will know and undoubtedly attack Marianne's niece."

Sue sighed, shaking her head. "I know, I know, but what the hell else can we do?"

Chloe continued, "If we do nothing, then yet more people will lose their money and, perhaps more importantly, their self-respect. I say we go ahead with the original plan, but we need to wallop them."

Emily said, "And Tom says they have more of his virus, or bugs or whatever. We can't allow them to carry on with their poisonous antics. I'm in. I'm scared, but I'm in."

Marianne wanted to explode, to tell them they had to do what she said. She was the boss. She'd give them what for. And then she stopped. And saw herself through their eyes. A demanding control freak who only thought about how something would impact on her. Little Mhairi Sinclair transformed into Marianne, an upwardly mobile, conceited bitch of the first order. Her throat constricted and she tried to speak, but her larynx burned. She cleared her throat and said, "Is that really . . ." And to her horror, her eyes blurred and she burst into heavy sobs that racked her body, hot tears spilling from her eyes and blinding her. Arms encircled her, and through her tears, she saw it was Sue.

"Marianne, hush, you have to open up and let people in. You are such a strong, intelligent woman, but you can't always make the decisions on your own."

Marianne took the rebuke. She knew what Sue meant. If she had confided in the others, taken their advice, then maybe she wouldn't have rushed to tell the scammers about Gavin and signed his death warrant. She sniffed, and Tom shoved a paper hanky in front of her face. She smiled, though it was more like a wobbly grimace, and blew her nose. "Okay, okay. Let's carry on, but the first one of us that gets hurt, I'm out."

Everyone was quiet for a moment, and Marianne could almost see the changing particles, relegating her to team member and not necessarily the leader—or should that be the dictator? She grimaced.

Tom sighed. "And bloody Adam is drawn into this yet again. We have James and Karl in the mix as well. I need to speak to our friend Cathy. You know, further our business relationship and see what else I can find out."

CHAPTER THIRTY-EIGHT

Tom watched Cathy as she stirred her cocktail, the multi-coloured, layers blending into a kaleidoscopic whirl. Evidently, it was the Regent's signature drink. She sipped, closed her eyes in apparent appreciation, then opened them and stared at him without blinking.

"I was pleased to get your call. What have you got for me?"

He adopted a cocky pose, leaning back in his chair and hooking his thumbs into the waistband of his jeans. "I'll give you an outline, but I prefer to talk money before I give the goods away."

"Of course, that's what I would expect."

"What if I told you that I could give you a virus that could strip a computer bare in less than fifteen minutes, copying all data, identifying external app passwords and all without leaving any trace that unauthorised access had taken place."

Her face gave nothing away. "I'd have to consider what, if any, use that could be to us." Her voice was cool.

Tom laughed out loud. "Let me help you with that. It would allow you to access a mark's computer time and time again. Move money from their accounts; find out their secrets without them ever knowing someone had been in their computer. The uses are limitless."

She licked her lips. "What do you want?"

"I won't be greedy. Give me £50,000."

Her laugh tinkled as if he had told an amusing joke. "Are you mad? We can't pay that much. I'll give you £20,000 and not a penny more."

He stood. "It's been nice knowing you, Cathy, but you can't afford me, love."

"Wait! Sit down."

He deliberately took his time before slowly taking his seat. He said nothing.

"Okay, look, I'll give you what you ask, but I want a guarantee you won't sell this to anyone else."

He shook her outstretched hand. "It's a deal. How do I get paid?"

She raised her brows. "I'll want to see the virus in action first. Do you want cash?"

"Usually I'd say yes, but I have substantial debts to clear that will only accept a bank account transfer, and there is no way I can pay £50,000 into my bank in cash. Anything over £5,000 is going to trigger money-laundering alarms."

She thought for a moment. "Okay. We have a company that legitimately pays for, and uses, development software. Bergen Enterprises will pay you."

He kept his smile hidden. "Thank you. That's great."

"I'll be in touch regarding when we'd like to see the demo."

"Sure. Hey, how is James?"

"He's fine."

"What is it he does again? I mean, I'm not sure how

Adam knows him."

She speared him with a look. "Quit the small-talk. You can go now, Tom. I'm done with you. For the moment, that is."

***

Tom's earphones hugged his head, and his hands flew across the keyboard. It seemed that Bergen Enterprises was a pretty big deal, with a website and social media sites that offered software solutions and a variety of apps. The idea of having a legitimate business as a cover for wrong-side-of-the-law dealings was not a new one, but Bergen seemed professional and well run. It had great reviews on consumer websites, and he despaired at their greed in running scams when they appeared to have a well-run business model that was appreciated by its legitimate customers.

Tom stretched his arms above his head, linked his fingers and rotated his shoulders to ease the muscles. This would be a long session. But he intended finding out everything he could about Bergen Enterprises and who was involved with it.

The first thing he would search was the ownership, and to do that he needed to know about Bergen's governance. It was a private company, and, he was not surprised to see, its country of registration was Panama. The South American tax haven had taken a beating in the international press over the past few years but had once been incredibly popular. Part of its attraction was the limited amount of information that had to be divulged. He wasn't going to find the beneficial ownership online. He ran a simple search and found a whole list of contracts and agreements that Bergen entered into. Even though it was a private company, some of its dealings were with public companies or organisations, and their details were often publicly available.

He selected a few of the agreements and went straight to the signing page, but he was unlucky in that the directors' names were not printed. All he could see were various scrawls. Then he hit pay dirt. Just over a year ago there was a contract to supply specific bespoke software to a range of private schools, which also obtained an element of public funding.

He would recognise that signature anywhere. It was Adam. His own brother was a director of Bergen.

He pushed back from the table, his shoulders slumped, and he held his head in his hands. He couldn't bear to contemplate the idea that Adam was involved in this whole dirty mess, yet how could he think anything else?

He checked the time. There was no point looking for Adam in the main house. He was usually out for most of the day. He grabbed his phone and searched WhatsApp for the right contact. The phone rang several times. Adam answered with a breathless, "Hello?"

"It's Tom. I need to speak to you."

"I'm at the gym, and then I've got a day of meetings. I'm out tonight as well. Do you fancy coming to a party with me? It's going to be pretty high-end. Karl Radinsky is hosting it. He has a pretty swanky place."

This sounded perfect. "Yeah, that would be great. Can I bring a friend? Maybe Marianne?"

"What is it with you and her? She's a looker but I'd

have thought maybe a little too old and, well . . . grownup for you?"

"Marianne's a good friend. It is allowed, you know."

"Yeah, sure." Adam sounded sceptical, but Tom let it go, let him think what he wanted.

Adam said, "Tell you what, Karl took a bit of a shine to your friend Sue. Why don't you ask her to come as well?"

"Sure, sounds good."

"Right, I'll send you a text with the address once I'm finished here."

The call disconnected, and Tom sat for a moment, trying to process what was going on. Adam was smart, but never in a million years would Tom have tagged him as someone who would go this far over the line. It was true—you never knew another person or what they were capable of.

Tom blasted up the volume on his music, the thundering notes crowding his mind and surrounding him until they faded into general background noise, blocking out any other distraction. He flexed his fingers as if he were a concert pianist getting ready for the event of his life. In some ways, he was. He was going into Bergen Enterprises.

**

Marianne called Tom several times, but there was no answer. She figured he had those damn headphones on again. She realised, with some shame, that she hadn't spoken to Adrian in several days. She dialled the number of the gallery and was soon connected to him.

"Hi, Marianne. What a lovely surprise."

There was no censure in his voice, but Marianne criticised herself; calling her fiancé should not be an out of the ordinary occurrence, no matter how difficult the circumstances she faced.

"It's good to hear your voice. I wanted to apologise for not calling you the last few days. Everything is a little crazy right now."

"Don't worry, darling. I know how busy you are. I'm not the possessive type, and what I adore about you is that you are one independent lady. I got back this morning. David signed the contract before I left, and I have exclusive access to all his new works for the remainder of the year."

"That's great. I'm glad it all went so well. I'm afraid I have a meeting tonight, but shall we meet tomorrow? I can cook us something, and we'll have a proper catch-up."

"I look forward to it. A few parties and events are going on. I'll keep myself occupied tonight. Take care and don't work too hard. I have to go. We're getting ready for next week's exhibition."

Marianne listened to the monotonous tone, signalling he had disconnected. A nagging, jabbing ache prodded at her temple. She was glad that Adrian was accommodating, but was that a natural reaction? Shouldn't he be having a moan and professing that he wanted to be with her? That he missed her and wanted some of her time for himself? Perhaps the question should really be: Why didn't she miss Adrian?

She shook her head, a physical reaction to the need to dispel these thoughts.

***

Bergen's security was good, exceptionally good. Tom was better. Not for the first time he considered how successful he could already be if he hadn't taken a detour to the dark side.

It had still taken him a few hours, but he was finally roaming through Bergen's files and private business. The first place he accessed was the corporate governance folder. He wasn't surprised, but he was disappointed to find a shareholders meeting where, in bold text, Cytech was named as the sole owner of Bergen. There was no doubt of Adam's involvement.

He, therefore, wasn't fazed to see Ryan's signature on various scanned-in bank transfer instructions. This meant nothing because the matters were related to Bergen's business. Adam wouldn't be the first person to use a legitimate concern in a way that was unknown to his general employees.

He needed a little more proof. He checked his notes from past meetings with the girls. Both Dave and Anita paid money to a company called Magpie. He ran a search on the name and wasn't surprised when he got positive hits. The related files were held under a higher level of security, and it took him a little while to gain access.

Magpie was created and closed within a relatively short period of time. He could see transfers going to a company called Bluecoat. Bluecoat apparently only received money to pay it out again almost immediately. If this followed traditional money laundering habits, then a labyrinth of companies would filter the money through various accounts to an untraceable destination. He checked Bergen's own financials, and the company was doing well.

It held substantial cash balances; a quick look showed accounts totalling over £2 million.

Tom was cloaked and invisible; he would leave no trace he had ever been there. This reminded him of when he tried to access the Cytech system but couldn't because of the level of security. Why didn't Bergen have the same trip wires in place? Was it because Adam expected Tom to go after his codes one day and wanted to prevent him from taking them? Yet the files had been deleted anyway. He shrugged. He was in. It seemed a shame, now he was here, not to finish the job.

He was going to place the virus at the heart of their system. The virus, if activated, would immediately destroy and delete all of Bergen's records. They would have no history, no applications, no financials and no way of recovering the information. They wouldn't even be able to access their online banking.

He needed to make the threat real. Once Marianne let the scammers know they were holding them for ransom, they would search for the bug. If anyone tried to remove it, the virus would start its trail of destruction.

Satisfied that everything was as it should be, he made to backtrack his way out of the system but stopped. Since he was in, he may as well leave a little something extra.

CHAPTER THIRTY-NINE

The party was at Karl Radinsky's home, the same address where he was photographed meeting with Cathy. Marianne whispered in Sue's ear, "What the hell does Radinsky have to do with all this?"

Sue's voice was muffled as she spoke from the side of her mouth, barely moving her lips. "Perhaps he just knows Cathy through Adam or James? And Tom's text said that he had loads to tell us and not to trust Adam. I don't know what, or who, to believe anymore. Careful, Karl's headed this way."

He was elegant, rich and, Marianne grudgingly admitted, sexy as hell. From the look on Sue's face, she was thinking the same. Her eyes sparkled, and twin spots of colour highlighted her cheeks, although she held herself a little stiffly. They needed to be aware of what was going on and keep their wits about them.

Karl stopped in front of them, and his smile was wide and welcoming. "I am glad you could make it. Thank you for coming." He spoke to them both, but his eyes were on Sue, and it was she who answered.

"Thank you, it was kind of you to let us come. Is the party for any special occasion?"

"Just to celebrate good friends and even better times." He paused for a moment. "You may query why I didn't invite you myself, but it is not because I didn't want to see you. It is that I will be busy with my guests tonight and I would prefer to get to know you better when we are alone. If I may say so, you look lovely." He paused for a beat and then obviously remembered his manners, for he turned to Marianne and said, "Of course, I mean both of you."

"Thank you," Marianne replied. "It was nice to see you in Monaco. Do you go there much?"

"I used to live there, but I have recently become resident in the UK. I still have good friends in Monaco, like Adam, so I try to get across at least every month."

Sue said, "How glamorous. I recall you never said what line of business you were in. You seem to have the flexibility to travel when you like."

"I dabble in many areas. Since moving to London, I have invested in the real estate market, but I also have interests in energy and technology."

"So you have that in common with Adam," Marianne observed.

"Yes, I do. I must go and greet my other guests, but please be reassured I'll be keeping an eye on you." His gaze lingered on Sue for a moment longer than was appropriate before he disappeared into the crowd.

Sue looked at Marianne, lingering flirtation evident in her eyes as she fanned her face with her hands. "He is gorgeous. The flippant part of me doesn't care if he is good or bad."

Marianne teased, "You probably hope he is bad. I can't figure out if his last comment was flirtatious or ominous!"

They shared a laugh, and Marianne marvelled that in the midst of all this drama they could still find something to laugh about.

Sue sobered. "I can't believe he is involved in all this, but he does have a connection to Cathy."

"Yeah, she gets around, doesn't she?"

***

Tom asked Marianne and Sue to meet him at the party and realised his mistake as soon as he arrived. The guests could freely roam all the downstairs rooms, one of which was what he assumed had once been the ballroom of the Georgian townhouse. God knew how they'd got the planning permission, but the glass wall at the rear of the enormous room slid back completely to flow onto the terraces and the expansive gardens beyond. People milled everywhere, talking, laughing, and drinking.

He needed to find them quickly. He had imagined a relatively small gathering, but one large enough that he could pull the girls aside and have a quiet word—for they all needed to be on their guard.

He did a double take as a famous actress strolled past, arm in arm with her co-star. Karl Radinsky certainly pulled out the stops—or called in favours—for his guest list. He grabbed a glass of champagne from a passing waiter. He'd hold on to it to blend in, but he needed to keep a clear head. He was moving towards the terrace when someone tugged on the back of his shirt.

"Come on," Marianne said. "We're over here."

He followed her to the corner of the room where Sue was waiting. "We thought we better not move about too much until we found you."

"Great. Have you seen Adam?"

Marianne shook her head. "No, but we did see our host. He was extremely affable. He couldn't take his eyes off Sue."

Sue blushed. "Don't be a beast, Marianne. He has always been friendly when we have met."

"Friendly my ass."

Tom didn't like this direction. "Yeah, well, watch it. He is a friend of Adam's and met with Cathy. We don't know which side of the line he is on."

Sue said, "I know, and isn't that just my luck. It's been refreshing to feel attractive again. No one can hear us here. What is it with Adam?"

He quickly explained. "So Bergen is owned by Cytech, and my brother is the only shareholder of that company. He has always been hands-on; no way he doesn't know what is happening."

"Did you find a connection to anyone else?"

"Only Ryan."

Marianne looked puzzled. "Who's he?"

"A guy I went to school with. He works for Adam now in finance and is the one who gave me access to my old folder in Cytech's system."

"Does he know about computers?"

"Yeah, but he's not as good as me."

Sue raised her brows. "I remember him. He was at Adam's party. So he's not as good as you? Cocky is as cocky does, mister."

He laughed. "I got right into their system, and I left the virus."

Marianne smiled, and for the first time in days, it lit her eyes. "So we're set?"

"Yeah, but we need to work out how to go about it."

"How do we do that?"

"Let's find Adam."

***

Adam smiled at Marianne as he grabbed her a glass of champagne from a passing waiter. "Here. That one is nearly done." She smiled her thanks. They had found Adam in the lower gardens in conversation with a surgically enhanced redhead. Marianne thought she was familiar, but since Adam didn't introduce her, she was none the wiser. Perhaps the woman was too famous to be introduced?

Adam moved his attention to Tom. "I almost missed you in this crowd. I didn't expect it to be this busy."

"Nor did I!"

Marianne joined the others in laughter, for it was their host who had spoken. Karl slipped in next to Sue. "You are enjoying yourselves, yes?"

The redhead replied, "Oh, it's wonderful, Karl. It was lovely to see you at the club last week. I may join. Perhaps we'll see more of each other." Marianne didn't know how it was possible for anyone to see any more of her than was already exposed by the gauzy skirt and bra-top she wore.

Sue was pretty in a fitted black cocktail dress and silver heels; her curly bob was wild and untamed. She was sexy and natural. An attractive, respectable woman. Sue's smile appeared fixed, and Marianne cursed young, gorgeous women who went for any man they could, irrespective of who he was or could be with. She didn't know if he could be trusted or not, but she hoped for Sue's sake he was genuine.

Karl's voice was polite. "I'm sure you'd enjoy being a member." He turned to Sue. "A new members club has opened in Mayfair. It has a fabulous rooftop garden. Perhaps you may be free one night, and we could have drinks there?" At her startled look, he hurriedly said, "Or lunch. We could do lunch?"

"Err, yes, that sounds nice." Sue sounded terrified.

"Hi, everyone."

Marianne froze. It was James.

***

Tom shifted closer to Adam. "How's business?"

"Good. Yeah, it's fine."

"I figured that. Two years ago you were doing well, but buying something like the villa would have been out of reach. You've surpassed that and more."

"I guess."

Tom was getting frustrated at his brother's short answers, all followed by an affable smile.

"So how do you know James?"

"We first met when he approached me about buying Cytech. Cathy introduced us. He's a good guy, so we hang out."

"You never did say how you know Cathy."

Adam lifted a brow. "Because you never asked. It's not your business, and why on earth would you care? Cathy works for a subsidiary of Cytech."

Tom couldn't believe how brazen Adam was. "And is Cytech for sale?"

Adam sipped his champagne, but his eyes flicked in a

tiny movement towards Karl. Was he interested in Cytech as well?

"No. The company isn't for sale." He downed his drink. "Why would I sell?" His accompanying shrug said he'd be a fool to sell a profitable business without good reason.

Something jogged at his memory. "But Ryan said he was at your party in London, then later in Monaco, because discussions were being held with an investor."

Karl said, "There is a world of difference between someone buying a company and investing into it."

"Yes, but Adam said James was interested in buying Cytech."

Adam's face darkened, and his brows drew together. "I said that is how James and I met. Not that I was discussing a sale to him. Just leave it. Okay?" his brother snapped, and Tom was taken aback. This wasn't the affable Adam he was used to.

Adam placed his empty drink on the tray. "Excuse me. There is someone I must speak with."

Tom watched him go. His brother was on edge, nervous.

CHAPTER FORTY

J ames was accompanied by a dressed-to-the-nines
Cathy, and Marianne didn't know where to put herself.
She avoided eye contact, breezed a "hello" to them
both and left the group, pushing her way through the
crowd.

She was hot, sticky and a little sick. She made her way
to the bathroom, which was an oasis of calm on the
ground floor of the house. An electric fan cooled the air,
but her cheeks remained warm and her face flushed. When
she first saw James, a rush of desire had threatened to
overwhelm her, and her body still bore imprints of the
heat that threatened to consume her. She ran the cold tap
and let the water trickle over her wrists, cooling the pulse
points. Refreshed, she tidied her hair and reapplied her
lipstick. God only knew why. She didn't want anyone, least
of all James, to find her attractive right now.

She would find the others and see what the score was.
It was getting late, so she assumed they would meet early
in the morning, ready to put the final plans into place.

The light was fading, and lanterns dotted the gardens.
An *Arabian Nights*-style tented area was proving popular.
She hadn't noticed it earlier, but the crowd was thinning as
people moved to the covered, heated areas. She was drawn
to the twinkling fairy lights and burning fire pits that lit the

area where she last saw Sue and Tom. The temperature of the night was falling, but the hormones were rising. Tipsy couples were canoodling in private—and not so private—areas. She saw Sue, still standing with the same group. James towered a head above the others. Every now and then he would glance around as if looking for someone. Then his eyes found hers, and she thought perhaps she had been the one he was looking for. Her palms were sweaty and her heartbeat accelerating. This would never do. She looked around, her head twisting from side to side. James started moving towards her. She needed to get out of there.

The tented area beckoned, and she headed into the light, the heat and the chaos of crowded bodies dancing to a pounding beat. It was a fashionable crowd in here. She knew some of them by sight. The trust-fund babies, entrepreneurs, celebrities and beautiful hangers-on who littered the London scene.

Her eyes were drawn to the corner of the room where a couple danced. The girl draped herself over the man in a seductive tease; his head was bent as he nuzzled at her neck, her mass of hair covering him from view. His hands cupped her buttocks as he pulled her tight against him, groin to groin. They gave off such sexual energy that Marianne couldn't take her eyes away from them. The girl pulled away, threw her head back and laughed as the man bent her over his outstretched arm into an old-fashioned dip. Good God, it was Lily. Marianne held her breath and stared at the man, a heavy weight in her stomach. Adrian. She guessed she had known the second she recognised Lily.

As if to dispel any doubt that they were just friendly, Adrian grabbed Lily's breast and kissed her. Oaf. Marianne knew at that moment that she hadn't been in love with Adrian for she was consumed by anger, not hurt. How dare he bloody treat her like this? She marched across to them and tapped him on the shoulder. He turned around, his ready smile sliding into a frown. His mouth gaped in shock for a moment, before quickly recovering himself.

"Hello, darling. What a lovely surprise. Lil, look who it is. It's Marianne."

Lily stopped her gyrating, but instead of surprise, remorse or shock, she smirked at Marianne from half-closed lids, a secretive smile on her thin lips. "Oh, Marianne, you do look funny. Don't be silly. Adrian and I go back a long way."

Marianne ignored her and turned to her soon-to-be-ex fiancé. "You can't talk your way out of this. It's over." She tugged and tugged at the stupid engagement ring, but it was too tight. Her fingers must have swollen with the heat.

"Don't be a fool. We were only having a little bit of fun. It won't be the last time one of us does that. We'll have a great marriage, and with your luck at making money and my connections and standing, we will do extremely well. Hey, come here, darling?"

He was unsteady on his feet, his hands grasping at her as he lurched forward. She took a step back and stumbled. Someone held her waist to steady her. She swore she knew who it was by the searing touch. She glanced over her shoulder and saw she was right. James.

"I saw them slobbering over each other. Is this the prat you're engaged to?"

"He isn't usually a prat. Go away. This is none of your business."

"Have you been playing at double standards?" Adrian said. "See, that's how it works. We'll be fine. You can have a fiddle with Mr Macho here, and it won't impact our life at all."

Oh Lord, how could she have imagined herself in love with this piece of shit?

"That's not how I roll, Adrian. It's best we call it a day." She turned to walk away when he grabbed her by the shoulder, his fingers digging into her flesh.

"You'll leave when I say you can. You're nothing but a little Scottish peasant. You might have the money, but I give you what you'll never have, and that is class and an entrée into a world you're not good enough for on your own."

Before she could speak, she was lifted to the side, and Adrian's hand was pushed from her. James stood in front of Adrian. "Don't ever lay a finger on her. Ever."

Adrian laughed, and spittle formed in the corner of his mouth. What had she ever seen in him?

"She's my fiancée. She does what I tell her."

James turned to her. "Do you want to stay engaged to him?"

She shook her head. "No, I don't."

"Give me your hand."

She did, and to her complete shock, he popped her ring finger into his mouth and sucked, wetting her finger with his saliva. It was wholly inappropriate but decidedly erotic, and a fierce bolt of desire shot through her belly. He took her finger in his hands and worked at the ring until it slipped loose. He handed it to Adrian, who pushed his hand away, and the ring fell to the ground.

James shrugged and turned to her. "Come on, I'll make sure you get home all right."

Suddenly, he fell forward onto his knees as Adrian jumped onto his back, his arms tight around his neck. James quickly recovered and in lightning-fast movements pulled Adrian's hands loose and hurled him over his shoulder. Adrian landed in an ungainly heap on the ground. He made to sit, and James knelt beside him.

"Behave yourself. If you ever lay a hand on Marianne again, I will hurt you more than you would believe possible, and I wouldn't even leave a mark." His voice was calm and even, his smile patronising. She remembered the angry, wild boy he had once been. Then, he could barely conceal rage born of passion; now, an easy smile and smooth moves accompanied his effortless dismissal of Adrian's clumsy attack.

He stood, dusted the earth from his trousers and, grabbing her hand, pulled her towards the house. Everything was a blur, and she couldn't see Tom or Sue. But she did hear Cathy. She was beside them, her voice low and furious. "What the hell are you playing at? Are you mad?"

James hissed, "Leave it. I'm not in the mood for any shit."

Cathy placed a hand on his arm. "Don't screw this up."

He shrugged her away. "I'll talk to you later."

Before Marianne knew it, they were through the house and in a cab. She stared at her ringless left hand and couldn't comprehend what had just happened.

CHAPTER FORTY-ONE

Emily turned to Chloe for reassurance for what seemed like the thousandth time. "So there is nothing else your mum mentioned in her communications with this guy? It is all on this piece of paper?"

"I spent all day making sure I covered everything. And remember, he has never seen Mum. Plus, I went into her Facebook account and deleted any messages about her passing away. There weren't many. Just a few random comments."

Emily nodded her head as she rocked forward in her chair. "God, I am so nervous. It was okay sending a message to Tony, and even fine when I replied to his message about the Skype call today, but I am freaking out about talking to him online."

"Don't worry. I'll be here. I'll wait in the kitchen. If we can get some information from this guy, anything at all, we can help the others."

Emily glanced at the digital clock on the TV. It was time. A ringing noise broke the quiet. It was coming from Anita's laptop. "Right, you go and hide. Let's get this over and done with."

Emily clicked to accept the call, and a grainy image appeared on the screen. She could see her own picture in a small square on the bottom right-hand side of the screen. Her nerves were in tatters, and blood was pounding in her ears. The man in the video picture looked almost, but not entirely, like the Tony Anita had been corresponding with. He was in a dark room, and Emily figured that was to slightly disguise his features. He had the same colour hair and build, but she couldn't make out his face. They must have ripped off someone's picture in identity theft. Perhaps the real guy actually was in the US Army.

When he spoke, his voice was low-pitched. He didn't sound American. "I am happy we finally get to see each other. It is Anita, isn't it?"

Emily smiled, trying her hardest to make sure her lips didn't wobble. She kept her hands tightly clasped in her lap to hide the trembling. "Yes. I was worried about you. How is everything?"

"Not good, I'm afraid. That's why I haven't been in touch. I am having trouble with the insurers. They have confirmed that they will pay the money. There is absolutely no problem there. But they have procedures to go through, and they need some signatures from human resources at my last posting. And then I got the latest news about my son."

Aha. He was straight to the point and wasn't wasting any time. This would be the request for additional money. Emily managed to keep the smirk from her face, delighted that she could see through this so completely. Weeks ago she would have fallen for it herself. "What happened?"

"My son is gravely ill and will need another operation." He leaned forward in his chair until his shadowed face was enlarged on the screen. Emily drew back; his posture was menacing. "But that is nothing to you, is it? Who are you?"

Emily's heart thudded. "I don't know what you're talking about. I'm Anita."

He laughed, but there was an edge of malice. "Anita is dead. I checked it out. For you were far too anxious to speak to Tony. I was brought in to check out the situation. Do a bit of investigation. The other girl's photo was posted all over Anita's account." He sniggered and spoke to someone off camera. "Hit the lights."

She blinked, and it took her a moment to realise what, or rather who, she was looking at. It was the driver of the blue car.

"Oh my God." Her hand flew to her mouth, and her heart pumped erratically. Her brain stuttered, and she froze.

"Now we know why you were following Cathy. Let this go and keep away from us, or you'll be sorry, bitch." He spat, saliva splattering the screen. Emily drew back in disgust. The call disconnected.

Chloe came rushing into the room. "I was listening outside the door. What the hell are we going to do?"

Emily was trembling, frozen by an arctic chill. "They set me up. Oh God, what have we done? We need to tell the others."

"Yes, we absolutely do, but they will still be at the party."

"There's no point in calling. They'll never hear it, and I can't explain this in a text."

"Email everyone. That way they will have all the details as soon as they open their mail. Shit, I can't believe what just happened."

"Yes, good idea." Her voice shook.

Chloe hugged her. "It will be fine. They've given us a warning, that's all. What's the worst that could happen?"

***

James didn't take her home. They went to his place. It wasn't the house he went into the night Chloe and Emily were keeping an eye on Cathy. She didn't know how to ask him about that place, but at the moment she didn't care. She tried to protest that she should go home, but he wasn't having it.

"I don't know why you brought me here in the first place."

James carried on opening a bottle of Malbec, pouring the dark red wine into two long-stemmed glasses. He handed her one. "I want to talk to you. And I don't want to be disturbed. If we had gone to your place, that ass might have appeared. I'm not in the mood for another run-in with him tonight."

She shrugged while he moved across the room and fiddled with a remote control. In seconds, low, melodic music filled the air. James had done well for himself. It was a traditional townhouse, tall and narrow. An extension opened the ground floor into one huge open living space. They settled on a comfortable sofa. She toyed with the stem of her glass, unwilling, or perhaps incapable, of making eye contact with him.

"You've done well for yourself, Marianne."

"By the looks of it, so have you, especially this place. Is it yours?"

"Yeah, I bought it a few years ago. To be honest, I

don't spend much time here."

"Why is that? I mean, do you travel for business?"

"Yes, the security business has exploded over the last few years. It keeps me busy."

She had no idea if she could believe a word he was saying. She realised she was staring at him. She was drowning in his eyes. Eyes that first drew her in when she was on the verge of becoming a woman.

"I thought you were headed for prison. I'm amazed you managed to turn everything around."

"So am I. If you hadn't left me, I would have carried on following the same path, the one of least resistance. I was an angry kid. I dread to think how I could have turned out." He looked away and gulped, his Adam's apple working furiously. "I loved you. Why did you leave me?"

She could have made something up. She could have said anything. But she figured she owed him more than that. So she told the truth or at least part of it.

"I was scared. I saw the older guys you were running with; I thought about their girlfriends and wives. Living hand to mouth when their man was in prison and enjoying the high life when he was out and had a few scams running. And their children, the children were going down the same path. The girls pregnant young and falling into the same old cycle. The boys in trouble before they were even out of school. I didn't want it. Didn't want that life."

He took her hand in his. "I could lie to you. I could sit here and say that would never have happened to us. That you were my world, my everything, and if you had told me how your fears, I would have walked away from that life and made a better one for us. But that's not the truth. I was a stupid kid. I thought my way was the right way. I wouldn't have listened to you. It's taken me a long time to say these words, far less to believe them. But I understand, I don't hold it against you."

This was not what she'd been expecting. The anger and rage had left him. Perhaps it was the years in the army, or maybe he simply grew up. The boy he had been began to fade from her sight, and in his place was the man who sat in front of her. He was caressing her hand, his thumb tracing a feather light pattern in rhythmic strokes. He was the most desirable man she'd ever met. She stilled, her breathing hard and laboured as her chest rose and fell, drawing his eyes to her low-cut neckline. He trailed a delicate caress across the fullness of her breasts.

"I've missed you, even though I didn't realise. I had no idea how empty my life was without your touch." His voice was roughened. He drew her hand forward and placed it against his chest; his heart was beating as erratically as her own. The air around them, the space between them, was charged with particles of life, desire and need. She touched his face, drew her fingers down the side of his cheek, across his jawline, gently rubbing the stubble. She moved closer. The last time she experienced such raw desire, this explosion of emotion, was when, as a scared seventeen-year-old, she made love with him one last time. She'd known she would be gone the next day, and every touch, every caress, each emotional cord had been multiplied a thousand fold.

Without breaking eye contact, he drew her to her feet and pulled her tight against him. He kissed her. She kissed him back. No hesitation, no holding back. Nothing else mattered right now apart from the two of them and this moment. Nothing at all.

He drew away and whispered, "Stay with me tonight, my love. It's been eighteen years, and I need you."

Marianne draped her arms around his neck and pulled him close. She needed him too.

He lifted her up, and as she hooked her legs around his waist, memories crowded her mind and blurred her vision. She was seventeen again, on the verge of womanhood and in love for the first time. Perhaps the only time.

James nipped at her neck, interspersed with gentle kisses. "Hold tight. We're going upstairs."

She laughed. "Careful. You're not eighteen anymore."

"No, but I can still handle you."

And he did. He lowered her to her feet and moved away as he unbuttoned his shirt and toed off his shoes. The bedroom was neat and tidy and beautifully decorated. Was this Cathy's touch? The thought provoked a flash of jealousy. She was shocked at its ferocity.

"I had the whole place done by an interior designer." There was laughter in his voice. He must have read her mind.

He was shirtless. Tanned, smooth flesh sprinkled with light chest hairs that she wanted to caress, to touch. Her mouth was dry, her heart hammering. He pulled her to her feet.

His palm settled in the small of her back as he drew her to him. His eyes never left hers as he reached behind to unzip her dress. He placed a hand on each shoulder, flicked her shoulder straps and slid the material from her shoulders and pushed until it fell, pooling at her feet.

She stepped out of it, still in her high heels. She kept herself in pretty good shape, but she didn't always make it to the gym. Her body was no longer that of a teenager, but that of a thirty-five-year-old woman.

The appreciative look in his eyes told her all she needed to know and gave her the confidence to carry on. She unclasped her bra and shrugged out of it, letting it fall to the floor to join her dress. She stood tall and proud, sharing all she had, all she was with this man, opening to him in a way she'd been unable to with any other.

He briefly closed his eyes, and his tongue flicked out and ran over his lips. When he opened his eyes, his gaze was burning hot.

"Mhairi, my love. Come to my bed." His voice was a hoarse whisper.

She kicked off her heels and tumbled onto the bed with him. She wasn't going to brood on the past or what she'd done to him. She was where she belonged—at least for one night.

CHAPTER FORTY-TWO

Marianne woke slowly, relishing those last, precious moments of twilight sleep before the day claimed her. Her body throbbed with the memory of the previous hours, of passionate coupling, frenzied touches and tender caresses. She rolled over, stretching out her hand to touch . . . nothing. Her eyes opened. James wasn't in bed.

She sat up, and the covers fell to her waist, exposing her nakedness. A rush of heat suffused her as she relived their night in her mind. He knew her body like no one else ever had, and their years apart, which rendered them semi-strangers, had melted away as their flesh connected and the barriers fell.

Her musings were interrupted by the sound of a whistling kettle and the dull creak of cupboards opening and closing. She threw back the covers and, searching the floor, found her underwear. She picked her dress up off the floor, pulled it on and grabbed her shoes. Eager to see him, she hurried down the stairs.

She stopped at the doorway that led into the open-plan area. James was talking. He was leaning against the kitchen island, his back to her as he spoke on his mobile.

"I know what I'm doing, Cathy."

Marianne froze.

"Of course I know what I'm risking. You don't have to worry."

There was silence as he listened to his girlfriend. Marianne's stomach twisted. She couldn't escape the fact that James had a partner. She glanced at her ringless left hand. She was now free, but he wasn't.

"Yes, we're at my place. No one would have seen us. Don't worry, Cathy. This won't change anything. I'll pick you up in an hour. We've come too far for things to be ruined now. Bye."

She gasped out loud. What had she expected? Even if he wanted a future with her, they could never have one, not with the secret eating away at her. And if he knew the truth, he would walk away in disgust.

He turned around, his mouth falling open in what she assumed was the shock at being caught dismissing her and their night together.

"You utter bastard."

He reached out to touch her, but she drew back. "Don't touch me." Her voice was a snarl. "Just leave me alone. I hope it's a lot longer than eighteen years before I see you again."

With that, she grabbed her bag from the coffee table and ran to the front door. She heard his footsteps as he chased after her, but she bolted into the road and hailed a passing taxi. As it took off, she looked back. He stood in his doorway, watching her leave.

***

Marianne had ignored her phone the night before and would now have to pay the price. She showered and changed into jeans and a T-shirt and pulled her hair back in a ponytail. She listened to her messages. Most were from Emily, becoming increasingly upset. Something about Anita's Facebook account, the pretend American army officer and how it all went wrong. Both Tom and Sue left several messages. They started out asking if she got home okay. Then she received texts from the whole lot of them asking if she'd read her email.

She opened her laptop and checked her emails, but there was nothing from Emily. She was debating who to call first when the doorbell rang. She almost laughed when she checked the intercom video and saw all four of them standing there. She pressed the buzzer. "Come on up."

They tripped in one after the other. Emily was ashen. "Where the hell have you been?"

Sue was pale. "Did you spend the night with James?"

"That is none of your business." Her face was burning. These guys didn't own her.

"I know you've got history, but he could be involved in all this. Hell, he could be the boss."

"There's as good a likelihood that Karl could be involved in this, but I guess you'd rather it was James."

Tom's voice lashed out like a whip. "Enough. We have bigger problems at the moment."

Marianne stilled. "What the hell has happened?"

Emily was trembling. "I Skyped Tony Anderson last night, pretending to be Anita. It was a setup. The guy online was one of the men who attacked me. He warned us to stay away from Cathy."

"Shit, that isn't good." Marianne was still puzzled. "You said you sent me an email. I promise you I haven't seen one."

Emily bristled. "I'm not lying if that's what you think. Here, look."

Emily held out her phone. The display contained a list of sent emails. She opened the top one and highlighted the address line. Pointed. "Look, just like I told you."

Marianne froze. She couldn't get her words out fast enough. "You bloody idiot. You sent it to my old email address. The one that has been corrupted. They are reading all my emails. What have you done?"

Emily drew back, stricken. Tom was the first to speak, his voice urgent, "Quick, give me your laptop, Marianne. I may be able to delete the message. I can't recall it because Sue and I have already opened the email."

She rushed across to her desk area, grabbed the laptop and entered her login and password details, moving out of the way as Tom took over. He tapped away, then stood back. He didn't look happy. "I've deleted it, but it was opened. They may have already seen it, or it could have opened automatically when you entered the email login details."

Marianne said, "We can't worry about it now. What we need to decide is what we do next."

Sue said, "We have the virus in place, now we need to work out how we let Adam know and get him to pull back from Marianne's business clients and leave Amelia alone."

Tom blew out a heavy breath. "We need to decide on the plan. I don't trust Adam at all now."

Nor did Marianne, and she agreed they should be careful. They needed a solid plan. She opened her mouth to speak, then snapped it shut as her phone rang. She quickly answered it when she recognised the caller ID.

Jenny was talking before Marianne could even say hello. "She's gone. They've taken Amelia." She was sobbing.

Marianne's heart was pounding. "What do you mean? Who's taken her?"

"The bloody maniacs you're involved with. They've taken my girl. Amelia never came home last night. We didn't think much of it because she often stays at her friend Katie's house. When she wasn't home early this morning, I called Katie's mother. Amelia didn't stay there last night. Katie complained she was tired and Amelia told her she would come home. Katie left her at the bus stop. That's when they took her." She ended on a sob.

Marianne gathered her strength and kept calm. "We don't know it's them, Jenny. Is there no way she could have gone to another friend's?" She knew the truth but wasn't ready to accept it yet. There had to be an explanation. It would be fine. It had to be.

Jenny continued talking, the words coming out in a rush and tumbling over each other. Marianne switched the call to speakerphone so they could all hear. "Thomas phoned the police. He has a cousin who works there. He's one of the detectives, and they examined the CCTV of the bus stop. Two men grabbed Amelia and bundled her into the back of a car. It's them, Mhairi. It's those bastards."

Marianne clutched at the phone as her sister's sobs breached every defence she possessed and laid bare a primal fear that consumed her.

Tom called her. "Quick, you've received an email."

She was shaking. "Jenny, I'll call you back. I promise."

She opened the video attached to the email. It was dark and the image distorted from lack of light. A match flickered, and a lamp was lit. "Oh my God, no."

Amelia slumped in a chair, tied by ropes and metal restraints. She wore jeans and a pale-coloured top, the sleeve of which was torn. A man walked forward wearing a mask and yanked Amelia's hair until she faced the camera. Her cheek was bruised, her lip split and her eyes were blank. "Your niece is okay. We've sedated her. You need to do as you're told, and no more crap from you, otherwise . . ." He grabbed Amelia's right breast and pinched hard. Little emotion showed on Amelia's drugged face. "I'll have a little fun before finishing her off."

If they hurt Amelia, this would be on her own head. She would be responsible for whatever atrocities she suffered. Yet again she was instrumental in determining Amelia's future. She fell to her knees and howled, a primaeval cry of despair.

CHAPTER FORTY-THREE

Tom found Adam at home. He was in the new games room he'd built in the basement. He should have known. Adam had been splashing the cash all over the place this past year. His brother acted like a European playboy, not some Internet gang leader, yet that was what he undoubtedly was.

Adam was hunched over the Xbox controller as he played the latest must-have apocalyptic survival game. "Damn. I'm dead again." He sat back. "Hi, Tom. Hey, that was some scene last night. Where did Marianne go with James?"

Adam's voice was pleasant and his smile, unless you knew better, seemed genuine.

"You can cut the crap and tell me the girl is all right."

Adams brow furrowed. "What girl?"

He was obviously playing dumb. "You know. Marianne Sinclair's niece."

"Your friend Marianne?"

"Yes, she is MJ Sinclair."

If Tom didn't know better, he could swear that Adam didn't have a clue what he was talking about. His brother shook his head and raised his hands in the air. "Who the hell is MJ Sinclair?"

Tom was getting fed up with this. He needed action,

and he needed it now. "I know all about it. I know that Cytech owns Bergen. I know the dodgy dealings it has going on. Don't lie to me, and don't try and hide what you've been doing. All we want is the girl. And for you to leave Marianne's business alone."

"Are you on drugs? You are acting like you are under the influence of something. What the hell are you talking about?"

"Don't give me that shit. I'm on to you. Give us the girl, and keep away from Marianne's business, or I will unleash hell on Bergen and delete every one of your contacts, deals, codes, bank and cryptocurrency accounts. And I mean everything."

"You fool. What have you done? I need to make a call."

Adam paled, jumped up and brushed him aside. Tom rushed him, pulled him back by the shoulders and slammed him against the wall. His forearm was against Adam's throat, right against his windpipe, pinning him to the wall. Adam struggled, but he was no match for Tom.

"I know that Cathy works for you. I've met her in Bulgaria. I know the scamming that is going on. And I know the damage it has caused. However, what you are doing in ruining Marianne's business and kidnapping and threatening her niece is too, too much. You've gone too far, Adam. Too far."

"What the hell . . . ?" Adam started to choke, his colour heightened and his eyes bulged. Tom pulled back, loosening his grip. Adam coughed and sagged against the wall. "I have no idea what you're talking about. I don't even own the bloody company anymore."

Tom stilled. "What do you mean you don't own Bergen?"

"Yes, well, no, what I mean is I don't own Cytech. I sold the company and its subsidiaries over a year ago."

"But everyone believes you still own it. You act like you still own it."

"I sold it for a premium. Believe me, I sold the company for much more money than it was worth on paper. But I'm not one to look a gift horse in the mouth. The only condition was that for another couple of years I didn't make it public knowledge and I continued to be the sole registered shareholder. But it's only a nominee arrangement."

"What do you mean?"

"The buyer was going through some legal squabbles and asked if the title could be transferred later."

Tom's head was in chaos. "Who did you sell the company to?"

"Karl. Karl Radinsky."

***

Marianne stared at Tom for what seemed like forever. "You are kidding me. It's Karl Radinsky?" She looked at Sue. "Thank God you never went on a date with him."

Sue was completely pale. "It goes to show that my track record of bad taste in men continues, abysmally."

Chloe said, "We have him. We have the guy whose business is responsible for everything that has happened. He seemed so genuine and charming. What a bastard."

Sue grimaced. "What if he knew who Marianne was all along? And was only pretending an attraction to me?

Maybe he got his kicks from meeting the people he scammed. Sicko." The last word was spat out.

Marianne was glad that Sue was furious. She'd done nothing wrong. She asked, "How do we let Karl know that we'll destroy everything he has if he doesn't leave me alone? And I need to know Amelia will be safe."

Tom's voice was gentle. "Don't worry. Your niece will be fine." He couldn't possibly know that for sure, but she accepted the words as they were no doubt intended: a soothing balm.

"I hope so. But what do we do? Dealing with your brother was one thing. Radinsky will be a much tougher nut."

Emily spoke. "There is Cathy. She's the only person in all of this that we absolutely know was connected all the way along. Cathy works for Bergen. And we know from Tom's meeting with her in Bulgaria that she is involved in the scamming."

"I thought of that," Tom said. "I've tried calling and texting, but there was no answer."

"I have Karl's number. I could call him? Perhaps arrange to meet?" Sue's voice wobbled a little.

Emily sighed. "That is the best option if you're up to it?"

Sue nodded and rummaged in her handbag for her phone. "Karl sent me a text the morning after we met saying he was making sure he had the right number for me." She peered at the screen as she scrolled. "I've got it. What will I say?"

Tom was quick to answer. "Not the truth, obviously. I want to catch him unawares. Say you'd like to meet with him, and try and organise something soon."

Sue bobbed her head in agreement and pressed the screen. She moved into the corner of the room.

After a few seconds, she spoke, "Hi Karl, it's Sue. Is that offer of a drink still available?"

There was a short silence, and then she said, "Okay. No, that's great. Tomorrow is fine. One o'clock at Scott's. Hope your meeting goes well."

She disconnected the call. "How was that?"

Tom said, "Good. Why can't he meet you today?"

"He said he has an important meeting and didn't know when it would finish."

"Okay, we can go with you, and then we'll speak to him."

Marianne thought about it and knew there was another option. One she hadn't wanted to take, but there were no other options. "I can't wait until tomorrow, I'm going to go see James. He is obviously connected to Cathy. I don't know how he is involved in this. I do know he was interested in buying Cytech. That either makes him an entrepreneur like Adam or a conman like Karl."

"And we don't know which one he is," Tom said. "There must be something else we could do. You can't put yourself in danger like that."

"Amelia is the one in danger, not me."

CHAPTER FORTY-FOUR

Marianne waited anxiously for James to speak. He seemed happy to see her when she first arrived on his doorstep. He didn't look pleased now.

James paced in front of the fireplace. "So let me get this straight. You, Tom, Sue and your friends Emily and Chloe have been acting as some type of Scooby Doo investigators to try and track people who scammed various parties. They also targeted your business and are looking to defraud your investors. And they have kidnapped your niece. At which point did you decide it was a good idea *not* to go straight to the police?"

"I tried. I didn't go initially because, well, I've sailed pretty close to the wind sometimes when building the business. I realised I had to involve the police. But they knew I was on my way there. And that's when they attacked Amelia the first time. I couldn't risk it happening again. I didn't have a choice."

"There is always a choice. Always. So what do you want me to do?"

"I don't want you to do anything personally. Cathy isn't answering her telephone, and Tom can't reach her. I have no idea if you know what I'm about to tell you—if you are in blissful ignorance or if you are part of it."

He leaned against the mantel. His pose was casual, but his demeanour was tense.

"Cathy is involved in online scamming." He started to speak, but she held up her hand to stop him. "We know she is. She met with Tom in Bulgaria and took him to see the operation."

James's face was impassive, but the tell-tale tic worked away by the side of his mouth. Damn. He knew about this. Oh God. She hadn't realised until that moment how much she wanted to believe in him. Was he behind this? Was it all about revenge?

"You don't seem surprised. It looks like you haven't changed your ways, have you? Is it you? Are you trying to harm me, hurt Amelia? Why? Because I left you?"

Her stomach was a hollow pit; her breathing quickened as she launched herself at him, clawed hands grasping.

"Shit. Stop it."

He held her wrists, and she flailed as she tried to reach him again.

"I may be many things, but I am not behind whatever is happening to you. I promise."

His voice was roughened and raw. His eyes pleading. She stopped struggling. "Then what the hell is your relationship with Adam and Karl?" Before he could reply she closed her eyes, moved away from him and waved her hands in a dismissive gesture. "Oh, forget it. I don't care about that. Not right now. A subsidiary of Cytech has been banking money from various scam operations. Adam sold the company over a year ago but has been acting as if he still owns it."

That got his attention. "Adam sold? Who owns it

now?"

"Radinsky. If it isn't you or Adam, then he is the one who has Amelia. I need to get her back safe. I don't give a damn what he does to the business. I don't care about the investors. I know I should, but I don't. I just want Amelia." And to her shame, she started to cry. Heavy, hot tears were running down her cheeks, and her breath hitched as she tried to stop the sobs escaping.

He clasped her upper arms, a reassuring caress that soothed. "I'll get in touch with Cathy. Leave this to me. I want you to keep out of this."

Even amid the fear and terror, disappointment crushed her that James hadn't changed one bit. It vindicated her decision eighteen years before.

"Thank you. I guess I should be grateful that you are still nothing but a criminal at heart."

"This isn't what you think. Please believe me. Leave it to me." His eyes beseeched as he took her hands in his. "I promise you everything will be all right."

She nodded. What else could she do?

He turned and scribbled on a notepad, tearing off the sheet of paper. "Here's my number. In case you need to get in touch with me."

She took it, and left, putting all her trust in a man she once betrayed in the worst possible way. But the question was: had he done the same to her?

∗

Marianne replayed the video of Amelia for over half an hour. She knew it was a masochistic punishment, but she deserved the torturous pain.

"Here, you look like you could do with this."

She turned to Tom, who handed her a cup of fresh coffee. "Thank you. I keep trying to see something, anything that can point us in the right direction. What if James goes to Cathy and Radinsky? What if they're all in this together, and he was just stringing me along?"

He shrugged. "All we can do is wait. If James doesn't come up with anything today, then we meet with Radinsky tomorrow."

Her eyes smarted with unshed tears, and her voice cracked as she spoke. "You don't understand. No one does. It's all my fault. I kept out of Amelia's life all these years only to bring her the worst kind of trouble. Trouble that could end her life."

Sue, Emily and Chloe came to join them, drawn by Marianne's obvious distress. Sue placed a comforting hand on her shoulder and said, "Don't be hard on yourself. How could you know they would go after your sister's child? This isn't your fault."

Marianne spoke without thought; her words blasting through the barriers erected eighteen years before. "Of course it's my fault. Amelia isn't my sister's daughter, she's mine."

Under other circumstances, their reactions would have been comical. Four mouths dropped open; eight eyes widened. Tom was the first to recover. "Oh God, no wonder you're in pieces."

A strange sense of release and relief enveloped Marianne; her darkest secret was out in the open, at least among this small group. "I'm telling you this in confidence. Amelia doesn't know. I made an agreement with my sister that I would walk away and never come back. That way Amelia would truly be hers."

She paused and considered their reactions before carrying on. "Please don't think badly of me. Part of me has always wondered if I did the right thing. But I couldn't have kept her. It would have ruined both our lives."

Emily said, "Don't be silly. You did the right thing. At least, what was right for you both under the circumstances."

Chloe said, "I hate to ask, but who is the father?"

Before Marianne could speak, Sue said, "It's obvious."

She turned to Marianne, who wanted to close her ears, clamp her hands tight against her head and not hear the truth that she knew was coming, the truth verbalised by another person. She'd opened Pandora's box, and there was no going back now.

Sue's eyes were kind. "James is the father, isn't he?"

There was a thunderous roar in Marianne's ears, and her stomach lurched. "Yes, yes, he is. But he doesn't know. And he mustn't ever find out. We were children. He was getting into more and more trouble. I hadn't long turned seventeen when I found out I was pregnant. If I'd told him, if I'd stayed, then I would have been bound to him and that life forever. I would have been a petty criminal's wife, living in my little house decorated with stolen goods and a partner who would have been in and out of prison. That was no future for me or my baby."

Tom asked, "How did your sister come into this?"

"Jenny was my saviour. I told her before I told our parents. Jenny moved to Edinburgh after she left college. I went to see her. She and Thomas had been married for a few years, but he'd suffered a childhood illness, and they knew he would never be able to have children. It was Thomas's suggestion. I'd already decided that I didn't want to get rid of the baby. I couldn't do that. Thomas said they would take the child. It was all so easy. I never went home again. Thomas had an aunt who lived on the outskirts of Edinburgh. I went to stay with her. The baby was born. I handed her to Jenny. A month later I left Scotland. Thomas gave me enough money to make a start in London. It all seems such a long time ago."

Sue hugged her tight, and she melted into the embrace. She was drained, with little strength left. She couldn't help but assume the worst would happen. The video still played in the background on continuous replay. In the silence, they heard the kidnapper's voice again.

Tom walked across to the laptop. "Let me turn this off. It is doing no good torturing yourself." He pressed stop, and the image paused. Amelia's head was pulled back, and her eyes were vacant. The picture was grainy, but her daughter's face was clearly illuminated from a small arched stained-glass window set high in the corner of the wall.

Tom stilled. "Oh my God. I know where this is. I've been in that room before. I recognise the window. That's where we used to crawl through and jump down into the wine store and raid the headmaster's booze collection. It's my old school." He turned to the others. "Ryan, my old friend who works for Adam, bought it. Or is it Radinsky he works for? What we do know is Ryan owns the place. That's where Amelia is. Or at the least, it's where she was."

CHAPTER FORTY-FIVE

The drive to the former Ardale College for Boys took over an hour in Emily's beaten-up old Range Rover. Marianne tried to call James again. No answer. She quickly left a message, then disconnected. She had done all she could. Hopefully, he'd listen to his voicemail.

Chloe sat in the back with Marianne and Sue. Tom bagged pole position in the passenger seat. He pointed straight ahead. "The school's main entrance is up there, but turn off on the next left. If I remember correctly, the track will take us to the back of the building. It was the old tradesman's entrance when this place was a private home."

Emily did as directed, and the car rocked along the overgrown track. It was nothing more than rutted, compacted dirt. "Sorry for the bumps, guys. It's a bit rough to navigate over the holes."

Marianne thought that might not be a bad thing. "At least anyone with a nice car will go through the main entrance."

The air was heavy with tension. They didn't know what lay ahead of them except that Amelia's life depended upon them getting it right. The foliage was thick on either side of the track, and huge trees spread their branches to create a tunnel from the canopy of leaves. Marianne squinted as a shaft of light hit the windshield. Suddenly, the pathway widened and opened onto a grassed area that lay behind a grey-stone, Victorian building. Its turrets and stone gargoyles cast a forbidding and stern glare over the gardens.

Tom pointed to the left. "Park there. If you reverse back a little, you will be hidden by the trees."

They got out of the car in silence. Marianne faced them. "Emily and Chloe, you stay here and keep a watch. We all have our phones on vibrate. If you see anyone or need to contact us, just send a quick text. Tom and Sue, you're with me. We go in and see if we can find Amelia. If we can get her out, we then let Radinsky know there is a virus inserted in Bergen."

Emily was pale. "And what if someone is there? God, I am so nervous."

Marianne smiled. "Then we bargain straightaway. Whatever happens, we get Amelia, and Radinsky backs away from my business, allowing him to keep his files and data intact."

***

Tom had come prepared with an assortment of tools, and he hefted the canvas bag higher on his shoulder. He'd packed a crowbar, and a battery-powered screwdriver, which he hoped would be enough to open the back entrance and anywhere else they needed to access. He needn't have worried. Out of habit, he tried the door handle and froze in shock as the door opened. He stopped, leaving it slightly ajar. There wasn't any noise from inside.

Sue said, "That doesn't look good. Someone must be here." Her voice was a hushed whisper.

Tom jerked his head in the direction of the door at the end of the long dark corridor. "That will take us through the kitchen, then into the main hall. Let's do this."

Marianne touched each of their hands and whispered, "Good luck to all of us."

Tom led the way. Holding the handle down tight, he carefully slid the door back. It squeaked, and he paused for a moment. Reassured there was no one in the kitchen, he opened the door wide enough that the three of them could get through.

They crept through the abandoned kitchen. It appeared clean but hadn't been modernised in years. The huge AGA was lit. A modern kettle was plugged in next to it, and the sink held dirty dishes. The heavy interior kitchen door, which Tom knew led into the main hall, was slightly ajar. He motioned for the others to follow him as he headed to the door. He opened it gently; there was no squeak this time. He stepped into the hallway and panicked, reversing back into the kitchen almost knocking Marianne over.

"I'm sorry. I heard footsteps." He pushed the door until it was almost closed. If someone came into the kitchen, they would have to deal with it. Through the slight gap, he saw two guys he didn't recognise. They were coming from the direction of the front door, and they looked like heavies. Both were muscled and mean-looking. They wore ill-fitting suits, and to his horror, there was a bulge over each of their breast pockets. These guys were tooled up and not trying to hide it.

Something pushed against his hip, and he glanced

down. Marianne was kneeling and peering into the hallway.

Radinsky was next, followed by Ryan, and, to Tom's surprise, Adam. So he *was* involved in this.

Radinsky was heading towards what used to be the headmaster's sitting room. He opened the door and called out behind him, "Come in here. We can be comfortable, and you can tell me about your proposition." Two more people walked across the hallway: Cathy and James.

***

Marianne tiptoed as she followed Tom across the dim hall, its walls covered in faded tapestries and hunting trophies. A low sideboard was littered with discarded sports equipment, tennis rackets and cricket bats. There was dust everywhere, and it tickled her nose. She prayed she wouldn't sneeze. She crouched slightly, and through the slit of the ajar door, she could see them all.

James and Cathy stood to one side facing Karl, Adam and Ryan.

James addressed Adam, "Thank you for agreeing to meet, although I have to say Mayfair would have been a sight more convenient. We also seem to have quite a party going on here. It's you I want to talk to, Adam, as you know, I'm interested in buying Cytech."

Marianne frowned. James already knew that Karl owned the company. Why was he pretending otherwise?

Adam's eyes flickered towards Karl, who smiled before speaking. "The time for pretence has gone. I am the owner of Cytech. Adam kindly agreed to stay on as the de facto owner to maintain my privacy. I'm not interested in a buyer, but I could be persuaded to have an investor. If you want to go ahead and get a share of Cytech, you'll be investing with me."

James looked at Cathy. "You didn't tell me, darling."

Cathy shrugged. "I didn't know. Well done, Karl. I thought you worked for Adam."

Ryan laughed, but it was more of a mocking smirk. "You don't need to know everything. That information was above your pay grade." The inference was clear. Ryan had been fully aware of the circumstances.

James said, "I am serious about buying the company. If that isn't an option, I could be persuaded to make a partial investment. I don't care who I deal with. And I am fully aware of its activities, especially those of the subsidiary, Bergen."

Karl stared at Cathy. "You have been busy, haven't you? You been telling tales? My business is my business, and you need to learn when to keep quiet." His tone and scathing look were insulting. "Maybe I'll be the one to teach you a lesson." He turned back to James. "If you know that much, then you are undoubtedly aware that a share of my company would come with a substantial price tag."

"Yes, I am aware of that, and I am prepared to pay a good price. It gives me access to a good working business with a proven track record. However, there are some things I don't dabble in. Your fake fund strategy, using MJS securities is, I believe, flawed. You are riding too high above the parapet. I also don't deal with kidnappers and don't want any taint of that."

Marianne tensed.

Karl drew back and laughed. "What the hell are you

talking about? I don't know anything about any fund. And I don't know anything about a kidnapping. Is this a joke? Because I'm a busy man, and it isn't funny."

Marianne couldn't take it any longer. This needed to be resolved, and now. They'd wanted a meeting with Karl, and now they had it. She glanced at Tom; he nodded. She turned to Sue and motioned for her to stay where she was. There was no sense in all of them being in the same room in case someone needed to go for help.

She strode into the room, Tom behind her, and held her head high. "Hello, everyone. I would love to say it's nice to see you, but it isn't."

The silence was thick and heavy as everyone turned towards her. Karl and Ryan were surprised, Adam bewildered, and James and Cathy furious.

She turned to Karl. "We know your game. You're running cyber scams and online attacks. You're screwing over the vulnerable and destroying lives. You killed Gareth O'Hare. And you have my niece. You're using her to keep me quiet while you pillage my address book of investors and try and sell them your non-existent fund. You crossed the line. We have as well. Tom, tell them what you've done."

Tom took centre stage, and Marianne had to forgive him if he seemed a little showman-like. From his cocky stance, she knew he was enjoying this moment, irrespective of the danger they were in. She hoped he didn't go too far.

"I have roamed through Bergen's online presence. I have been inside all your files. And I left a little present behind. I have inserted a clever little bug that will be activated the moment I send an email message to Bergen, and I have already prepared one in draft, ready to go." He held out his hand and indicated his phone. "That email will immediately hit your inbox, and it doesn't even need to be opened to connect with the virus and delete everything. And I mean everything. You lose details of contacts, bank account information, investment information; all of your private details and records will be gone."

Karl was ashen as he turned to Ryan. "Is that even possible? Is he lying?"

A dark red flush crept along Ryan's neck and across his face, his eyes narrowed, and a vein throbbed in his forehead. "I have never come across that. But that doesn't mean anything. You know as well as I do that when I got you to buy Cytech, Tom had created coding and bugs that were unique in the hacking game. So yes, in answer to your question, the little shit may very well have created something like that."

Karl addressed Tom. "Look, I don't know what your game is, but I have done nothing against you or your friend here." He pointed to Marianne. "But if you activate that bug, I will create such a vendetta against you that you will wish you'd never been born."

"Enough of your bravado. We know Amelia is here. Let Marianne's niece go, walk away from the fake fund, and I will never send that email. I will also go into your system and remove the virus. Your little puppet, Ryan, can even watch me do it."

Karl shook his head, his waving hand a dismissive flick. "I seriously don't know what you are talking about. What girl? You can search this place. It belongs to Ryan. I'm sure he doesn't have the girl hidden away somewhere. Tell them, Ryan. This is bloody ridiculous. And who is Gareth O'Hare? I've never heard of the man."

Ryan sighed. "I've been running a small sideline. I didn't want to tell you before because it was a little bit riskier than our usual business. But this is going to be a helluva payday. I needed a little extra security. The girl provides that. The O'Hare guy was threatening to stand in our way. I had to do something. It's fine."

Karl's face was red, and he sputtered as spittle shot from his mouth and spread across the room. "You little fuck. How dare you endanger my business? You tell them where the girl is, and we end this NOW."

"No. You are a low-life criminal who happened to have money to spare. I'm the one who set everything up. I'm the one who knew the value of Cytech and Tom's code. We are not throwing away the best opportunity we will ever have to make serious money."

Karl stood still but didn't say anything. He didn't have to. He merely glanced at his two heavies, who each pulled out a gun and trained them on Ryan. Ryan slowly backed away, edging toward the battered chesterfield sofa at the end of the room.

"Oh, come on, Karl. Don't be stupid. I have a good number going here. I did it for the business—for us." There was a plea in his voice.

"No one screws with me. Boys, he's all yours."

Suddenly, Ryan reached into his jacket and pulled out a gun. With one smooth movement, he fired, and the gunshot ripped through the air. Everyone froze. The bullet tore into the nearest thug, who fell to the ground as an arterial flow of blood sprayed everything in proximity. Marianne pressed herself against the wall, her heart pumping and her mind a blank.

CHAPTER FORTY-SIX

The two coolest heads in the room were James and Cathy, or so he imagined. James engaged autopilot and knew Cathy would do the same. It's what they'd been trained for, after all. He pulled his Glock standard issue from his shoulder holster, took aim and hit Ryan in the shoulder.

The force of the bullet spun Ryan around, and his arms flailed. Ryan dived behind the sofa, firing erratically as he disappeared from sight. His shots went wide, but one caught the thug a glancing blow. Surprised, the man dropped to his knees. "Cathy, on him. Ryan's mine." He raised his voice and called out, "Special Services. Drop your weapons."

The thug's pistol-arm was unharmed, and he fired at Cathy. Cathy dropped low and fired rapidly. She hit him once in the knee and again in the throat. The guy started to gurgle, a deep-throated death knell, and collapsed.

Time stood still as everyone froze. James quickly assessed the scene. The two thugs were down. Karl had backed himself against the windows. Tom was tucked into an alcove by the door, and an ashen Marianne pressed herself against the wall. Adam backed into the corner of the room, his hands raised in surrender. "This has nothing to do with me. All I did was sell my company." His voice ended on a whimper as he crouched and covered his head with his arms.

James was disgusted by Adam. What a pathetic excuse for a man. To think he'd once considered him the mastermind of the hacking scams. His gaze was caught by a blurred motion to the side of him. Ryan darted out from the sofa and ran towards the door. James followed.

***

Marianne was backed against the far wall and didn't have a clear run to the exit. Tom was by the door, and she motioned for him to get out, but he stayed put, although he did move deeper into the safety of a recessed bookshelf.

She cried out in pain as her hair was yanked and her head wrenched back. Ryan fisted his hand tighter around her hair as he pushed her in front of his body, before shifting to pin her to him, his arms tight around her throat and waist. She was trapped against his torso—nothing more than a human shield.

Ryan called out, "Cathy, you're a bitch, and I knew you weren't to be trusted. I had guys following you, but you played the part well. Did you fuck James? Was that part of the act? And, James, it must have been a shocker when your old girlfriend turned up."

He pulled Marianne closer to him, so close she could smell his body odour. He bent his head to her ear as if to whisper, but his voice carried across the room. "All you had to do was shut up and do what you were told. But no, you had to get your little vigilante gang together and stick your nose in it. What happens to the girl is on your head, just remember that. You forced me into this." The words were a savage bite that she accepted. She knew it was her fault.

Ryan shouted at Karl, "For Christ's sake, help me. Get one of the guns and cover her." He pointed to Cathy.

James kept his gun on Ryan. Out the corner of her eye, Marianne saw Karl bend over and scramble on the floor. He came up clutching a pistol that he aimed at Cathy.

"I've got it under control over here, Karl. You need a hand with her? She is just a girl." Ryan's voice was mocking.

Marianne froze as Sue's voice came from behind them. "I'm a girl too, son. You'll need a hand with me."

Startled, Ryan loosened his grip and turned towards the voice. Marianne knew this was her chance. She swung her leg out and, bringing it back with force, smashed her heel into Ryan's kneecap. He yelled and bent over, and Marianne slipped free.

"You fucking bitch. Come back here."

He grabbed the sleeve of her jacket and held tight. She struggled to get away. Sue was in the doorway, a cricket bat held aloft in both hands. She brought it down with force against the side of Ryan's head. He crumpled to his knees and was still, for a moment at least, but then he moved and rose to his feet. It wasn't over.

James ran across the room towards them, firing at Ryan and shouting, "Tom, take Marianne and Sue out of here. Go and find the girl. Hurry."

Marianne ran to the door, stopped and looked back as a fierce cry rent the air. Karl had got off a lucky shot and hit Cathy in the thigh. She collapsed onto her back but didn't falter as she took straight aim, and her bullet blasted into Karl's chest.

James's bullets hit their mark. Ryan howled as his hand exploded with shattered bone and ripped flesh. James jumped the space between them and punched Ryan in the throat. His eyes bulged, and he gasped as he collapsed.

James looked up saw her and yelled, "Hurry up. Go get your niece."

***

Emily turned to Chloe as yet more gunshots boomed from the house, echoing in the quiet. She was sure the look of horror on Chloe's face would be mirrored on her own. Her mind was a blur, and before she could speak there was a thundering noise as at least a dozen men came running along the track towards them. They wore masks, dark clothing and carried automatic rifles. Emily was frozen to the spot. The men ran towards the house, barely giving them a glance except for the last two in line, who headed directly towards them.

Emily screamed, "Quick, Chloe, get in the car."

They did, and thankfully Emily had left the keys in the ignition. She was a finger-tip away from escape when the driver's door was yanked open, and the key was ripped from her grasp. She looked at Chloe and saw to her horror that the other man, eyes cold behind his mask, stood by the passenger seat door. They were trapped.

***

Marianne followed Tom through a labyrinth of corridors until he stopped before an unassuming wooden door.

"This is it. It's the door to the wine store."

He tried the handle. His luck didn't hold out this time because the door was locked. He still carried the canvas bag and threw it to the ground. He knelt and rummaged about inside. He drew out the electric screwdriver. "This should do the trick."

"For God's sake, hurry."

It seemed like an age, but Tom managed to loosen the bolts and disable the lock. He wrenched the door open.

It was dark inside, and musty air escaped. Tom reached out and fumbled against the wall, and Marianne heard a click as a light switched on. Marianne turned to Sue, and whispered, "Stay here and let us know if anyone approaches?"

Tom ran downstairs, and she followed him. The room was no longer used as a wine cellar. A small bed was pushed against one wall, a commode by its side.

Amelia was tied to a chair in the middle of the room

and was completely still. Marianne ran to her and gently lifted her head. Her eyes were closed. Marianne's heart thudded. Were they too late? She shook her. "Amelia, Amelia. Wake up, wake up. We've come to get you. I'm your Aunt Marianne." Then she thought better of her words. "Darling, it's your Aunt Mhairi. Open your eyes like a good girl."

Was that movement? Marianne saw a tiny flutter as Amelia's eyes slowly opened. She was bloodied and bruised, but Marianne had never seen a more beautiful sight. Amelia coughed and spluttered, and Tom ran across to them. He held a glass of water while Amelia slowly sipped. There was a noise behind them, and Marianne turned in fear. Then her heart soared. It was James.

He came to her, pulled her into his arms and held her tight, whispering into her hair, "You bloody magnificent fool. But you did it."

"What about the others? Is everything okay?"

"Yes. The rest of the team arrived. The two heavies are dead, and Karl and Ryan are in handcuffs. Cathy is okay too. So is Adam. Not that he bloody deserves it." He looked at Amelia, smiled and walked over to her. Her head drooped, and her face was hidden behind a curtain of tangled hair. James gently swept it to the side, and when her battered face was exposed, he stood back and stared. "Bastards. Who could do this to a young girl?"

Pounding feet battered down the steps, and three black-clad men appeared. Two of them rushed to Amelia while the other approached James.

"Sir, the incident area is secure, as is the perimeter."

"Thank you, Gallagher. The girl will need urgent

medical attention."

"The paramedics are on standby, sir. They're being airlifted in now."

"Excellent. Good job."

Gallagher moved to assist his colleagues in carefully carrying Amelia upstairs. Marianne made to follow, but James placed a restraining hand on her arm. She cocked her head to one side, "What is it? I want to go with Amelia."

"You can see her at the hospital. The paramedics will need to check her out and don't need you in the way."

She opened her mouth to protest, but his words stopped her. "It's for Amelia's sake. Let them tend to her."

They were alone, Tom having left with Gallagher and his men. She stared at him. "Who the hell are you? What was that all about?"

He sighed. "I officially left the army 5 years ago, unofficially I moved into a newly created department. We specialise in undercover investigations. This is one of the largest, and longest, we have been involved in."

"And Cathy?"

"She's a trusted colleague and good friend. She has been deep undercover in Bergen for almost a year. No mean feat, but she's a strong woman." He smiled. "You'd like the real her."

She snorted. "I'm sure. So what you said about owning a security company was a lie?"

"No, I have a few ex-forces guys on the books who I occasionally set up with jobs. Perhaps, one day I'll run it full-time."

She shivered and hugged her arms across her chest as a

chill overtook her. The cellar was damp and the air heavy.

James shrugged off his jacket and draped it around her shoulders. His hands lingered on her for a long moment. He stared at her, and she matched him gaze for gaze. Her heart pounded as he spoke. "Look, I wanted to say . . ."

"Sorry, sir. The Commander is here, sir. He wants to see you." Gallagher's booming voice shattered the moment, breaking the invisible coils drawing them together.

James briefly dipped his head. "Of course. I am on my way." He gestured to the staircase and smiled at Marianne.

"Come on, the medics will want to have a look at you. Gallagher will make sure someone accompanies you all back to London."

CHAPTER FORTY-SEVEN

Marianne's stomach lurched as she waited in the hospital corridor. Amelia had been taken into a private room the day before, and Marianne had been refused access until this morning. She'd spent a sleepless night tossing and turning, worrying about Amelia mixed with confusion over James.

A middle-aged man approached her. "Miss Sinclair, I'm Dr Amani. I bet you're anxious to see Amelia."

"I am. How is she?"

He smiled. "Considering what she has gone through, she isn't bad at all. Once the blood from her split lip was washed away, she cleaned up pretty good. There is some bruising over her right cheekbone, but apart from that, she has no other injuries. There is, naturally, some faded bruising from the attack in Edinburgh, but overall she is good."

"What about the drugs?"

"There was little left in her system when she was brought in. I assume they gave her enough to appear drowsy and out of it when they recorded her. To make you more fearful, perhaps. There won't be any lasting damage."

"That is such a relief. May I see her?"

"Of course. Her parents have given permission for you to visit. They should be flying in this morning."

Marianne smiled. When she had called Jenny, she had been far from accommodating, and Marianne's ears had been battered by every Scottish curse she had ever heard and some she didn't know existed. Jenny's genteel mask had slipped, but Marianne couldn't blame her.

He indicated the door to their right. "Shall we?"

Marianne's mouth was as dry as the Sahara and her stomach a churning mess. Amelia was sitting up in the bed, her long dark hair washed and dried. Dr Amani was right. She was bruised, but the dried blood had made everything look much worse than it was. Her busted lip was covered by a scab. She had got off lucky.

Amelia's eyes were dull, but she forced a polite smile. "Oh shit, that hurt." Her hand flew to her split lip. "Sorry about the language."

Dr Amani laughed. "I did say smiling would be a chore for a few days. It seems a bit odd making the introductions, but this is your Aunt Marianne."

Amelia frowned. "Mum said on the phone you'd be coming to see me. I thought you were called Mhairi?"

"That was my name a long time ago. You can call me that or Marianne. Whatever you prefer."

Dr Amani said, "I'll leave you two to have a chat."

The door closed behind him, and Marianne had to take a deep breath. How the hell was she going to handle this? She started with, "How are you?"

Amelia's eyes clouded, "Okay, I guess. I spoke to the men from . . ." She paused. "I don't know where they were from, but I think they were the police or something. I told them what I knew, but it wasn't much. I got bundled into a car while I was at the bus stop, then I don't remember anything until I was in the room you found me in. Dr Amani said I was drugged. I guess I should be grateful the worst never happened to me."

As a woman, she could understand the young girl's fears. Luckily, Ryan hadn't been as evil as he painted himself. At least not in that respect.

The door opened behind her. Amelia's eyes widened, and she mouthed an "oh." Marianne turned to see who it was, and her blood chilled.

James came in, preceded by a huge teddy bear, an enormous bouquet of flowers and a carrier bag. He smiled at her.

"I thought I'd come and introduce myself to Amelia. Hi, honey, these are for you. There are some books in the bag as I am sure you're going to be bored soon."

He handed across the gifts, and Amelia blushed. "Thank you." She tilted her head to one side. "I know you. You were there, weren't you?"

"Yes, I was. I'm James MacLean. I hear you gave a helpful report to my colleagues, and I thank you for that. I bet you'll be glad to see your mum and dad."

Marianne choked back bile.

"Yes, they must be worried. It's lovely to properly meet Aunt Marianne." She stopped and stared. "It's funny. We don't look alike at all. I don't even look like my mum and dad. I used to say I must be adopted." She laughed, her eyes crinkling and her features lifting. She held her mouth and giggled. "Ouch, there goes my lip again."

Marianne had a glimpse of what a lovely, happy girl Amelia usually was. She turned to James and froze.

His stance was rigid, and all humour had left his face.

"Amelia, I have to go now. But you take care, honey." He pulled a card from his pocket. "These are my numbers in case you ever need me. You need anything, you let me know."

Amelia held the card, and her mouth wobbled as her eyes filled with tears. "Thank you."

The door opened, and Dr Amani came in. "Sorry, but my patient needs some rest before her parents arrive."

James was quick to speak. "We're leaving. Come on, Marianne."

She bent and kissed Amelia. Her skin was smooth and peachy, and she braced herself. This was the first time she had touched her daughter in seventeen years. Amelia's hair smelled of apple-scented shampoo, and Marianne knew she would always associate it with her. She held herself together and drew back. "Take care."

She followed James out of the room and along the corridor, ready to say farewell and go their separate ways. She had to accept that they were two old lovers with an ocean of time between them. They had come together for a moment, but that had passed. She stopped by the elevators, but James grabbed her hand and pushed her through the door to the stairs. They were on the eighth floor. She was about to protest that she wasn't going to walk, but the look on his face stopped her.

"What have you done? Amelia is the spitting image of my late mother." His voice was hoarse, and his eyes disbelieving.

Marianne took a step back and stared at him in horror. Her heart pounded "I don't know what you mean. You're crazy." She took another step and stopped as she bumped into the wall.

He advanced. His face was ashen. "Don't lie. I get it now. Shit, she's mine. Amelia is ours. You utter bitch."

He drew back his arm, and his fist lunged forward, hitting the wall beside her head.

"I have never hit a woman in my life, and I never will, but shit, Mhairi, you've driven me near insane."

His eyes were wet with tears, and he looked vulnerable and lost. She touched his arm. He immediately shrugged her away and drew back. "I get it now. You left me because you were pregnant. Why? I loved you. I would have taken care of you both."

"James . . ."

"No. Leave me alone. I swear, Mhairi, just leave me. I never want to see you again."

He hunkered on his haunches and held his head in his hands as his sobs filled the air.

"I'm sorry, Jamie. Please believe me."

He glared at her through red-rimmed eyes. "Fuck off. I never want to see you again."

When she didn't move away, he screamed, "Go! I can't stand the sight of you."

It took a moment to find the strength, but she opened the door and ran. Ran from the past and into a future she had never wanted.

CHAPTER FORTY-EIGHT

Marianne left her meeting with the regulator. It hadn't gone as bad as she had expected. She got a major ticking off for not bringing in the police, but the circumstances were understood. She didn't have an option once they attacked Amelia.

Amelia had been airlifted back to Edinburgh with her anxious parents. She had been discharged from hospital a week ago. She had apparently been told that her aunt was mixed up in an Internet scam and Amelia got caught in the fallout.

Her business may or may not recover. Time would tell. A few investors had liquidated their holdings, but she was keeping her head above water. Her heart was an entirely different matter.

She hurried along the road. The restaurant was only minutes away. The others were waiting for her. It had been strange, but they had gone from people who had spent every day together to getting back into their normal lives.

The small Italian restaurant was empty as it was not yet noon. There was already wine on the table, and Tom quickly poured her a glass. He raised his in a toast. "Here's to us."

They clinked glasses, and Marianne said, "And to Anita and Dave. We got our vengeance."

Chloe said, "And some. I have a mystery benefactor. Money was transferred into the account of the business Mum worked for. Apparently, it came from a well-wisher who said it was in Mum's memory. Her boss dropped the civil case to get the money from Mum's estate as he got everything back."

Emily said, "Shit. You too? My solicitor called to say they had received the money for the flat. I have no idea how that happened as I had sent it to an account with completely different details. But I'm not going to look a gift horse in the mouth."

Tom asked Sue, "Have you received any unexpected money?"

"Ha-ha, I wish."

"Check your account?"

"What?"

"Check your online banking. On you go. Humour me."

Sue sighed and pulled out her phone and tapped away. "I hope I can remember the password. I changed everything, as you said. Okay, I'm in."

She went white, all colour leaching from her face. "I've had a deposit. It's the exact amount that my Dave transferred. Oh my God, how could this happen?"

Marianne looked at Tom, a suspicion forming and blooming. "I assume that if I check, I will have received back the money that was taken from me?"

At Tom's delighted nod, she laughed. "What did you do, you naughty boy?"

"I worked on something years ago, but the tech wasn't right at the time. That has changed. I had to have something I could talk to Cathy about that was probable. I finessed what I had. I left a second virus in Bergen's records, and I activated it. The police will find all the original Bergen files. They will have enough to lock up Karl and Ryan for a long time. What they won't have is any actual money or assets. As soon as I activated the virus, it trawled Bergen's records, files, applications—everything, in fact. It started a series of instructions transferring anything of value into a new account, one I used for monies I wanted kept private. I've taken all their money and have had a copy of all Bergen's files put on my system. I can plunder anything else they have at will. And there is no trace whatsoever. No one will ever know."

Sue said, "And what did you call this one?"

Tom laughed and raised his glass. "I named it after you all: CyberSisters."

Marianne laughed and toasted him. "Funny, but apt. You've stolen their illegal gains? Oh, you are a devious swine, but I don't know what we'd have done without you. What a team."

And they were a team and maybe, just maybe, friends for life.

CHAPTER FORTY-NINE

Marianne basked in the morning sun and sipped at her black coffee as she took in the atmosphere. Saturday morning locals and tourists milled around the crowded Edinburgh street. Her small table was in a prime position outside a popular cafe. She had got there early to bag the exact spot for their purposes. Several empty tables bore reserved signs, and she kept her eyes on one reserved for three people.

A shadow fell across her table, blocking out the sun, and a chill made her shiver, and hug her arms tight across her chest. She looked up. The sun was behind him, and she couldn't see his face, but she knew who it was.

"You're late."

James smiled, his eyes crinkling. "Sorry, I got home late last night and got the early flight. I was in the Middle East."

"I guess it's best not to ask what you were doing there?"

"I guess so." He beckoned the waiter, ordered a refill for her and a cappuccino for himself.

He drummed his fingers on the tabletop and looked around, while they waited for their drinks.

"Are you nervous?"

His fingers stilled, and he bit his lip. He seemed boyish

and anxious and so much like the Jamie she had first loved. "Yeah. I've done some things in my life that would make the hardest quake in their boots, but this—well, this is on a different level. I'm terrified."

"So am I." She rubbed her hands together. Her palms were sweating, and she was nauseous; her stomach an empty, gaping pit. She glanced at her watch. "They should be here soon." She paused, looked at him, and knew she had to speak. "I am sorry, you know. Thanks for taking my call and giving me the opportunity to explain."

He held his hand up to quiet her. "You did what you thought was right. I've done a lot of thinking, though it kills me, I have to admit that you were right. I would have stayed a thug and got into deeper trouble. Your life and Amelia's would have been destroyed."

"Thank you." There was awkwardness between them, but then, what did she expect?

He was looking over her shoulder, out towards the busy square. "They're coming. Jenny has barely changed. I'd recognise her anywhere. Christ, I can't look." He closed his eyes, and when he opened them, she saw pain mingled with tension.

The trio walked passed them, towards their own table, which was the table with the reserved sign that Marianne had been watching. Thomas was closest, and he must have seen her, must have seen Jamie. Yes, they were older, eighteen years of living written on their faces, but the essence of them remained the same.

Thomas appeared the epitome of the prosperous lawyer that he was. When Marianne had last seen him, he had been a young man fresh from law school and starting to work in his father's legal practice.

Amelia sat between them, all three laughing and joking as they perused the menus and chose their brunch. The bruising was gone entirely. She looked even more beautiful than Marianne could have imagined.

Even after all these years, Marianne recognised how Jenny curled her hair around one finger when she was nervous. Jenny turned around, looked straight at her, closed her eyes in seeming resignation and briefly dipped her head in acknowledgement.

Jamie's voice was low. "So what's the plan again?"

"When Jenny called me a week or so after it all happened, she was changed. She got upset, said that something could have happened to Amelia or one of us and she would never have known her real parents. Would never have known that she was adopted."

"So what's the plan?" He repeated, his voice ragged and thick with emotion.

"We go over to the table, say hello and explain that we've come to see how Amelia is. Jenny will ask us to join them . . . and we take it from there."

He pushed his drink to the side. "Okay, let's do this."

Amelia jumped to her feet as soon as she saw them and wrapped her arms around Marianne. "What a brilliant surprise." She turned to Jenny, her eyes sparkling. "Mum, you must've known. I didn't know you were so good at keeping secrets."

Jenny smiled, but her lips wobbled a little. This would be hard for her sister, but she had instigated it. "Everyone sit down."

Thomas looked at them both. "Good to see you,

Marianne, and a pleasure to meet you, James. Thank you for what you did for our girl." His look was unwavering, but his tone held a slight distance. He would be the toughest nut to crack. He was staking his claim to Amelia as his daughter, which she always would be. All Marianne and James wanted was a little bit of her. But could you ever just have a tiny piece of someone. Was it all or nothing?

Amelia was chattering away. "James, thank you for the books. They made the time in hospital fly past. I love reading."

James's smile was tender, and a dagger stabbed at Marianne's heart. Look what she had taken away from him. "It was nothing. My mum was a great reader as well."

"And you're not? Nor is Dad, are you?" She playfully tickled her father and snuggled into his side. Thomas met their eyes over Amelia's head. Then he stared at Jenny for what seemed the longest moment. He cleared his throat. "Why don't you stay with us for a few days? We have plenty of room." He spoke the words he had been primed to say.

Before Marianne could speak, James got to his feet, pulling her with him. "That is a kind offer, but we only wanted to say hi. We're off to spend a few days at a small place I have in the Highlands. I'm sure one or both of us will pass through here again at some point. We'll always come and say hello."

Jenny was rigid, the changed script immobilising her. Not so Thomas. He was on his feet in seconds. "What a shame, but we don't want to keep you. Do we, girls?" His tone was jovial, but Marianne could sense the sheer relief.

She had no idea what James's plan was, but she had to play along.

Jenny rose and hugged James, and Marianne could hear her whispered thank-you. She repeated the gesture with Marianne, and she could see the bewilderment in her sister's eyes.

Amelia came round the table and gave Marianne another hug, hard and tight. "Don't be a stranger, Aunt Marianne. Maybe I could come and see you in London?"

"Of course, if it's okay with your mum." Marianne was sure Jenny would have enough excuses to see them through the immediate future.

Amelia went to James and briefly hugged him as well. "Thank you for saving me, both of you. I owe you my life."

Marianne couldn't help her dry thought that Amelia didn't know the half of it.

James took her hand, and she glanced at their entwined fingers before her eyes asked him what was going on. "Let's go."

They walked away, and Marianne held her counsel until they were clear of the cafe and couldn't be overheard. "You want to tell me what that was all about?"

He stopped and took both her hands in his. A frisson of desire coursed through her.

"Amelia isn't ours. We didn't bathe her, change her nappies or read her night-time stories. We didn't teach her right from wrong or ferry her to swimming and riding lessons. We haven't sat up half the night with worry when she had a childhood illness, nor were we filled with anxiety when she had her first day at secondary school. She belongs to them. Amelia is Jenny and Thomas's daughter. Let's not take that away from her. Not right now. Maybe one day the time will be right, but this is too soon."

"I do agree, you know. I've lived all these years knowing she existed. I've had time to accept that she is better off not knowing. But I never gave you that chance."

"I forgive you. Honestly, it was for the best. I was no good back then. You leaving shook me, threw me. I wanted to better myself, to be someone you would want. I dreamt of meeting you again, showing you who I had become, seducing you and then, in my dreams, I'd discard you the way you had done with me."

That hurt, but she didn't blame him. She drew back, gently removed her hands from his. "Look, I better be off. I can change my flight to one later today. Take care, James."

She held her head high and walked away, only to be swung around as he grabbed her hand and drew her in tight. His head descended, and he covered her mouth with his. Sensation exploded, and she melted into the kiss. It wasn't soft or gentle, but fierce and claiming. When he drew back, her head was reeling.

His smile was seductive, drawing her in. "But I could never do that. The second I saw you again, all I wanted to do was protect you, be with you, and love you."

Anticipation bubbled. She was stepping off a cliff. But she didn't care. "What happens now?"

"We both have time off. And I genuinely have a place in the Highlands. There will be a train leaving in a bit. Let's get our stuff and just head off. Get to know each other again and see where this goes."

She closed her eyes, and when she opened them, she walked by his side, into the future but embracing the past.

THE END

ABOUT THE AUTHORS

Kelly Clayton and Grant Collins remain happily married, despite writing a book together! They live in the stunning Channel Island of Jersey, where they spend their time in a home overlooking the sea.

Kelly has also written three contemporary crime thrillers:- Blood In The Sand, Blood Ties and Blood On The Rock.

She also writes romance as Julia Hardy, and Fortune's Hostage was published in 2018. This historical romance is laced with murder and mystery.

Grant first had the idea for Cyber Sisters when watching a TV news programme, which highlighted the rise in online crime, especially involving more mature victims and online romances.

He had one of those "what if?" moments, and this story was born. We very much hope you enjoyed reading about the Cyber Sisters. If you have a spare moment, we'd be grateful if you could leave a review on Amazon or Goodreads.

You can find Kelly on Facebook, Twitter and Instagram.

Printed in Great Britain
by Amazon

38258437R00179